Bat out of Hell

Bat out of Hell

AN ANTHOLOGY OF NEW MYSTERY SHORT STORIES BY

ANDREW CHILD • RICK BLEIWEISS • HEATHER GRAHAM

DAVE BRUNS • JOHN GILSTRAP • DON BRUNS

CHARLES TODD • C. J. KUDLACZ

EDITED BY **DON BRUNS**

BLACK STONE PUBLISHING

Published in 2025 by Blackstone Publishing
Cover and book design by Kathryn Galloway English

Printed in the United States of America
Originally published in hardcover by Blackstone Publishing in 2025

First paperback edition: 2025
ISBN 979-8-212-87797-8
Fiction / Mystery & Detective / Collections & Anthologies

Version 1

Blackstone Publishing
31 Mistletoe Rd.
Ashland, OR 97520

www.BlackstonePublishing.com

TABLE OF CONTENTS

ANDREW CHILD

BAT OUT OF HELL

Lucas Croker was all alone.

That was nothing new to him. He was used to it. He liked it. It meant no one could hurt him. He was in the dark. He didn't mind that, either. It meant no one could find him. So no one could steal from him. He was in a new place, which he also didn't care about. He was forever moving on. Or getting moved on. The only thing that was bothering him was the heat. He'd taken off his shoes. His socks. His shirt. His pants. His head was starting to spin. It was an effort to catch his breath. His throat was rough and raw. And he was sweating so hard he half believed his body was starting to melt.

Charles Clifford was two miles away from Lucas as the crow—or, as Clifford preferred, the vulture—flies. He was also alone. Also in the dark. Also battling the heat. But he didn't have the chance to strip down to his underwear. Not yet. Because he was out on the street, lurking in the shadows, watching a couple who had just staggered out of a bar.

Clifford knew the town was called Maynard's Creek, though he hadn't seen any bodies of water in the eight hours he'd been there. He'd read that the place had been pretty lively in its heyday, back when the nearby copper mines had been running at full pelt. All bars and brothels and gambling and gunfights. Now there was just a handful of streets that still had occupied buildings, all hemmed in by rail tracks to the west and scrubby desert to the east. The bricks-and-mortar equivalent of a broken-down athlete, Clifford thought. Once mighty, now stuck in a retirement home, short of breath, skin like paper, eyesight fading, waiting for the final grain of sand to tumble through the join in the hourglass.

Clifford couldn't tear his eyes away from the couple. The girl looked barely twenty-one. The guy was maybe five years older. The girl was having a hard time walking straight. The guy put his arm around her waist and steered her to the east. Toward the desert. To some predetermined, secluded spot, no doubt. Clifford grinned in the darkness. He started to follow. The fingers of his left hand stroked the textured grip of his pistol. His right hand closed around the smooth wooden handle of his knife. He glided smoothly in the couple's wake, unheard, unseen, as always. Then he stopped. Got a hold of himself. He could do this anywhere. Anytime. It wasn't what he'd come to New Mexico for. One 911 call from a worried parent or an anxious roommate and the whole town could be crawling with cops. His contacts could pull the plug. Go to ground. There was no way he could allow that to happen. The trip was so expensive. So hard to arrange. So great an opportunity. He had to keep his eyes on the prize . . .

Jack Reacher had spent most of the day walking so when he arrived in Maynard's Creek that evening, even though he was hungry, he took a room—one night, paid in cash—at a small, old-school motel he passed at the north end of the town. He showered, dried himself, did his best to dry his shirt with the anemic hairdryer he came across in the bathroom, then headed out in search of food. He found a diner two blocks farther south. It was a basic, no-frills establishment. Just the kind of place Reacher liked. It had a linoleum floor with an indistinct pattern, worn thin in places. A dozen wooden tables. Wooden chairs. WPA national park posters on the walls, some a little faded. And a menu that covered all the essentials. Reacher took a seat in the far corner, and when the waitress approached a minute later, he ordered two cheeseburgers and a mug of coffee.

There were three other people in the place. An old couple sharing a table and an older man eating alone on the other side of the room. The man struggled to his feet and staggered toward the door just as Reacher was finishing his first burger. The couple left as he finished his second. The waitress reappeared from the kitchen and asked if he was ready for his check.

"Depends," Reacher said. "How's your pie?"

"The peach?" The waitress wrinkled her nose. "Beyond saving. Don't go near it. You might survive the apple."

"I'll risk it. And another coffee."

"At this time of night? Your funeral, I guess."

Reacher stretched over to the next table and retrieved a newspaper someone had left there. It was some kind of regional publication, folded open to the arts page. There was an article about a new opera that had been performed that week in Santa Fe. Apparently the *New York Times* critic had loved it. The local guy was less impressed. Reacher struggled to summon any enthusiasm. He flicked through some other pages and set the paper down when the waitress returned with his pie and a fresh mug. He started to eat, then his attention was taken by a set of headlights on the street outside. They belonged to a white panel van. It swooped toward the diner's window, shuddered to a stop, the lights went out, and a woman jumped down from behind the wheel. She started to hurry away but stopped a moment later when another headlight—a single one—silhouetted her against the side of the van. She stood, frozen, for a second. A rough, rumbling engine sound grew louder. The light got brighter. Then the woman snapped out of her trance. She turned and ran inside the diner. She was maybe in her mid-thirties, five foot eight, thin, with long blonde hair. Her face was pale and pinpricks of sweat were showing on her forehead.

The woman called out, "Patsy? Juan? You there?"

The waitress poked her head around the kitchen door and said, "Blythe? What are you doing back here?"

A motorcycle pulled up outside, next to the van. Something dark and wide. A Harley, Reacher thought, or maybe an Indian. The driver killed the engine, heaved the bike onto its kickstand, and climbed down. He started toward the door to the diner, taking big, angry strides. The woman who had just arrived took a step toward the kitchen and then changed course. She ran to the opposite end of the room, where there were doors to a pair of restrooms. She pushed her way into the women's and slammed the door behind her.

The guy from the motorcycle barged through the entrance. He looked to be around six foot four, maybe late twenties, probably north of two hundred pounds. He was wearing motorcycle boots, greasy jeans, a white wife-beater with an ace of spades on the front, and his hair hung halfway down his back. He glared at Reacher, then the waitress. The waitress ducked back into the kitchen and let the door swing shut. Reacher took a mouthful of pie.

The guy turned and hammered on the women's room door. He yelled, "Blythe? Come out."

Blythe didn't answer.

Reacher ate another piece of pie.

The guy hammered harder. "Blythe? I know you're in there. Open the door."

The door stayed shut.

Reacher drained the last of his coffee.

The guy kicked the door. The lower corner flexed but the lock did its job. It held. The guy yelled, "Enough of this. Out. Now."

A small voice from inside the restroom said, "No. Go away. Leave me alone."

The guy slammed the door with an open hand. "Come out. You can't stay in there forever."

The voice said, "I can. Go away. I'm never coming out."

Reacher stood up, dropped some cash on the table, and started toward the door. He paused when he drew level with the motorcycle guy and said, "Question for you. The woman asked you to leave. So why are you still here?"

The guy opened his mouth but didn't speak for a moment. He looked at Reacher, as he had when he first walked in, but it was like he was only just seeing the size of him. How his arms were the width of most people's legs. His chest was like a bank vault. His fists were as big as baseball mitts. And with his face scorched by the sun and his hair wild from the shower, he looked like he was a heartbeat away from going fully berserk.

The guy wobbled but recovered. He said, "Why do you care?"

Reacher said, "If you have to ask, you wouldn't understand. Answer the question. Why are you still here?"

"I'm here because I want to be. What are you going to do about it?"

"This isn't about me. It's about you. And what you're going to do. Because you're going to leave in the next thirty seconds. The only question is, are you going to walk out of here, jump back on your hog, and ride back to whatever rock you hide under? Or are you going to be carried out in a bucket on your way to the hospital? And if you're wondering, either way works for me."

The guy was silent for a long moment. Then his Adam's apple bobbed up and down a couple of times and he spat out, "Fine." He moved to the door, skirting around Reacher and giving him a wide berth. "But this isn't over."

"Over?" Reacher said. "It never even began."

Reacher watched the guy walk to his bike, roll it back, climb on board, fire it up, and roar away down the street. He waited to make sure the guy didn't have any dumb ideas about circling back around the block, then tapped on the restroom door. He said, "Coast's clear. You can come out now." Then he made his way out to the sidewalk and strolled toward his motel.

Lucas was no longer feeling quite so hot. He had no idea what time it was, but figured that maybe the sun had set outside. He thought he might be in the desert based on the brief glimpse of the landscape he'd caught when he was being moved from the vehicle he'd been riding in, and he'd heard somewhere that it gets cold in the desert at night. Really cold. He felt himself shiver. He unwrapped the bundle he'd made of his clothes and slipped them back on. That wasn't difficult. He was used to getting dressed in the dark. But it wasn't pleasant because the waistband of his pants and basically all of his shirt were damp with the sweat they'd absorbed before he took them off. The cotton clung to his body. He shivered again, harder. Then his stomach got in on the act. He hadn't eaten since the day before. Still, going to sleep hungry was nothing new. He crouched down and stretched his arms wide, patting the ground around him and checking for anything sharp or dirty. He found nothing to worry about so he lay down and curled into a ball. It was a day like any other, he told himself. There was nothing to do but be thankful he was still alive and pray that the next day would be better.

As always, the outlook for the next day was beyond Lucas's control. It was the people around him who would determine how things played out. And they were confident that the day would turn out to be excellent. For them.

Reacher had covered half a block when he heard footsteps behind him. They were fast and light. He glanced over his shoulder and saw the woman from the diner hurrying after him. She was carrying a small yellow backpack that she hadn't had before. Reacher slowed to let her catch up.

The woman skipped around in front of him and held out her hand. "I'm Blythe."

"Reacher." He held out his hand, and they shook, briefly. Then Blythe pulled free and shot her hand up to touch his biceps and chest.

"Sorry," she said through a crooked smile. "I had to check if you're real. And I wanted to say thank you. You got me out of a jam with that guy back there. That's for sure."

"He looked like he had bad intentions."

"He did. Very bad. The worst."

"Why? What's his beef?"

Blythe looked around her like she thought the guy might suddenly reappear. Then she said, "Let me buy you a drink real quick. Thank you properly. And I could put you in the picture at the same time."

"You aren't worried he'll come back? Maybe bring reinforcements?"

Blythe touched Reacher's chest again. "Why would I worry when my knight in shining armor is standing right next to me?

I'm talking about one drink. I know a place where he'll never find us. And you could walk me to my ride when we're done?"

"I'm no white knight. And I'm not sticking around. I'm leaving town in the morning. Maybe you should do the same. Maybe you should go before then."

"Maybe. But first, let's get that drink."

Blythe led the way to the end of the block, took a right, and then turned into the next alleyway they came to. She continued halfway to the next road, stopped in front of a green wooden door, knocked, and waited. There was no name or number or sign to show where they were.

Reacher said, "What is this place?"

Blythe said, "Patience. You'll see."

A moment later the door opened. A stocky guy in a black suit and white dress shirt blocked the way. He said, "Blythe. Good to see you. Who's this?"

Blythe said, "A friend. His name's Reacher."

The guy turned to Reacher and said, "Weapons?"

Blythe said, "Come on. Look at him. He's a walking weapon. He's not carrying anything. I'm vouching for him."

The guy said, "OK then, I guess. But any problems, it's on you."

The guy stepped back and Blythe pushed past him. Reacher squeezed by, too, and followed her into a narrow vestibule, then down a flight of cement steps that opened into a rectangular basement. The space was airless and low—too low for Reacher to stand upright—with rough stone walls and a cement floor. There was a makeshift bar made out of old packing cases at the bottom of the steps and a bunch of tables and chairs scattered around in no discernable order. None of them matched. About half were taken. There was no sign of the guy from the diner, and no other bikers. The clientele seemed to mainly be in their thirties and looked either very relaxed or very bored. Or oxygen deprived, Reacher thought. He had no intention of winding up like any of them, which meant he wouldn't be staying very long.

Blythe shimmied through the crowd to the far end of the room, took hold of the last table, and pulled it as far away from the others as she could. She said, "What do you want? Beer?"

Reacher said, "Sure. Anything in a bottle."

Reacher moved a chair so that he could sit with his back to the wall while Blythe worked her way across to the bar. On top of the lack of headroom and restricted ventilation, there was only one way out—the steps they had used to come in—and no viable cover. A terrible situation. Reacher figured this was going to be a very quick drink.

Blythe returned a couple of minutes later with two bottles with labels Reacher didn't recognize and a smile on her face. She set the beers down and said, "You're a good luck charm. They have the good stuff today."

Reacher lifted his bottle. He said, "Cheers," and took a sip. It wasn't as bad as he'd expected. He said, "What is this place? A preserved speakeasy?"

Blythe laughed, almost choking on her first mouthful of beer. "Not a chance. No one took the Eighteenth seriously down here. No. This place is new. It's what economic reality looks like. The town's circling the drain. A few of the older businesses, where the families own the buildings, they can still make it work. But if you're starting out? Rent, tax, building codes you have to conform to—forget it. You have to get creative."

Reacher nodded. He didn't approve, but he understood. "And you?"

The smile left Blythe's face. She sighed and set her bottle down. "If you're looking for something original you're going to be disappointed. I just want to get out of this dump. Go somewhere interesting. Santa Fe. Albuquerque, even. Get a good job. Community college, maybe. So for now, I work at the diner. Just to earn money, so I can leave."

"How does working at the diner put you at odds with that biker?"

"That guy—he's called Eric. He's got three buddies. They all ride bikes. They all look pretty much alike. They've got a piece of property a couple of miles to the west of town. A ramshackle kind of place. Used to be a maintenance shop for a silver mine that closed down eons ago. They run a welding operation out of it. But they don't fix vehicles. They make sculptures. They get pieces of old machines and tools and truck engines—anything metal, basically—and stick them together to make giant animals. Moose. Elk. Bison. Things like that. They sell them on the internet. Make, like, fifteen, twenty grand apiece. No other work around here pays like that. They don't come to town much. Why would they? But they have to eat and they don't like to cook. So they phone in to-go orders to the diner pretty much every day. They're our best customers. And it's my job to deliver the meals."

"So you were out in a remote spot, and this Eric tried something on . . ."

"No. Nothing like that. They're always quite sweet to me, actually."

"What then?"

"Yesterday, when I was over there dropping off a pot roast for their dinner, I saw something. Something I shouldn't have."

"Not a giant metal critter, presumably."

"Right."

"What was it?"

Blythe turned her head away. "Something so bad, so horrible, I don't want to say. I can't say."

"Listen to me. I was a military cop for thirteen years. I dealt with the worst things the worst people can do. You can tell me. You're not going to shock me."

Blythe shook her head. "It's not about you. It's about me. I don't need that image in my head."

Reacher didn't respond for a couple of minutes, hoping the awkward silence would loosen her tongue, but she stayed resolute. He said, "It was something illegal?"

Blythe nodded.

"They know you saw it?"

Blythe sniffled. "They do."

"Now they want to shut you up. Make sure you don't tell anyone."

"It's too late for that. I dialed 911 from the delivery truck while I was hightailing it back to town."

"Do they know you did that?"

Blythe paused. "Good question. I don't know. I guess it depends on whether they've been raided yet. That would pretty much let the cat out of the bag. But either way, they'll still come after me. To shut me up, or pay me back. Either way ends with me, dead."

"So what do you want to do?"

"The way I see it, I have two choices. Run, or hide. But hiding's no good. Either they'll get me before the cops get them, or they'll wind up in jail and send somebody else here to get me. Which would be worse because I wouldn't know who to look out for. So really I have no choice. I have to run."

Reacher was silent for a moment. Blythe was right. Her analysis was bang on the mark. He knew that. And he hated it. He couldn't stand to see an innocent person run out of their home by some lowlife lawbreakers. But there was nothing he could do about it. He said, "If you're going to run, why wait? That only increases the danger you're in. Go now. Don't even finish your drink."

Blythe shook her head. "Can't. I need to get my money."

"Some things are more important than money. Like staying alive."

"What do you need to stay alive? Food. Shelter. Clothes. And how do you get those things? Money. And anyway, I earned it. It's mine. I'm not leaving it behind."

"Where is it?"

"In the bank. I'm not an idiot."

"Which bank? It must have branches in other towns. Go to one of those."

"It's not just cash. I have a deposit box, too. With some silver in it."

"What, like jewelry? Candlesticks? How much can it be worth?"

"Not trinkets. Raw silver. Worth a fortune. Probably."

"You're a prospector as well as a waitress?"

"You have to understand, the kids around here, there's not much for them to do. So the teenagers like to sneak out to the old mines. Poke around. See what they can find. Sometimes they find leftover explosives. Dynamite. Gelignite. I don't know which kinds, for sure. But I know that when they find explosives, they throw them at each other. The boys do, anyway. Sometimes nothing happens. Sometimes they explode. So one evening a while ago I was driving back to town from the welders' place—it was a Saturday, June, hot—and I saw some kids hurling things around. One went up in smoke. The kids ran. I stopped to check in case anyone was hurt. There was a crater, like ten feet across. Dirt and boulders strewn everywhere. And right there, in a kind of pocket just under the rim, I saw a bunch of rocks that were full of silver. I dug them up. Kept them. Stashed them at the bank."

"You didn't get the silver refined? Weighed? Valued?"

"No way. I couldn't. Mineral rights—it's complicated. The silver probably belongs to some landowner, technically. Or failing that, the BLM. I'm not sure. The only thing I do know is it didn't belong to me. Technically. So I liberated it. And kept it secret."

Technically you stole it, Reacher thought. Although he couldn't see many people in Blythe's shoes turning their noses up at a stroke of good fortune and handing over the loot. Not to an absentee landlord. Or a government bureaucracy. If they could even find out who to give it to. He said, "So, first thing in the morning?"

Blythe picked up her bottle. "First thing. Then I'm out of here. Going to hit the highway like a battering ram. There'll be no stopping me. You'll see."

"You have a car?"

"A bike. A silver black Phantom." Blythe sat back and waited for Reacher to respond. He didn't, so she added, "OK. A repro. A knockoff. I can't afford the real thing. Who can? But it looks the same. And it goes like a bat out of hell. I can promise you that."

Reacher took a moment and tried to think of something suitable to say, but he came up empty.

Blythe said, "More of a car guy, huh? Shame."

"Not really."

"So what are you doing here? Tell me you're not one of those bomb nuts?"

"Bomb nuts?"

"You know. Oppenheimer. The Manhattan Project. Any time there's a movie or documentary it brings out the tourists."

"This town wasn't part of the Manhattan Project."

"I know. But there was a uranium mine nearby. The mayor had a crazy campaign to big it up. Tack it onto the legit places."

"Did it work?"

"No."

"Was anyone surprised?"

"No. Well, maybe the mayor. But she's an idiot. So, if not the bomb, what?"

"Sepulcher."

"What's that?"

"A ghost town. Five miles northeast of here. I went, yesterday."

"Why?"

"I like ghost towns."

"Oh. OK. I guess. And when you're not wandering around abandoned places, where's home for you?"

"Depends."

"On what? I'm not the IRS."

"On what day it is. Today, it's here. Tomorrow it'll be somewhere else."

"You mean, you're homeless?"

"I don't own a home. There's a difference."

"But you were in the army. You were a cop. Drifting around—isn't that a big step down?"

"Most things are a step down after the army, but going where I want, when I want? After having no choice for thirteen years? Always going where the army sent me? To me, that's a step up."

Blythe was quiet for a moment, then she said, "How do you choose? Where to go, I mean. Because it just struck me. I've only ever lived here, in this town. My whole life. Tomorrow I'll be somewhere else. Somewhere new. How do I pick?"

"You don't. You get on your bike. Get on the road. See where it takes you. Don't go fast. Look around. Sooner or later you'll spot something interesting. Or you'll find somewhere beautiful. Then you stop. Spend the night. The next day, you do it again. If you find a place you like, you can stay and put down roots. If you like that kind of thing. Me, I have to keep moving."

"Why?"

Reacher shrugged. "It's how I'm wired."

"Don't you get lonely? On your own all the time?"

"Who says I'm always alone?"

"I mean at night . . . oh." Her face reddened for a moment, then a gleam appeared in her eyes that Reacher hadn't seen there before. A smile spread across her lips. It was part bashful, part something else. She held his gaze for another second then drained the last of her beer. She said, "Another?"

The security aspect of the room wasn't so bad, Reacher thought. If any bad actors burst in, they wouldn't open fire. If they had a conscience they'd be afraid of hitting bystanders. If they had a brain they'd be afraid of triggering panic and losing control of the scene. The smile returned to Blythe's face and Reacher realized he didn't want the evening to end. Not yet. He said, "Sure. Why not."

Blythe made her way back to the bar. She moved a little faster than the previous time, and when she returned, she was carrying four bottles of beer. The good kind. She put two down in front of Reacher and said, "You know, I only have one night left in this town. I'm going to make the most of it. Want to help me?"

Charles Clifford passed four people on his way back to his hotel at the southern fringe of Maynard's Creek, and another two were loitering in the lobby as he made his way through. So six people saw him, but if they had been asked, none would have been able to give a convincing description. Some might have mumbled about his average height. His average build. His unremarkable face. His short, tidy hair, maybe gray, maybe sand colored. His anonymous clothes. A couple might not have been able to recall anything distinctive about him at all. Clifford took pride in the way he could pass unnoticed. It was a characteristic that had been marginally helpful back in his working days. He had been a tax consultant, and that was the look a sizable subset of his clients expected. But it was invaluable when it came to his hobby. His full-time hobby, now. The ability to go wherever he wanted, and do whatever he wanted, and never leave a witness. He thought of himself as a ghost—separate from other people. Separate, and untouchable.

Clifford let himself into his room and crossed to his suitcase which was perched on the luggage rack at the end of the bed. He worked the combination, opened a concealed compartment, and slid his gun and knife inside. He would take them tomorrow, although he shouldn't need them, and in the meantime, he wanted to keep temptation out of reach. He grabbed a book, closed the case, and moved to the shabby armchair next to the window. But before he could start the first chapter, his phone made a sound. An unfamiliar chirp. His chest tightened. It was the alert he'd allocated to a new email app. It was run by an obscure outfit in Switzerland. It was said to be highly secure. Fully encrypted, end to end. Unhackable. The guys he would be meeting tomorrow insisted on using it. Initially, for all the back-and-forth involved in setting up the arrangement, but at that stage, it should just be for emergencies. Now a message had come, so there must be an emergency. Clifford could feel his dream slipping away. Being torn away. He listened for sirens in the street. For heavy footsteps in the corridor. He heard nothing. Forced himself to breathe. Opened the phone. Read the words on the screen. And exhaled, long and slow. There was no crisis. The sky wasn't falling. There was just a slight tweak to the plan. He wasn't to go to the diner to pick up his ride to the venue, as originally instructed. He was to wait at the hotel. Another message would come in the morning, confirming the time. That was no problem at all. He could stand in the lobby all day long and no one would notice him. He was sure about that.

Reacher and Blythe stayed in the basement bar for another double round then made their way to the surface and started toward Reacher's motel. The temperature had dropped while they were inside. The air was noticeably cooler. Blythe snaked her arm around Reacher's waist. He wrapped his around her shoulder. They moved slowly at first, each with a kind of exaggeratedly casual gait. They talked about nothing important. As they grew closer to Reacher's room they picked up the pace. Their bodies tensed. The conversation died away until the door was locked behind them, and after that, no words were needed at all.

Blythe was gone when Reacher woke up the next morning. He hadn't felt her get out of the bed. He hadn't heard her take a shower or close the door. For a moment he wondered if he'd imagined that she'd been there at all. Then he realized he could smell her hair on the pillow next to his. He stretched out his arm and felt the slight hollow she'd left in the saggy old mattress. He lay still for a moment, smiled, then pushed the covers back and stood up. The clock in his head told him it was a minute before half past eight. He started toward the bathroom, then stopped dead. He had heard a sound. A motorcycle engine. It was growing louder. Coming closer. Maybe it was the guy from the diner. The welder who had gone after Blythe. And if he now knew where Reacher was, that meant he had found her. Reacher picked his pants up from the floor and pulled them on. He pressed himself against the wall to the side of the window and craned his head around until he could see the stretch of forecourt outside his room. The motor grew louder. He caught sight of a bike. It was heading straight for him. But it wasn't the machine from last night. It was narrower. Sleeker. And the rider was smaller. More petite. And wearing a helmet.

Reacher opened the door. Blythe parked her bike and unhitched a pannier from a rack at the back. She held it up and said, "Went to the bank, as planned. No problem there. Got my bike. Started to leave town, but couldn't do it. After last night I just felt so alone. So here I am, crawling back like a sinner at the gates of heaven. Well? Do you forgive me? Do you feel the same?"

Reacher crossed his arms. He said, "I feel worried. Every second you're here increases the risk of you getting caught. By the welders, or someone they send in their place. You're damned either way."

Blythe stuck out her jaw. "Maybe I am damned. Maybe that's my destiny. Maybe I deserve it. Which is fine. I accept it. If I have to be, then I want to be. But more than that, I just want to be here with you, one last time. Come on. What do you say?"

Reacher said nothing. He just stepped back and opened the door a little wider.

Lucas Croker heard a loud *click*, and at the same moment, a sharp pain stabbed into both of his eyes. His lids snapped closed and he realized that someone had switched on a light. A bright one. He waited for his vision to adjust then coaxed his eyelids open again, slowly, a tiny fraction at a time.

Lucas saw that it wasn't just one light that had come on. It was a whole string of them, stretching away along a kind of rocky corridor. There was a bed, ten yards away. A kind of old-fashioned camping cot. Lucas felt a flash of anger. It didn't look comfortable. It didn't look very clean. But it was a sight better than the hard floor he'd been forced to sleep on. Next to it was a bucket. Lucas figured it was there to be used as a toilet.

He was glad about that. He was desperate. He hurried over and relieved himself, and just as he finished, he heard a harsh metallic *clank* behind him. He spun around and saw that a flap had opened in a metal door. Two things had appeared on it. A bottle of water and a white paper bag. Lucas rushed across and grabbed the bottle. He tore off the cap and sucked down half the water in one giant swig. Then he investigated the bag. There was a sandwich inside it. The biggest one he had ever seen. The bread was a little dry, maybe, but he wasn't about to complain. The thing was stuffed with slabs of cheese, different kinds of meat, and some kind of green vegetable he didn't recognize. He tried to take a bite but the sandwich was so tall with all its fillings that he had to squash it some to get his teeth around it. The riot of flavor filled his mouth, and suddenly, he no longer cared about having had to sleep on the ground.

Blythe left the motel again after ninety minutes, and this time, she didn't come back. Reacher brewed a mug of coffee with the little machine he found in one of the cupboards, took a shower, and left the room, too. He smiled as he pulled the door closed behind him. He would take happy memories of the place away with him. That was for sure.

Reacher didn't have a particular plan. He just figured he would make his way south to the highway, which must only be three miles away based on what he remembered of the map—four at the outside—and hitch a ride. As for the destination, he didn't care. He would go wherever the first driver who stopped was happy to take him. It was a method he'd used countless times over the years and he'd always lived to tell the tale.

Reacher didn't make it to the highway. He had walked less than a mile when he came to a sudden curve in the road. A sharp left. He could see tire tracks on the asphalt. Two sets. One single.

One double. The single set started farther from him and continued over the edge of the shoulder, all the way to the ditch that ran alongside the road. The double set started sooner and came to a stop before they left the highway. Reacher had worked enough vehicular homicides during his years in the military police to know what had happened. He could read the tracks like a confession. A car had come up behind a motorcycle, heading into the bend. It had pushed the bike to go too fast to avoid getting rear-ended. Then the rider had braked, too hard, too late. The bike had careered off the road. The car had stopped in time. The only question left in Reacher's mind was what had happened to the rider. He sprinted toward the ditch. He saw a bike lying torn and twisted, down at the bottom. It was Blythe's. Reacher recognized it from earlier that morning. Its panniers were missing, presumably full of Blythe's silver. And there was no sign of Blythe herself.

Reacher climbed down to the wreck. He crouched and probed the dirt with his fingers, seeking blood. He couldn't find any. That was good. Blythe had been wearing a helmet. That was also good. But Reacher couldn't believe she would have been in a state to walk out of there after a spill like that, even without the weight of her treasure to carry. He changed his angle. Scanned the ground around the bike again. And this time picked up a pair of dry tracks. They were parallel. Shallow. Shoulder width apart, for a petite person. Left by a pair of heels. Not a gurney. They extended up the bank. The driver of the car must have dragged Blythe, unconscious, back to the road. Then he had taken her somewhere. To the hospital? No. Reacher knew where. He clambered out of the ditch, started running toward the town, and didn't stop until he got to the diner.

Charles Clifford woke early—he'd been too excited to sleep well—and got dressed. He checked that his boots, coveralls, gloves, and mask were all squared away properly in his day bag. Then he settled down to wait for the secured email to arrive. He waited. And waited. He began to get angry. Who were these jokers to keep him waiting like this? Then fear took hold. What if something had gone wrong? The police? The FBI? They could be coming for him. He was a sitting duck. He should run. He got to his feet. And paranoia took over. Maybe he was getting ripped off? He'd paid in full, in Bitcoin. There was no way to get it back. He'd never met the guys at the other end of the email chain. He didn't know them. He shouldn't have trusted them. But maybe this was what they wanted? For him to run? To disappear, so they could keep the money and give nothing in return?

Clifford sat back down. Some degree of reason returned. He knew what was happening. Whenever there's an information gap, the human mind will fill it, and never with a best-case scenario. It always goes to the other extreme. He had no reason to distrust the people he was doing business with. They'd kept their word every step of the way, so far. Some temporary problem must have cropped up. A bump in the road. Nothing more. They would be working to fix it. He just had to keep the faith.

Clifford's faith was rewarded a few moments later. His phone made its sound. He opened the message, read it, and almost wept. It said, *Outside the hotel, blue Chevy Cruze, ten minutes. Apologies for the delay. We have a bonus for you, to make things right.* He checked the time. There was no rush. This was one appointment he was not going to be late for.

Reacher was hoping for two things: The white panel van Blythe used for deliveries would be where she had left it the evening before; and that she had been in too much of a panic, running from the welder on the motorcycle to have thought to take the keys. Reacher knew how to hot-wire a vehicle. He had done it before, but not for several years. He was rusty. Figuring out which wires he needed, stripping off the insulation without any tools, and fixing them together securely would all take time. But more of a problem was that Reacher wasn't sure how old the van was. He knew that after a certain year manufacturers had upped their game when it came to security. Mechanical safeguards had been added. Electronic ones, too, like transponders in the keys. Countermeasures that he didn't have the skill or experience to defeat.

Reacher rounded the final corner and saw that his luck was in on the first count, at least. The van was still parked outside the diner. He hurried to the driver's side, wiped the sweat from his eyes, and tried the handle. The door opened. He leaned into the cab and found he was two for two. The key was in the ignition. It was attached to a fob shaped like a robot that had been made out of some kind of delicate, mechanical components, welded or soldered together. Clock parts, Reacher thought. He paused for a moment. Examined the thing. Then racked the seat all the way back and climbed in behind the wheel.

The van's engine coughed to life on the second try. Reacher backed out into the street, turned to the north, then took a left at the first intersection. Blythe had said that the welders' place she delivered to was a couple of miles west of town. That would mean crossing the railroad. Reacher paused when he got to the street that ran parallel to the tracks. He looked both ways. Only one bridge was in sight, to his left. He took it and leaned harder on the gas once he was on the other side. The road was arrow straight, but the pavement gave way to dirt after a quarter mile. There were no buildings on either side. Storage racks in the back shook and rattled as the surface grew rougher. The incline grew steeper and the approaching foothills filled the windshield, spreading like fingers as they rose toward the mountains.

Reacher hammered the van through another mile of bumps and ruts. He could see a tall cloud of dust billowing in his mirrors. It was trailing behind the van like it was physically attached. Which meant there was no chance of a covert approach, if anyone was watching. Reacher kept up the speed for another half mile, then eased to a stop at the crest of a slight rise. The dust cloud caught up and enveloped the van. Reacher waited for it to clear then scanned the area ahead. To the right of the road, a couple of hundred yards ahead, he could see a cluster of buildings nestled close to a shallow cliff face. A large wooden structure, dilapidated and ramshackle, similar in style to pioneer barns Reacher had seen before in the West. Four double-wide trailer homes lined up, parallel, on the right. And a squat, metal shed on the left. A place to work, places to live, and a place for a generator, Reacher guessed. If they had a water supply and a fuel dump, the little camp would be pretty self-contained. Reacher could also see some vehicles. A pickup truck—black, dual wheels at the back, crusted with mud—with a trailer hooked up, between the barn and the first trailer. Four motorcycles parked in a crescent in front of the barn, facing out. And a small blue sedan, facing in.

The smart move would be to turn and drive away. Reacher knew that. He was up against a force of unknown size in an easily defensible position with no opportunity for any kind of reconnaissance. But he also believed that Blythe was there, no doubt in mortal danger. Which meant he had only one decision to make. To approach on foot, or in the van.

Reacher went with the van. He approached fast and parked behind the sedan, climbed out, and crept toward the barn. It had a single, wide door in the center of the wall facing away from the cliff. It was standing open an inch. Reacher moved in close. He stopped. Listened. Aside from a low thrumming from the generator hut, he could hear nothing. He nudged the door, bracing for the ancient hinges to protest, but it swung back smoothly and silently. Reacher crouched and peered inside. He saw no one. He straightened up, stepped inside, and dodged to his left to avoid being silhouetted in the open doorframe. The interior of the barn was lit by a row of overhead work lights. The air was heavy with the smell of oil and burned ozone. The space was divided into four areas. The front left corner was fitted out with industrial-style metal shelves, floor to ceiling, stacked high with all kinds of mechanical components. A bunch of engines and tools in various stages of disassembly were lined up in the back left corner. Workbenches crowded the front right corner, four of them, each with an oxyacetylene rig at their side. And the back right corner had been walled off to form a room within a room. It was square, maybe twenty feet by twenty. An office, possibly. Or a store for more valuable items.

Or something else altogether.

The walled-off section had one door. It was closed, but Reacher heard voices from behind it. The first was a man's. It was raised and angry. It said, "The hell is this? I didn't order a woman. The hell are you trying to pull?"

The second voice was also male. It was quieter. More conciliatory. It said, "Have no fear. She's the bonus I promised you. A freebie. The main course is yet to come, exactly as you specified. You're not going to be disappointed. I guarantee."

There was silence for a moment, then the second voice continued, "Unless you don't want her? Which is no problem. We can take care of her ourselves. I just thought, since you're here, and you're something of a connoisseur . . ."

The first voice came back. "Yes. Thank you. Why not? Let's lose the gag, though. It's no fun if we can't hear her beg."

Reacher crossed to the shelves. He selected one that was full of old hand tools. Picked up a twelve-inch screwdriver, then an adjustable wrench. A solid, heavy one. The mechanism was jammed with rust, but that wasn't going to be a problem. Not for what he had in mind. He strode across to the wall of the inner room that didn't have a door. He stopped three feet back from the corner and ran the head of the wrench up and down on the rough wood surface. It made a deep, grinding sound. He kept it up for three seconds. Four. Then he paused. He listened. There was no response from inside the room.

Reacher started banging the wall with the wrench. Five, six times, hard, like he was trying to bust all the way through. Then he heard the door open. Footsteps approached. They were soft. Tentative. Then a man launched himself around the corner. He looked to be around six foot even, and maybe in his mid-thirties. He had on black work boots, black jeans, and a Motörhead T-shirt. A blue paisley bandana was stretched over his head. And he had a matte black pistol in his right hand. He raised it, trying to bring it to bear on Reacher's chest. Reacher swung the wrench down, hard, smashing it into the guy's wrist. The guy screamed. He dropped the gun and pulled his hand back to his chest. Pain jolted up his arm and flooded through his body. His knees wobbled. He stretched his good arm out to the wall for balance. Reacher scooped up the guy's gun. He tucked it in the waistband at the back of his pants. He slid the wrench in at the other side. Grabbed the guy. Spun him around. Stepped up close behind him and clamped his left arm across the guy's chest, holding him tight. He jammed the screwdriver blade into the guy's neck. Then he marched him back around to the inner room's doorway.

There were five people inside the inner room. Blythe, with a ball gag in her mouth, strapped to what looked like a dentist's chair, which stuck out a forty-five-degree angle from the far corner. The biker Reacher had faced down at the diner the previous night, plus another guy, were to her left. The new guy was about five foot ten and had short, neat hair and bland, tidy clothes. He reminded Reacher of someone he'd caught helping a crooked quartermaster cook the books at an army vehicle depot, years before. And to Blythe's right were two more bikers. One was around six foot four, the other at least six foot six. There was a light suspended from the ceiling on an articulated arm. A circular drain in the floor, about nine inches in diameter. A sink against the wall, behind the biker, with a coiled hosepipe hanging on the wall above it. A set of stainless steel shelves on wheels, covered with all kinds of surgical tools with bright, shiny edges. And a second set of shelves with two cordless drills plus a bunch of hammers and chisels and pliers.

Reacher stepped into the room, keeping the guy with the broken wrist clamped tight to his chest. He pulled the screwdriver away from the guy's neck then jabbed it back, hard. It ripped through the guy's skin and his carotid artery. Reacher tore the screwdriver out, shoved the guy forward, and at the same time tugged on his shoulder. The guy stumbled into the center of the room, spinning around, blood hosing out of his wound like sparks from a Catherine wheel. Everyone who could move twisted and dove to evade the sticky spray. Reacher pulled out the captured gun. He shot the two taller guys first, center mass, and watched them drop. Then he turned. The biker from the diner was holding the bland guy out in front, like a shield. A bright scarlet swathe stained the front of the guy's shirt. Reacher shot him in the heart. He hoped the bullet would go right through and continue into the biker behind him, but it didn't. It must have taken a freak deflection from one of the guy's ribs because it popped out of his side, spiraled away, and buried itself in the wall. The biker launched the guy's body toward Reacher and dove for the doorway. Reacher batted the corpse aside, raised the gun, and pulled the trigger. The gun clicked. It was dry. Reacher cursed. An old instructor's voice echoed in his head: *Never rely on a weapon you didn't load yourself.* But there was no time for recriminations. Reacher ducked down and grabbed a gun from the six-foot-six guy's waistband. He spun back to the door, gun raised. And was too late. The biker was gone.

Reacher crossed to the chair and wrestled the gag out of Blythe's mouth. She was writhing and struggling against her straps and her face was scarlet.

Reacher said, "Are you—"

"Go!" She cut him off. "Stop him. There's one more. There's a kid . . ."

Reacher sprinted out of the barn. The delivery van was still there. So was the blue sedan. And the pickup. And all the bikes. Reacher turned to the trailers. He took a step toward the nearest one. Then stopped. He'd heard a sound. A deep, metallic *clang* from behind the barn. He ran around to the far side and saw an iron door set into the cliff face. It was ancient and rusty. Reacher guessed it was the entrance to the old silver mine that Blythe had mentioned. A light flickered on inside it. He heard a scream. It was high-pitched and desperate. Reacher ran toward the opening. He heard the sounds of scuffling. He closed to within ten feet. Then the biker emerged. He was gripping a young boy by the neck and pressing a gun against the kid's temple. The kid was pale and skinny. There were dark streaks on his face and his hair was long and matted. Reacher guessed he'd be about eight but he wouldn't have sworn to it. It can be hard to judge with street kids due to the malnutrition they often suffer.

The biker stopped, then started to grin like a hyena. He

said to Reacher, "On the ground, fool. Face down. Lace your fingers behind your head."

Reacher didn't move.

The biker said, "On the ground, or I shoot the kid. Then I shoot you."

The kid let out a long, low, whimper. Reacher looked directly at him and said, "What's your name?"

The biker said, "Don't talk to him. Listen to me. Get on the ground."

Reacher said, "Son? Your name?"

The kid's voice was little more than a whisper. He said, "Lucas."

Reacher said, "OK, Lucas. I want you to close your eyes. Close them, and keep them closed until I say you can open them. Understand?"

Lucas nodded and closed his eyes.

Reacher raised his gun and took aim.

The biker said, "Nice bluff. We both know that gun's empty."

Reacher held his breath. There was no margin for error. He fired. And didn't miss. The bullet went straight through the biker's mouth and sliced his brain stem before any signal could reach his trigger finger. His head rocked slightly, then he folded onto the ground like a puppet with its strings cut.

Reacher moved forward. He said, "Lucas, I'm going to pick you up, OK? Keep your eyes closed."

Reacher lifted the boy and made his way around to the front of the barn. He'd carried bags of groceries that were heavier. The boy's bony torso and skinny limbs were rigid. His shirt was damp and he smelled like it was a while since he'd seen the inside of a bathroom. Reacher tried to move gently so as not to scare him. He crossed to the blue sedan and set the boy down so that he was sitting on the hood.

Reacher said, "OK, Lucas. You can open your eyes now."

Lucas's face immediately scrunched up, then relaxed a little. His right eye opened a crack, then all the way, and finally his left eye opened, too.

Reacher said, "Are you hurt?"

Lucas shook his head.

Reacher said, "Where are you from?"

Lucas said, "Seattle."

"How did you get here?"

"A lady brought me. And a man."

A lady. Reacher glanced over to the entrance to the barn. He said, "What did she look like? The lady?"

Lucas shrugged. "Tall."

"What about her hair? Was it long? Or short?"

"Long."

"What color was it?"

"Light color."

"Did she tell you her name?"

Lucas shook his head.

Reacher said, "Do you remember anything else about her?"

Lucas said, "She lied. Lying's bad."

"What did she lie about?"

"She said she'd take me to my mom. But she didn't. She made me come here. I don't like her."

"I don't blame you. And you're right. Lying is bad. Can you remember anything else?"

"She had a spider."

"What, like a pet?"

"On her hand."

"When?"

"All the time."

"A real spider?"

Lucas giggled. "A picture. On her hand. It was nice."

Reacher glanced back at the barn. He felt his chest start to tighten. He said, "Lucas, I need to go into that building for a minute. I need you to stay here. Right here, sitting on this car. OK?"

Lucas shrugged.

Reacher said, "This is important. Stay right here. Tell me you understand."

Lucas's eyes widened. His lip trembled. He half curled up, half leaned away.

"It's OK. You're not in any trouble. Just don't move from this spot."

The door to the barn was standing open, just as Reacher had left it. He crept through. Looked around. No one was there. Nothing had changed. He moved forward toward the inner room and heard a voice. A woman's. But not Blythe's. It said, "I'm going to kill you, you stupid bitch. I'm going to rip your heart out. You're going to die, and the last thing you're going to see is your own heart, still beating . . ."

Reacher made it to the doorway. He saw Blythe, still strapped to the chair. Her shirt had been sliced open. Her bra had been cut through. A woman was looming over her. She had black boots with stiletto heels. Black leather pants. Blonde hair cascaded over a black leather vest. Her right arm was raised high over her head. She was holding a scalpel, ready to plunge it down into Blythe's abdomen. And on the back of her hand, Reacher could see a tattoo. A spider.

Reacher stepped forward and said, "Stop. Drop the knife."

The muscles in the woman's shoulder tensed and rippled. Her bicep bulged. The tip of the scalpel twitched. Reacher fired. The bullet hit her below her left armpit. The impact knocked her sideways. She dropped onto the shelf of power tools but kept hold of her blade. She tried to roll sideways, back toward Blythe. Reacher fired again. A headshot, close range. The woman flopped back and slithered down to the floor. Her eyes were open but unseeing. Her mouth was wide and her tongue flopped out. Reacher jabbed his toe into her temple. There was no reaction.

Reacher turned to Blythe. He covered her torso with the remains of her shirt, then picked up a fresh scalpel from the tray of surgical instruments. He went to slice the strap restraining her left wrist, then paused. He said, "You were part of this?"

Blythe didn't answer.

Reacher pulled the scalpel back and said, "I could walk away. Leave you here. You want that?"

Blythe scowled then said, "Yes. I was part of this. Emphasis on *was*."

"For how long?"

"Eighteen months. Closer to two years, I guess."

"People were brought here? Tortured? Killed? For money?"

Blythe nodded. "But I had no part in that. I was just a driver. Like a taxi service. The clients came to the diner. I drove them here. They did their thing. I drove them back."

"You must have known what was going on."

"Not at first. It's like I told you. I needed to get out of here. I was desperate. I needed money. You know how much you earn waiting tables in a town like this? Not minimum wage. That's for sure. There is a way to earn more, if you know what I mean, but I wasn't going there. No way. Then, one day, I drove out here to deliver some food, like I did all the time, only the guy offered me money. Cash. Under the table. No questions asked. More than I was earning in a month. All I had to do was give a stranger a ride. Who wouldn't jump at that?"

"The delivery van was cover."

"Right. The guys here wanted no physical connection with

their clients. Their vehicles were off-limits. Taxis would raise red flags a mile wide. But the diner's delivery service? Already established. Totally plausible."

"Where did they get their clients from?"

"I don't know, exactly. Some dark web thing. Untraceable. Payment through crypto."

"And the victims?"

"Also on the dark web. There are hubs in all the big cities. Menus, basically. You specify what kind of person you want—nothing is off-limits."

"Including kids?"

"Kid. Only one. This one. Which was beyond the pale for me. I only found out last night when I was here delivering food. Just food. I found out and said, *No way.* And that's when the shit hit the fan."

"You said you called 911. That wasn't true."

"Of course it wasn't. I'd have been grassing on myself. I wanted out of Maynard's Creek. Not into jail for the rest of my life. But all the same, a kid? I couldn't go there. So go on. Hand me your phone. I'll call 911 now."

"I can't."

"Why not?"

"I don't have a phone. But there is a little boy outside. Life's dealt him nothing but crap so far. He needs someone to change that. You up for that kind of challenge?"

Blythe didn't hesitate. She said, "Damn straight. Put your faith in me and I'll lead us both out of this hell."

RICK BLEIWEISS

YOU TOOK THE WORDS RIGHT OUT OF MY MOUTH

In the waning days of the summer of 1910, Pignon Scorbion, the brilliant, unorthodox chief police inspector of the English countryside market town of Haxford, arrived for supper at the Bridgehouse Inn, one of the main eateries in the hamlet. There were few customers in the somewhat darkly lit dining area of the establishment, so Scorbion was able to sit at a table next to the fireplace at the rear of the room.

Roland Mack, the innkeeper, approached Scorbion. "It's a bit warm in here to fire up the hearth. It mainly functions during the cold and damp that permeates the winter. I hope that meets with your approval, Chief Inspector."

"It does," Scorbion replied. "I like the positioning this table enjoys more than having any expectations of additional warmth. It affords me a view of the entire expanse of the room and allows me to observe the actions of the others who are here this evening."

As Roland started to ask, "Do you know what you'd be havin' tonight?" Billy Arthurson, printing press mechanic and chief reporter for the *Haxford Morning News*—and Scorbion's chronicler and protégé—walked into the room, spied Scorbion, and hurried over to him. "Do you mind if I join you?"

"Not at all," Scorbion answered, "I would be delighted to have your company. Would you like a stein of stout or ale?" When Billy enthusiastically nodded his assent, Scorbion turned to Roland. "Please bring us two mugs of your finest brew. After that, please be so kind as to place before us whatever you consider to be the most delectable meal the chef can conjure up."

Roland scratched his ear. "Just so I'm makin' sure I understand you right, you want the *chef* to choose what you two will be eatin' tonight?"

Scorbion affirmed, "That is correct. We will partake in whatever savory concoction he prepares for us."

Billy smiled at Roland. "I've never not known what I'd be eating, but being familiar with your cook, I'll wager anyone that it *will* be tasty."

Roland began walking away and called over his shoulder, "Two stouts and two mystery dishes coming up."

Billy and Scorbion both laughed at Roland's pronouncement, and then Billy turned to face his dining companion. "Calvin Brown's barbershop is a very unusual place to hold the types of examinations and interrogations that you conduct—especially considering you do them with Calvin and his staff, Thelma Smith, and me assisting you. Have you ever previously done anything similar to that in another unique location and with the involvement of regular citizens?"

Scorbion waited until Roland put their glasses of stout on the table, and then raised his mug. "Here's to uncommon locations, unusual associates, and unknown repasts."

After they clicked their glasses together and each downed a gulp, Scorbion answered Billy. "I utilized a barbershop once before, but never any other exotic locale."

Billy was intrigued. "When was that?"

"It occurred when I was a constable in Chamfield, and Calvin was an apprentice at Nathaniel Talbot's barbershop in that market town. It was in the year 1888. Would you care for me to relate the story of that first use of the barbershop as my place of inquiry and interrogation?"

"Please do," Billy responded.

"Well then, here's the tale—"

Once every fortnight, I arranged my schedule so that during my rounds I reached Nathaniel's barbershop exactly at noon. On those days, I passed up my midday meal to have my hair trimmed and my nails buffed by Calvin, the only barber I would allow to touch my locks. Even as an apprentice, I believed Brown to be the best tonsorial artist with a razor and shears who existed in all of England—as I still do.

In those days, I never missed a cut of my hair or a shave of my neck. I participated in physical activities regularly, and my uniforms were always pressed and spotless. So much so, that my superior, Chief Police Inspector Horace Raymond, told me that I was the most fastidious, immaculately dressed, and physically fit constable ever to serve under his command.

I was also so dedicated to detail that whenever I entered Talbot's shop, I performed two rituals.

First, I would gaze at the clock on the wall to determine if it was accurately displaying the time. On those rare occasions when it wasn't, I would manually adjust it so that it was correct to the second.

Then, I looked next to the timepiece at a promotional calendar given to Nathaniel by the Chamfield Funeral Home—which proclaimed itself to be the finest mortuary in England—to confirm that the square for each day on that month's sheet had been marked off up to the current date.

On Friday, May 4, 1888—two days before my twenty-second birthday—as I stood inside the front door to the shop, I noticed that the prior day's box on the calendar had not been filled with an X. I directed Talbot's eyes to it. "You have left off yesterday, Nathaniel. If I were not as aware of my surroundings as I am, I would think that today was Thursday, the third of May."

Talbot walked closer to the calendar and confirmed to me, "You're quite right, Constable. Blimey, I missed crossing it out."

Talbot drew a large X through the date with the charcoal crayon he kept for that purpose. Just as he did, the page was fluttered by a breeze coming from the direction of the shop's front door when Calvin walked through it. After hanging his cap on the wall hooks at the entrance, he strode next to me and lightly laid a hand on my shoulder. "Ah, Pignon, you've arrived ahead of me. I beg your forgiveness. I was taking a late breakfast at Sloan's Tavern and lost track of the hour. They do have the most scrumptious fry-up of any establishment in this town, and I was enjoying it at too leisurely a pace to be here when you arrived."

"It is not an issue, my friend," I responded. "I have just appeared here myself. I would have waited longer if necessary. There is none other who does your magic with the scissors, razor, and now the emery."

Calvin smiled and removed his hand from my shoulder. "You flatter me, but I'll not argue with you."

"Speaking of nourishment, are you available for us to dine together this evening—that is if you have nothing else pressing on your schedule?"

Calvin replied, "I'm unbound by any other commitment, so

it would be a pleasure to break bread again, my friend. I truly do enjoy our suppers, and the lively, stimulating conversations we engage in, especially when we discuss both world events, local goings-on, and news such as the Whitechapel murders. But if I must be perfectly honest, my favorite part of the evenings is finishing off each meal with the fine brandy you regularly provide. Do you have another good digestif for us to sample tonight?"

I grinned. "I have recently acquired a splendid French cognac produced by Hennessy, which I will break out post our consumption of the meal. As Hennessy has recently come into vogue and is regarded highly, I am eager to sample their offerings. But for now, let us get started on my hair and nails so I may return to my rounds in a timely manner."

Before sitting in the barber chair, I surveyed the shop, and after not seeing who I was looking for, I asked Nathaniel, "Where is Johnny? As you are aware, just as I solely allow Calvin to touch my hair and nails, Johnny Mann is the only bootblack I will permit to work on these black and white shoes I have custom-made in Liverpool. I trust no one else to keep the two areas of each shoe separate and free from the polish of the other color."

Talbot walked closer to me. "Johnny won't be here with us today. He came in just after Calvin left for the tavern and told me that his cousin, who arrived from London only two days ago, was savagely attacked earlier this morning and has been transported to the charity hospital in Crooked Woods. The act was so violent his cousin is comatose."

Of course, my curiosity was piqued. "I am sorry to be asking so many questions in rapid succession, but has Johnny reported what occurred to my superiors? Did he mention if he knew who assaulted his cousin and why they might have committed such an act? Were there indications of a struggle—was his cousin an older fellow who was not capable of resisting, or a younger person who might have attempted to fight off his assailant?"

Talbot, not disconcerted by my barrage, answered me in full. "After telling me of the incident, Johnny departed. He said he was going to your station to file a formal report—you might still find him there. Before leaving, I asked him similar questions to the ones you just raised, and he indicated he had no idea who would do such a thing to his cousin. In fact, he told me it made no sense to him. And most strangely, at least to me, he related that his cousin was not a *he*—rather, he was a *she*—and she was but a child in her late teenage years. However, he described her as alluring beyond her age."

While I mulled over Talbot's revelation, Calvin asked, "Did Johnny mention if his cousin was alone when this aggression took place?"

Talbot answered, "His twenty-two-year-old brother, Alexander, was accompanying the poor girl at the time. They were apparently on their way to Hickford's Emporium when two sizable fellows blocked their way, and then a third burly sort joined them, and the three lashed out at them both. Johnny's brother reported that he fought back and suffered cuts and bruises and a slight concussion in the melee, but before the blokes ran off, they had inflicted a great deal of harm on his cousin. Once Alexander saw that she was unconscious, he hurried home, told his parents of the attack and of his cousin's condition, and they took her in their cart to the hospital."

I considered what Nathaniel had said. "That is a curious set of circumstances, is it not? Why would a young woman unknown in Chamfield be so set upon during the daylight hours?"

Then I addressed Calvin. "We shall forgo having you perform your customary services upon me today, and instead, I will return to the station so that I may learn more about this unfortunate transgression. Hopefully, I can be of assistance in determining who did this deed and what their motivation was for doing so. In fact, I will request that I be assigned to lead the investigation based on my long-standing relationship with Johnny."

As I walked toward the front door, Calvin hurried up to me. "Please keep us abreast of your findings, and if there is anything we might do to assist, do let us know."

Talbot added his agreement. "If it becomes convenient for you to utilize this shop in any way—possibly if you need a location other than the station to question someone, do not hesitate to do so. I will clear any customers if necessary."

I nodded, thinking it a fine suggestion. "I may indeed take you up on that generous offer. Calvin was quite helpful to me when I was recently bemused regarding the theft of Leonard Church's mare, and his, and your, involvement may prove to be valuable in this instance as well."

Billy nodded his head and said understandingly, "So that's how it started with your using a barbershop. Well, you've answered that question, but now I'm intrigued by what happened. Please, will you continue?"

Scorbion went on—

When I entered the station, Johnny was sitting in front of Chief Inspector Raymond's desk, both deep in conversation. After quickly walking the short distance to where they were seated, Raymond looked up at me.

"Constable Scorbion, you must be a reader of minds. I was about to send Sergeant Thames to fetch you, as I'd like you to take on this incident Johnny Mann has been reporting. You're familiar with him and his family to the greatest degree of anyone in our precinct, and you've shown quite the propensity to see solutions that elude the rest of my officers. Therefore, I believe you are best suited to head the inquiry into the matter. I'm temporarily making you acting detective constable."

I was quite pleased with Raymond having such faith and trust in me, as well as my being afforded the opportunity to help Johnny's relatives, but I attempted to adopt an inscrutable countenance so that I did not appear overly enthusiastic or unprofessional.

"I learned of the ghastly attack on his cousin and brother from Nathaniel Talbot at the shop in which Johnny works, and I am prepared to take whatever actions are necessary to find the assailants, determine the motive for their actions, and bring them to justice."

"Brilliant," Raymond exclaimed. "You may utilize the unoccupied desk near the entrance to the holding cells. Have Mr. Mann recapitulate to you everything that he's told me. I'll assign Constable Wolfe to patrol your district so that you may dedicate yourself to this affair until you've resolved it."

Raymond's attention was diverted to the station's front door when another constable entered, lugging a drunkard who was riotously singing "My Bonnie Lies over the Ocean" at the top of his lungs. "Smitty's sotted again," Raymond observed. "Those two blokes in the cells next to the one he'll be housed in will get no peace and quiet while he's there."

Raymond went to assist his officer with booking Smitty, while Johnny and I moved to the unoccupied desk, where I began to quiz him. "Please tell me everything your brother related to you about the assault."

Johnny started, "To begin with, Alexander said he didn't recognize the three brutes who set upon him and our cousin Anna."

"What is her family name?" I inquired.

"Ford. She's the stepdaughter of our mother's sister, and Alexander and I've visited with her many times since we were all tykes—here and at her home. Alexander told me that both he and she fought the blokes, but were easily overpowered as they were large men, much heftier than either Anna or him. He said they wore heavy boots with thick hobnailed soles. One sported grey trousers with a stripe running down the side of the leg, while another had on black trousers. They were both wearing dirty white cotton shirts. One of the men was light haired and had on a dark blue cap. The other sported a mustache and was bald. The third man was dressed similarly, with dark trousers."

"Alexander said," Johnny continued, "he and Anna had just passed the church and turned into Grosvenor's Alley when the two men appeared at the other end of the passageway and came toward them. Then the third fellow joined them. When they reached Alexander and Anna, the thugs blocked them from going any farther and started shoving Alexander and telling him that if he didn't give up all his money, they'd beat the living daylights out of him. Then they turned to Anna and started making lewd remarks about her womanhood and how she'd enjoy their manliness. One of the blokes grabbed her wrist and started to pull her and grab at her clothes, but she fought back, as did Alexander. Unfortunately, they were overmatched, and it only ended when the bald fellow shoved Anna. She fell backward and struck her head on the pavement. When she didn't stir, the thugs must have thought they'd killed her and ran off, leaving Alexander bleeding and Anna unconscious."

When Johnny did not add any other details, I told him, "I must speak with Alexander, and it is imperative that we find these ruffians and interrogate them. Additionally, I will travel to the hospital in Crooked Woods to learn if Anna has awakened. If she has, I will attempt to converse with her to learn if she can provide any information beyond that which Alexander has told you and will tell me when I sit with him. In fact, I will begin with a trip to the hospital. Are your parents still there with your cousin?"

Johnny responded, "No. They were told it would probably take some time for her to regain consciousness, and they should leave and return later this evening."

I thought for a moment—just a short one—and then reflected, "In spite of that, I will still journey to the hospital to see for myself the extent of her injuries. I will ask Talbot if Calvin can be released from his duties for the remainder of the day so he may transport me to the facility in his cart. Therefore, please accompany me back to the barbershop."

Before we left the station, I asked Raymond if he would instruct the constables and sergeants to be alert for anyone who fit the description of the thugs who attacked Alexander and Anna and report their location if they were sighted. Raymond confirmed he would immediately do so.

Johnny and I left the station and walked the four blocks to the barbershop. When we arrived, I made my request of Talbot, who readily agreed and said, "My horse and buggy are three streets away. Calvin knows where they're housed. While you're gone, I'll service any of Calvin's clients who happen to come here."

"Thank you for your assistance and your conveyance," I replied, and then Calvin and I departed to harness Nathaniel's steed to his cart. After doing so, we left Chamfield.

Roland appeared at the kitchen door carrying four plates. As he strode toward them, Scorbion said to Billy, "Aha. Now we shall learn what flavorful items the chef has prepared for us."

When Roland reached their table, he set two dishes in front

of each of them. One contained a large portion of hearty beef stew with suet dumplings, while the other held their dessert—a large dish of cold fruit pie.

Scorbion viewed the food before him on the table, while Roland hurried away. "I would wager that our esteemed innkeeper does not want to learn what we think of the repast the chef has cooked, lest we not prefer it. Well, I, for one, rather enjoy a good stew, especially when it comes from a roast that was cooked the prior Sunday, and when it is accompanied by suet dumplings."

Billy added, "Oh, and I do appreciate a fruit pie that's filled with overripe sugary apples and blackberries."

As they began to eat, Billy asked, between bites, "Would you go on with the account you have been telling me? I'm curious as to who the thugs were and which of them was most to blame."

Scorbion put his fork down. "I shall stop the tale every now and then, as I just have, and take a mouthful so my stew does not get chilly from remaining uneaten. However, I will commence telling you more of the incident right after I consume this first forkful."

Once Scorbion swallowed the food, he continued the tale.

As we approached Crooked Woods, even prior to entering the town proper, Calvin and I saw the three-story-high charity hospital, the tallest building in the vicinity. Its bleak, weathered, grey stone facade, crumbling from age in numerous places, and its dearth of windows gave it a foreboding appearance that was both unpleasant and ominous.

Calvin observed, "I'd rather not be among the infirm housed here."

"Nor I," I confirmed, as we reached the path that led to the large double-door front entrance.

Once Calvin tethered Talbot's steed to the hitching ring, we proceeded inside and were instantly inundated by overpowering smells of antiseptics, feces, illness, decaying stone, and rotting wood, and by an unintelligible cacophony of moaning, screaming, agony, and shouted orders.

A nurse in a blood-splattered uniform approached us as we lingered inside the doorway. "May I assist you?"

I addressed the tired-looking, matronly woman. "I am Acting Detective Constable Pignon Scorbion of the Chamfield Police, and this is my associate Mr. Calvin Brown. We have travelled here to speak with a young woman who was transported to your facility earlier today. Her name is Anna Ford."

The woman brushed a grouping of dried vomit off the white apron she was wearing over her grey uniform. "I am the head nurse, and I regret to inform you that your journey here was for naught, Constable. You'll be unable to speak with Miss Ford as she hasn't regained consciousness."

She pointed to a woman dressed in a hospital gown lying on a cot two beds away from us. "That's her, and as you can see, she doesn't stir."

As I began to walk toward the girl, I told the nurse, "Then we must look at her person, her clothes, and any of the belongings which accompanied her when she was admitted, to determine if they can tell us that which Miss Ford cannot."

The nurse accompanied us to the bed, reached into a small, plain wooden cabinet standing beside it, and handed me a pile of clothes and two shoes. "She had only these garments. There were no other articles of any kind with her when she arrived."

Further conversation was halted when a woman three beds away screamed out in pain and the nurse turned in that direction. "I must attend to her. Please excuse me. When you're finished with Miss Ford's things, please return them to that cabinet."

While the nurse was walking to the other patient, Calvin took in the entire room and bemoaned, "This is a most distressing place, is it not, Pignon? There is no privacy. This long, dark, cavernous room is not appealing in any manner, and everywhere within it are the sounds and sights of pain, suffering, and precursors of death. I cannot wait to be back out in the fresh air."

I placed the clothes neatly on the top of the cabinet. "I agree, my friend. I assure you we will not tarry in this facility one moment longer than is necessary. If you wish to leave now and bide your time for me outside, I will not think any the less of you. But I will remain here. We have come to learn what we can about the unfortunate Miss Ford, and that is what my duty, and my curiosity, compel me to do."

Calvin seemed befuddled. "I don't understand how that will be possible as the poor lass can't speak with us."

I moved next to the bed before responding. "Then we must allow her body and garments to speak in the place of her mouth. Let us determine what they have to say. To begin with, Johnny described her as being more alluring than her peers. He said that she was in her teens, yet from what I can see under that flimsy gown, she has already developed the stature and shape of a mature female. That is unusual, but not unheard of. I can imagine that she has been mistaken, possibly regularly, to be five to ten years beyond her actual age."

I leaned down so that my eyes were only inches away from Anna's head, and then I slowly examined her, starting at her hair and ending at her toes, closely peering at her exposed face, arms, and legs. I noted discolorations on each of her upper arms.

"These could have occurred if she was being held to prevent her from moving," I suggested.

After completing my scrutiny, I gently rolled her onto her side and inspected the back of her legs and head. When I parted her hair, it revealed a red area the size of a fist embedded in her cranium. "This must be where she impacted the ground," I suggested to Calvin.

When I placed Anna onto her back again, I was preparing to gently lift and roll away her gown and examine her naked body, but that made Calvin uncomfortable. "Do you really have to do that, Pignon? It makes me feel like we are lecherous old codgers staring at an unclothed young wench. What would the nurse think if she were to see us doing this? That just isn't proper."

I considered what Calvin said and called out loudly. "Nurse! Might I entreat you to come join us here at Miss Ford's bedside so that you may make an examination of her person for us?"

The nurse tucked the sheet under the chin of the woman she was assisting and marched over to us. "What is it exactly that you wish me to do?"

I responded, "It is most important that we learn everything that Miss Ford can tell us before we depart, which includes observing any lacerations or wounds upon her person."

Then I turned to Calvin. "In spite of the examination being carried out by this fine woman, if you still find the process disagreeable, you may stand away or return outside. However, I must look for anything and everything that might declare itself for Miss Ford. I feel that to be my duty to her, no matter the mores and customs of the age in which we live. Personally, I would look at her with the same eye as I would look at a cadaver—Miss Ford's brain is no more responsive than that, even though she still breathes—however, bowing to you and your sensibilities, I defer to the nurse to conduct the scrutiny."

I gently took hold of the nurse's forearm and looked at her name tag, "Nurse Sloan, please look for anything that is not natural. Any bruises, contusions, scrapes, or other marks upon her person. When you locate one, please describe to me what you see and exactly where it is located."

Nurse Sloan nodded her assent to my request and began her examination at Anna's groin. She reported, "There are two reddish welts just below where her abdomen meets her legs, and a scratch alongside one of the bruises."

Calvin asked, "To what do you ascribe those, Pignon?"

I replied, "Taken on their own, I cannot yet make a judgment. I am anticipating, however, that as the nurse inspects the rest of her, we may see either a pattern or a correlation to other things that are found."

When Nurse Sloan's view came to rest on Anna's sternum and the top of her chest, she witnessed three similar contusions, and when she reported them, Calvin inquired, "Could those have occurred when she was shoved?"

I replied, "Very possibly . . . or not." Then I directed Calvin to look at her face. "You will note there is no bruising to her face, nor any scratches."

Once Nurse Sloan completed the examination of Anna's body, she carefully draped the gown back over it.

After she was so covered, I lifted Anna's right arm as far as it would raise and then bent over the bed to obtain a closer look at her fingers and nails. After I studied them, I gently put her arm down and then walked around the cot and repeated the sequence with her left arm.

"I have observed traces of blood and skin under the nails of her fingers on both hands. That may ease our task of identifying her assailants, as I suspect one or both will have scratches upon their faces and or arms. Her fingernails, while not ragged, are not as well taken care of as many of the females I've encountered recently. They more than likely did some damage to those who attacked her, although it might be minor."

I proceeded to go around to the other side of the cot. "I do not believe her person will yield any further useful information, so let us now examine her clothing to see if her garments tell us anything that her anatomy has not revealed."

Nurse Sloan left us to go to a woman four beds away on the far side of the aisle who had suddenly started crying out.

I reached over to the bedside cabinet, picked up the items lying on it, and laid them out on the cot next to Miss Ford.

After I accomplished that, I told Calvin, "And here we have a basic black dress typical to the daily fashion of today's young women. You'll note that it is well kept, yet it is creased near the hem and again in the middle of the skirt—as though it had been grasped in each place, and the fabric was unable to relax back into its natural shape."

"I see that," Calvin replied.

I laid the dress back down and picked up her knickers. "This is most strange and inconsistent. Why would there be a gathering of fabric in her knickers as well?"

"Could it simply have been from use and not related to the assault?" Calvin asked.

I unfurled the dress so that it laid flat along the sheet next to Anna and placed the kickers over it, attempting to match the waistband of the knickers to where the top and skirt sections of the dress met. When I was confident I had done just that, I moved the knickers to the side of the dress, and told Calvin, "Notice how the area that is creased in the dress matches the location of the crease in the knickers. It is curious that they would be there from the assault if most of the blows and shoves were to Miss Ford's chest."

I picked up the camisole on the cabinet and examined it front and back. "I see nothing outstanding in this garment." Then I handed it to Calvin. "Would you mind looking at it to make sure I have not missed anything?"

Calvin took the undergarment and inspected it carefully. "I see nothing unusual either, Pignon, although I'm not a student of women's underthings, being a bachelor through and through."

That brought a short-lived smile to my face until Calvin handed the item back to me.

Then I picked up the two shoes that remained sitting upon on the cabinet. "These are far more scuffed than I would have expected them to be."

I showed the shoes to Calvin. "Do you see the cuts and abrasions at the front by the toe boxes? Given the overall well-kept condition of her dress and the rest of her shoes, I find it incongruous that the front of her shoes would be so scraped."

Nurse Sloan returned from the patient in the other bed. "Have you completed the remainder of your examination?"

When I responded that we had, she folded Anna's clothing and put it, along with the shoes, back in the cabinet. Once she completed the task, I addressed her. "Might I entreat you to contact the police station in Chamfield at once when Miss Ford regains consciousness?"

"I absolutely shall," the nurse responded, "but I've seen a number of situations similar to hers, and they don't always recover and become responsive again."

Calvin scowled. "I pray that doesn't happen to this unfortunate young lass."

Nurse Sloan crossed herself. "Amen."

Then Calvin and I exited the hospital and departed in Talbot's buggy for our journey back to Chamfield.

Scorbion stopped to take a serving of stew and a bite of a dumpling, which he followed with a swallow of stout. Billy was much further along in his meal than Scorbion, so he chastised Scorbion, "You must eat some more of this delicious stew." Then he softened his tone, "But I want to hear the rest of the account. Are you fine with continuing?"

Scorbion answered only after he had swallowed two more forkfuls. "I shall commence the next part of the story."

Upon reaching Chamfield on the trip back from the hospital, before Calvin returned the cart and horse to where they had been stabled, he dropped me off at the station house.

Once inside, I was struck by the noise level, which was at such a high volume it hurt my ears, even though they are generally not sensitive to loud sounds. Smitty had changed songs and was boisterously singing "Bobby Shafto." The bare, hard walls of both the cell area and the main room of the station amplified his voice and caused it to resound throughout the building. Another detainee was incessantly calling out to be released from the holding area in which he was housed, citing that Smitty's caterwauling was giving him a headache, and two constables were taking reports at their desks from squawking locals who were reporting minor crimes. It was a cacophony of blaring, disagreeable sounds.

I located Chief Raymond near the back of the room and did my best to tell him, over the din, what I had learned at the hospital. After I completed my shouted account, I asked if any of the station's officers had any success finding the three thugs. Raymond indicated they had not but were still looking throughout the town for them.

I advised Raymond that my next action would be to interview Alexander Mann.

I left for the barbershop to meet up with Calvin, hoping Johnny would be there to inform me where his brother was. To my good fortune, when I arrived, Johnny and Alexander were both in the shop, deep in conversation with Calvin and Nathaniel.

"My dear fellows," I called out to get their attention, "how propitious it is that you are all in attendance. Especially, you, Alexander, as it saves Johnny or Calvin from having to venture out to locate you and bring you to this establishment. I am filled with inquiries to which only you will have the answers."

Alexander involuntarily touched the plaster on his left cheek, one of three on his face. "Whatever you want to know, I'll tell you, Constable, but Johnny's already told you most everything I could. I'd wager there's not much more I can tell you. But if you want to hear it from me, should we head off for your station?"

I did not hesitate to reply. "That building is quite filled with a cacophony of deafening sounds, so if Mr. Talbot does not mind, I would like to take him up on his offer to use this shop as the location in which we speak."

I witnessed Nathaniel's chest swelling. "Yes. Please do remain here." Then he shut the door and turned the sign on it to Closed. "If anyone comes while you're speaking with each other they'll have to return."

I walked over to the wall with the guest chairs and dragged five of them into a circle in the middle of the room. "Let us all sit down and do this together."

That appeared to surprise Calvin. "Really?"

"Yes," I replied. "As you, Nathaniel, and Johnny are here, we shall all work on this."

Once everyone sat down, I began my questioning. "Alexander, why was it Johnny who reported this incident to Chief Inspector Raymond rather than you?"

Alexander answered, "After the assault, my wounds were being attended to, so me and Johnny thought the sooner the incident was made known to the police, the better."

I next asked him to recite everything he could think of pertaining to the incident, but after the thirty minutes that it took Alexander to complete his account of the attack, I had learned nothing new that Johnny hadn't already related.

"In light of your being able to shed no additional information, allow me to inquire what the circumstances were under which you received the bruises, lacerations, and scrapes that the dressings cover on your face and arms."

"I was pummeled by both the ruffians, at first, and then a third man joined in with them," Alexander described. "I tried to retaliate, but they were overpowering. They took turns lashing out at me."

"When did they change their attacks to Miss Ford?"

"As soon as I stopped having the strength to fight back. I somewhat crumpled to the ground after a time. I'm decent-sized, but those brutes were so much bigger that I was no match for them. When they started in on Anna, I tried to help her, but they kept pushing me aside."

I nodded. "It must have been a terrible experience for you, one that was compounded by your inability to defend your cousin. Might I entreat you to remove your shirt so that I may observe any contusions on your torso?"

When Alexander took the garment off, all eyes looked at his bare chest. Calvin seemed surprised. "I must say I expected there to be more marks on your body than the one or two that we see. Were you not shoved or hit on your chest by the hooligans?"

I turned away from Alexander to Calvin. "That is an astute question, my friend. I, too, would have anticipated seeing additional signs of the assault there as well."

Alexander put his shirt back on. "They mostly went after my face and arms. I can't tell you why, but that's what they did."

"That is most curious," I advised, and then added, "may I assume that you will be able to identify the men once we apprehend them?"

"I certainly will," Alexander confirmed.

Before another question could be asked, a rapping was heard at the front door. We all turned in that direction and saw Constable Wolfe stiffly standing outside. Nathaniel arose from his chair and let him in.

Wolfe walked straight to me. "Inspector Raymond dispatched me to locate you. He believes we have found two of the blokes who assaulted Mr. Mann and Miss Ford. He would like you to return to the station house at once."

I took no pause before responding to him, "While I am not in the habit of disobeying my superiors, I am concerned that if the volume of the hubbub at the station has not diminished, it will make it extremely difficult to interrogate the suspects. Has Smitty ceased belting out his melodies, and has his cellmate stopped his protestations?"

Wolfe shifted on his feet. "Unfortunately, no. If anything, it has gotten louder and more irritating."

"In that case," I directed, "please tell the chief I would like to interrogate them here, in this shop."

Wolfe appeared nonplussed by that pronouncement. "Here? In a barbershop?"

I was firm in my response. "Yes. Here. It is an environment much more conducive to hearing everything they will say, without the distraction of all else that is taking place at the station. Additionally, as Alexander is here, it will expedite our confirmation that these are indeed the fellows we have been searching for. Inform Raymond it is my request, and as I am heading the inquiry into this matter, I would appreciate it being done in the manner that suits me best."

After telling me that he was not sure how Raymond would respond to my request, Wolfe left.

Within fifteen minutes, Raymond and Wolfe appeared at the barbershop, escorting two oversized ruffian-looking blokes. When they entered, Raymond addressed me. "This is highly irregular, Acting Detective Constable. However, I dare say I'm eager to witness the methods you use to uncover those things which none of my other men appear able to discern."

I gave a slight bow to the chief inspector. "I appreciate your confidence in me."

Then I turned to Nathaniel. "Would you please add four additional chairs to the circle so that we may all face each other during this process? Oh, and another if the third fellow should be apprehended as well."

While Nate was positioning the seats, Raymond questioned me. "Is it your intention to have these barbers," indicating Calvin and Nathaniel, "be part of these proceedings?"

"As unconventional as that may be, sir, yes, I do. They, especially Calvin, are astute observers of human nature, and I anticipate they may both contribute valuable insights."

Raymond wryly snickered, "Perhaps I should add them to my staff. They may prove to be more useful than some of the unimaginative personnel I currently have under my command." When he realized that Constable Wolfe had heard his words, he added, "Not you, Constable Wolfe. I'm sorry I didn't make that clear."

When all the chairs were positioned, everyone sat down, except for me. I stood in front of the bald man with the mustache and looked down at him. "What is your name? As I do not recall seeing either of you in this town at any prior time, I also ask where you hail from and for how long a period you have been in Chamfield."

The man bolted upright in his chair, looked me directly in the eye, and didn't hesitate to answer. In a firm voice, he responded, "Chauncy, sir, Chauncy Howard. Me an' me chum, Robert, we came here to work a fortnight ago. We ain't really from any one place. We go to where there's jobs and then move on when they're over."

"And what is it that you're working at here?" Calvin asked.

Robert answered. "We're doin' bricklayin', mate. Renovatin' the postal buildin'."

I turned to Robert. "Mr. . . ."

"Platt, Robert Platt."

"Mr. Platt," I began, "it has been alleged that you and Mr. Howard, and another man not yet known to us, set upon Alexander Mann . . ." I stopped and pointed to Alexander. ". . . and his cousin, Miss Anna Ford, earlier today and did significant bodily harm to them both. Do you deny doing that?"

"Holy bejesus," Howard interjected indignantly, "who said that? It's a load of crap, that's what it is."

"Then how," I asked, "do you account for the bruises you and Mr. Platt both sport on your faces?"

Platt answered. "We was in a scuffle outside a tavern last night. Two blokes started cussin' at us for no reason . . ."

Howard continued the narrative, ". . . jest because we ain't from around here and didn't know where the beer shop was. Some of these local buggers seem awful ready to get into a row. Didn't make no sense that *that* would set them off."

Platt resumed the account. "When we left, them fellows followed us outside and we got into quite a skirmish."

Calvin cocked his head. "That appears to be quite a convenient story. Did anyone see it happen? Were there any witnesses?"

"No," Howard responded, "it was jest us and the two of them."

I moved to stand in front of where Platt was seated on the chair. "Do you deny being in Grosvenor's Alley this morning?"

Platt looked up. "I don't deny that. We was there."

"And what did you do while you were on that street?" I asked.

"We was walkin' . . ." Platt replied, ". . . headin' to work."

I crouched down until I was at eye level with Platt. "And did you not set on Mr. Mann and Miss Ford while you were there?"

Platt's face began to turn red. "We may have bumped him as we passed, but we didn't do him no harm."

Howard added, "And we never touched the bird. She were a pretty one, though."

My back started to ache a wee bit, so I stood up. "I must say that I do find your having bruises from a supposed fight to which there were no witnesses, and Mr. Mann having cuts, scrapes, and lacerations that he accuses you of inflicting upon him, and Miss Ford lying in a hospital after being pushed to the ground, to be a bit much of a coincidence. So much so, that I am not comfortable with your account of what did, or as you allege, did not occur earlier in this day."

Alexander arose from his chair. "They're lying, all right." He touched the plasters on his face. "Look at me. I didn't do this to myself."

I politely but firmly asked Alexander to sit down. Once he was seated, I spoke. "I agree. It is not practical to believe that Alexander could have inflicted those wounds upon his own person. However, before we proceed any further, I would like to confer with Mr. Brown and Mr. Talbot outside the shop. If everyone else would remain seated, I shall return quite shortly."

Calvin, Nathaniel, and I stood up, walked outdoors, and stood on the pavement in front of the shop. Those inside could see but not hear our conversation, and what they observed was me appearing to give an instruction to Calvin, after which he turned and walked down the street away from the shop while Nathaniel and I returned inside.

Nathaniel went to his chair in the circle but I remained near the door and addressed the group. "I have dispatched Mr. Brown to return to the hospital at Crooked Woods to determine if Miss Ford has regained consciousness, and if so, to take down her account of this morning's events. While he is gone, I wish to conduct an experiment so I might better understand exactly how Alexander Mann's injuries were caused."

I moved to an open spot behind the barber chairs. "Mr. Howard and Mr. Platt, I ask you to stand up, remove your shirts, come to where I am now positioned, and attack me."

Raymond shot up before the two men rose. His voice was filled with concern and disbelief. "You want them to do *what*, Acting Detective Constable? *Attack* you? I dare say, is that a wise thing to do?"

I assured Raymond I would be fine. "I wish to see the fighting style of these fellows. Thank you for your concern, Chief Inspector, but I engage in rugby scrums on a regular basis, and they are as brutal as anything these two could inflict on me. Additionally, when I was a lad, I had training in bare-knuckle fisticuffs. I assure you I will not be harmed in any meaningful manner."

Raymond sat down. "Whatever you say, Scorbion. It's your bloody body." He added, "Hopefully, not literally."

I directed my next instructions to Platt and Howard. "Please accommodate me by disrobing and then coming to where I am standing and attack me. Please do it in the same manner that you employed when you fought those two fellows outside the tavern."

Howard shrank back and resisted the idea. "I don't fancy

that setting on an officer of the law will lead to any good. Why must we do this?"

I responded, "As I am requesting you do this, you have my word that no matter what happens, nothing will be held against you. However, do be prepared for me to defend myself from whatever onslaught you may throw at me."

Having said that, Howard and Platt stood up, removed their shirts, draped them over the backs of their chairs, and strode up to me, stopping a foot away.

"Good," I told them. "Now assault me."

Neither man moved.

I chided them. "Have you not got it in you to go after me?"

When neither moved again, I decided that I had to provoke them. "Are you afraid I will knock both of you on your behinds? Might your brawl at the tavern never have occurred, and you are only capable of victimizing a smaller lad like Alexander Mann and a defenseless young girl?"

Despite my attempts to evoke a reaction from Howard and Platt, they both stood motionless. So I leaned into Platt and pushed him so forcefully that he staggered back and fell to the ground. Then I turned to Howard. "I will do that to you and your pal again and again. You will eventually have no choice but to defend yourselves. Would it not be faster and more expedient if you would just set upon me?"

While Platt was rising from the ground, Howard unexpectedly threw a right cross at me, which narrowly missed my jaw as I ducked out of the way at the last second. "As you have just witnessed, my reflexes are top-drawer and most probably superior to yours, and your jabs will miss your mark if those are the only weapons you have in your arsenal."

Just as I completed that last word, Howard and Platt charged and drove me backward against one of the barber chairs, slightly knocking the wind out of my lungs. They began pummeling me with their fists, but after only a few seconds, I had recovered my stamina and pushed back against them and forced them away from me. I had blocked most of their jabs—which were mostly aimed at my chest, arms, and abdomen—although a few managed to get through and reddened my upper arm.

Then the two men charged me again, throwing roundhouses and punches that connected with only air.

I lowered my head as I would in a scrum, and wrapped my arms around their bodies, causing them to struggle to get free of my restrictive hold. While I was engaging Howard and Platt in that manner, I whispered to them, "Thank you for accommodating my request. You may now relax your fists and we will return to the chairs. I am afraid that any further struggle on your part will be unnecessary and fruitless. Despite your superior size, my superior pugilistic skills and rugby training will keep you in check no matter how long or how hard you attempt to assault me or break free."

Both men dropped their hands, their bodies untensed, and they disengaged from my hold. As Howard returned to his chair, he called over his shoulder, "I'll have you on my side any day, in any melee, Constable. I don't know how you did that, but you bleedin' stopped us cold."

I brushed off my shirt and trousers and when I got back to the circle of chairs, Raymond asked, "What did that accomplish, Constable? Is there something you learned from that fracas that has totally eluded my comprehension?"

I leaned in close to him and said, so that only he could hear, "I most assuredly did. I learned that neither man had any scratches upon their bodies and that they tend toward fisticuffs aimed at the torso rather than brawling, pushing, shoving, or aiming their jabs at one's face."

Raymond didn't understand the significance of any of those revelations. "And why, might I ask, are those important to have ascertained?"

I responded, "It somewhat discounts their tale of last night's supposed melee, but, that said, it will all become understandable when Mr. Brown returns from Crooked Woods."

Raymond's face took on a look of surprise. "Do I take that to mean that you know what is going on here?"

I affirmed, "I believe I do indeed. However, we must hear more from these men and from the third fellow, whomever he may be, for me to make certain my assumptions are correct. If they are, then what happened to Miss Ford shall become as clear as a cloudless day to all in short order. In the meantime, I will continue to interrogate Howard and Platt."

Raymond sighed. "As you wish, Constable. It's fully in your hands."

Howard and Platt had put their shirts back on and were seated on their chairs.

I asked them, "Would you please identify the third fellow who joined you in the alley?"

Platt responded, "His name's Ham. Ham Twitchell."

I immediately shot back, "And who might I ask is Ham Twitchell? And how are you acquainted with him?"

Howard answered, "He works on the same job we're doin'. He's a carpenter, and he wasn't with us. He came into the alley after us. We was all headin' to the jobsite."

Platt added, "And he left the alley after us. He coulda been the one who done all that to the bird and this here fellow."

I turned to Constable Wolfe. "If it is satisfactory to the chief, would you go immediately to the postal building and bring Mr. Twitchell here? As it is just beyond the corner of this block, you should be able to return with him in no time at all."

Raymond nodded his approval and Wolfe left.

I thought back to Platt's last statement for a moment before continuing. "Why should I believe either of you, and your claims that you are innocent of invoking any harm on Mr. Mann or Miss Ford? Your tale of last evening's melee is suspect, you admit to being in the alley at the time of the alleged attack, you told us you came into physical contact with them in an unpleasant manner, and Mr. Mann sports wounds that he could not have possibly inflicted upon himself. Again, I ask, why should I believe what you say?"

Platt looked up. "Because it's the truth, guv'nor."

I responded, "And do you continue to maintain that you never touched Miss Ford and solely made comments to her about her womanhood?"

Howard equivocated. "I might have put a hand on her. But it weren't nothin' heavy. No way did I push the bird hard enough to drop her to the ground. Mind you, it was jest a light touch on her arm. She were a fit bird though."

"She were," Platt confirmed.

I asked, "Did you lay your hands on Mr. Mann as well? In a heavier manner, possibly?"

Platt responded, "Like we tol' you earlier, we knocked into him as we passed, but it weren't no big thin'. Just a jostle."

Howard added, "We didn't do anythin' that woulda caused him to have those plasters on his face. An' if he's sayin' we did, that's tosh."

I glared at both men. "If I understand you right, you are saying you bumped into Alexander Mann but did no more than that to him, and you may have said something inappropriate to Anna Ford, and put your hand on her arm, but nothing else. And the bruises on both of you were a result of the supposed altercation outside the tavern the prior evening. Is that correct?"

"It is, guv'nor," Howard confirmed.

Platt added, "We kept going outta the alley to our jobs at the postal office this morning. You can ask the headman at the site if we was late, 'cause we wasn't."

Howard added, "And you can ask Twitchell when he gets here too. He'll tell you we left before him, and that bird was fine when we did."

Alexander shot up off his chair. "They're lying. Everything they just said is pure pork pie. They pummeled me, and after they knocked me to the muck, they set on Anna. You don't believe them, do you, Constable?"

I flicked my thumbnail as I thought. Then I answered his question with a question of my own. "And what about Mr. Twitchell? Could he have been the one who damaged you and Miss Ford to the greatest degree?"

Alexander responded. "It is possible. I was lashing out—and being lashed at—indiscriminately, and I really have no idea exactly who was doing what to whom. So, yes, that's possible, but these men were in on it."

Before anyone could say another word, the door opened, and Constable Wolfe strode in along with a large surly-looking bloke who I assumed to be Twitchell from the partially dried mortar on his hands. I quickly assessed him, noting that he had scratches on his stubbled face and was missing his two front upper teeth, his collarless white shirt was covered in splotches and streaks of dirt and mud, his dark, baggy work trousers were ripped at both knees and held up by a rope tied tightly around the waist through the belt loops, and his nondescript black cap fit too tightly, sitting higher on his head than it should, which led me to believe that it, like much of the rest of his outfit, was secondhand. His scowling face held an expression that I sensed to be a cross between anger and defiance.

I walked over to him. "May I assume you are Ham Twitchell?"

He answered, "I am. Me full name is Hammond, but everyone calls me Ham. And who are you?"

I responded, "I am Acting Detective Constable, Pignon Scorbion, and you have my apologies for having taken you from your labors and employment. However, we have a matter most pressing that we believe you may have had some involvement in."

"Whatever that is, it's a complete load of shite," he replied. "I ain't been involved in nothin'. I been mindin' my p's and q's since I got to this town a fortnight ago. I got nicked last year and spent me some time inside a chokey, and I ain't never goin' back in. No sir, I'm walkin' the straight and narrow these days."

I then asked him, "And for what crime were you incarcerated?"

Twitchell softly replied, "Assault."

I escorted Twitchell to one of the chairs, asked him to sit, and told him who everyone in the barbershop was. Then I asked, "Were you not in Grosvenor's Alley this morning?"

He responded immediately, "I was in some alley walkin' to my job, but I ain't got no idea what its name was."

I asked, "And when you were there, did you come across anyone who is now in this room?"

Twitchell looked at the men seated in the circle. He pointed to Alexander, Platt, and Howard. "Him, him, an' him."

"Was there also a young woman there as well?" I questioned.

"There was," he confirmed.

"In that case," I asked him, "would you tell me what took place when you were there?"

He pointed at Platt and Howard. "Those two blokes were shovin' and grabbin' at the wench and that fellow." He motioned toward Alexander. "And him an' her was resistin' pretty good."

I then asked, "And what did you do?"

He answered, "Nothin'. I jest kept on walkin'. I didn't want to be late. I already got one warnin' for not bein' on time two days ago. An' like I just said, I'm keepin' me nose out of anythin' that could cause me trouble."

I cocked my head to the side for some unexplained reason and then responded to him when I straightened up. "So, your testimony is that at no time did you engage with any of the others in the alley?"

"Right as rain," he replied.

Platt looked up from his chair. "That's complete bollocks. He was doin' his share pretty good."

Howard added, "And he was still there when we left."

I turned to Twitchell. "What do you have to say about that, sir?"

He snorted. "Shite. They're talkin' shite."

"Well," I observed, "we have a conundrum now, do we not? Alexander Mann says you three were all assaulting him and Miss Ford. Yet Messrs. Platt and Howard claim they did not do any significant harm and left prior to Mr. Twitchell's departure, who claims that he had nothing to do with any of this affair. But that Platt and Howard were indeed assaulting both Mann and Ford."

I stopped and thought for a moment before I continued. "Mr. Twitchell, what condition were Alexander and Miss Ford in when you were in the alley alone with them?"

"When I got there, he was a bit bruised, but nothing special. But no matter what, this here Alexander, was quite cack. I don't think he could've hit anythin' the way he was flailing about. But I didn't say I was alone with them."

Before anyone could utter another word, the front door opened. Calvin stopped in the doorway and motioned to me to join him. When we walked outside and stood talking on the pavement just by the front window, we could see everyone inside the shop watching us intently. After five minutes of animated conversation, mostly by Calvin, I patted him on the shoulder and then we both reentered the shop. Calvin sat on one of the empty chairs. While I stood behind it, I placed my hands on the backrest and addressed the group.

Scorbion stopped speaking so that he could finish his stew and sample the fruit pie. "Delicious. It is all delicious."

Billy coughed after taking too large a gulp of his stout, which caused it to run down from his mouth. He put the mug on the table and wiped his chin with his serviette. Once he had regained his composure, he said, "I can't believe you are stopping the tale there. Crikey, Scorbion, did you really know who assaulted Anna at that point?"

"I did," Scorbion affirmed. "Who is it that *you* think perpetrated the act which caused Miss Ford to be rendered unconscious?"

Billy thought for a moment before answering. "I think it's that Twitchell fellow. Everyone else's accounts match each other, except his. And if he was alone with her and Alexander after Howard and Platt left, then he most likely did it. Plus, he had been incarcerated for assault."

Scorbion leaned in toward Billy. "That is fine deducing on your part. You quickly reached the core of the matter—who was last with Anna Ford who would have pushed her to the ground? Was it one man, two, or three? May I continue?"

Billy nodded, "Absolutely."

Scorbion continued the tale.

When Calvin and I stepped back inside the shop, I spoke from the doorway, "I am pleased to disclose to you all that Mr. Brown has returned with a favorable report. When he arrived at the hospital at Crooked Woods, to his great relief, he found Miss Ford awake, and learned she had regained consciousness . . ."

Calvin broke in, "Although she was still in a bit of a foggy condition."

We both moved to the circle of seats, and I continued, "As I was saying, she had regained consciousness less than a quarter of an hour earlier, but she was lucid enough to tell Mr. Brown her remembrance of this morning's events."

I noticed everyone was still and silent as they waited to hear what Anna Ford had said to Calvin. So, I began to relate Calvin's account of Miss Ford's story.

"Anna Ford told Calvin that while she and Alexander Mann were beginning to walk down an alley just past the church, two large men did indeed enter the street from the opposite end. She described the men in enough detail, so there is no doubt the two men were you, Mr. Platt and Mr. Howard."

Howard said, "We don't deny that."

"Miss Ford went on to tell Mr. Brown that shortly thereafter, a third man joined the other two—a man with two missing front teeth. When the first two fellows reached her and Mr. Mann, they made crude remarks aimed at Miss Ford and one of them laid his hand upon her arm. She reported that after she pulled away from him, the second man purposefully jostled Mr. Mann, causing him to lose his footing. But no more than that. She also related that the third bloke did nothing to her in any way and did indeed leave the alley shortly after the first two men departed and neither she nor Alexander Mann had further contact with any of them."

Alexander stood. "That's not all that happened. Anna must have lost the memory of everything else that occurred after she fell and hit her head."

"Actually," I countered, "Miss Ford apparently acutely

recalled the events that took place after that, and she related them in great detail to Mr. Brown."

Raymond asked impatiently, "And what did she say, Acting Detective Constable? Don't leave us here in anticipation and to speculate for ourselves."

I replied to Raymond, "I will tell everyone now. Through tear-laden eyes, she told Mr. Brown that after the men had gone and were out of sight, her stepcousin, Alexander Mann, told her that since she had arrived, he had been smitten with her, and he could restrain himself no longer. He set on her, trying to force himself upon her. She said she resisted his advances, but he was forceful, and she had to fight him off, scratching his face with her nails numerous times. When he grabbed hold of her dress, started to lift it, and at the same time grasped her knickers, she fought even harder and kept kicking at him. She said was not able to connect with his legs and mostly only scraped her shoes on the stones in the road. When he forcibly pulled her toward him, she fought back and gashed his face one last time. After she did so, he pushed her away, and she fell to the road and smacked her head against it. She told Mr. Brown that she has no memory of anything after that impact."

Everyone in the shop looked at Alexander for his response.

Raymond stood up and towered over him as he sat on his chair. "Do you still maintain your version of what occurred and contest this report by Miss Ford? Do you have the gall to do that, young man?"

Alexander stared at his feet. "I'm not saying nothing."

Johnny turned to his brother. "How could you have done that to our cousin? I thought I knew you, but I don't know *that* person. The one who could have done *that*. Tell me, did you really do it, Alexander? And why?"

Alexander looked up at Johnny, but before he said anything,

a tear dislodged from his eye and ran down his cheek, and then he lifted his hands to his face and started crying into them. "I don't know. I don't know why I did it. I didn't want to hurt her. I only wanted to show her how much I liked her. I thought she liked me too."

When Raymond sat back down, I squatted in front of Alexander. "Thank you for being honest with us and saving these men"—I pointed to Howard, Platt, and Twitchell—"from being wrongfully accused of perpetrating the deed that you committed."

Then I paused before continuing. "Unfortunately, Alexander Mann, it is my duty, which I do not relish, to arrest you. For murder."

Raymond shot out of his chair. "*Murder*?! *What* murder?"

I stood and faced Raymond. "The murder of Anna Ford."

Raymond responded, "But you said that she told all that to Mr. Brown. She would have to be alive to do that."

I answered, "I am afraid that one part of the story I have just recounted is not truthful—the portion in which I said that Anna Ford had regained consciousness and related those events to Mr. Brown. When he arrived at the hospital, he was informed that shortly after we left there earlier today, she passed away from her injuries."

Raymond appeared confused. "So how did she tell him all the things she did? Everything you just detailed?"

"Actually, sir," I reported, "she told Calvin none of it. I had sorted out the events that had actually occurred, and when Mr. Brown returned here and told me that she had died, we arranged to create this ruse together. I took it upon myself to speak for her."

Raymond asked, "But how did you know exactly what happened? You related it in such detail, and so accurately, that Alexander Mann confirmed it all."

Constable Wolfe cuffed Alexander as I began my explanation. "When I examined Anna Ford and her belongings at the infirmary, I noted that she had skin and blood under her fingernails. The only person involved in this affair who has scratches consistent with being gouged by her is Alexander Mann. When Mr. Platt and Mr. Howard disrobed to have their tussle with me, I noted that their bodies had no scratches, solely bruises which one would have as a result of being punched—as they were in their row last night. And regarding Mr. Twitchell, he has scrapes but not any scratches consistent with being clawed at."

"Getting back to Miss Ford and her garments, I observed that her dress, which appeared to be generally neatly laundered, had sections which were creased, near the waist and at the hem, in a manner consistent with what would occur if someone were hastily trying to lift it. Her knickers had the same creases in almost the exact same location as the dress, which, to me, indicated that someone hastily grabbed her knickers while lifting her dress—and in a somewhat clumsy manner. That was confirmed by the nurse on duty who witnessed bruising in her groin area, which, I am certain, occurred after her dress and knickers were seized. The toe boxes of her otherwise well-kept shoes were scraped and discolored. I can only ascribe that to her repeatedly attempting to ward off her attacker by kicking at him but hitting the stones in the road instead."

I continued, "When the nurse at Crooked Woods examined Miss Ford's person, she reported no signs of her having been assaulted by Mr. Howard or Mr. Platt, both of whom—as you witnessed when I was finally able to get them to set on me—tended more to pugilism than to brawling."

Twitchell broke in, "That's me style too."

I agreed. "I am quite certain it is. The marks and bruises on Anna Ford's body, such as the ones on her upper arms, appeared to come from an attempt to forcefully restrain her, and compel her to engage in an unwilling sexual relationship—they are not consistent with her being punched, bashed, or shoved. There were additional clues as well, but those that I have just recited painted enough of a picture of the scene as it actually happened to enable me to surmise what had occurred—which was exactly how Mr. Howard and Mr. Platt, and later Mr. Twitchell, described it, and quite different from the account that Alexander Mann gave."

I turned my attention to Johnny. "I feel badly for your double loss today—that of your cousin who is now deceased, and of your brother. I do believe that it was an accidental death and that he did not mean to kill her. However, despite that, I do expect he will be incarcerated for a good period of time."

Raymond arose and stood next to me. "I am dumbfounded. Your telling of the incident as though you took the words right out of her mouth was so convincing that even I believed she had said those words. And I had no idea that was what had happened. I would have sworn that Howard, Platt, and Twitchell were all fabricating their stories. I am truly glad to have witnessed your performance, Acting Detective Constable. I can assure you that what you did will be communicated to London so that the Met may know of your talents. I see a long, illustrious career ahead of you. I am almost embarrassed to have you return to your regular beat, but I do need you patrolling the area. At least for now."

A rare smile lit up my face as I responded, "Thank you, sir. I will apply my talents whenever you require them, but in the meantime, I am quite satisfied remaining in this sector of Chamfield and continuing to have the opportunity to be in this establishment during my rounds."

Johnny left, accompanying Raymond and Wolfe as they

took Alexander to the station house, while Howard, Platt, and Twitchell departed to return to their jobs. When only Talbot and Calvin remained in the shop with me, Nathaniel asked if I would still like to have my hair taken care of.

I looked at the clock, and replied, "Thank you, but I must attend to my rounds. I will return tomorrow, and Calvin may take care of my hair then. And Calvin, I look forward to our dinner tonight, and sampling that Hennessy."

As I left, Calvin called out, "Me as well."

And then Talbot added, "Tomorrow is on the house. It's my way of paying you back for the amazing experience that took place in this shop today."

Scorbion tore into the dish of fruit pie as Billy took a swig of his stout. When he had swallowed and savored the last bit of the liquid, Billy placed the mug and both his hands flat on the table and leaned into the backrest of the chair. "My goodness, Pignon, I had it all wrong. How *do* you get such insights that none of the rest of us can see?"

Scorbion paused between forkfuls. "I believe it is a gift our Creator has bestowed upon me. It is the only explanation I can discern. While I have studied the ways of Holmes, and the methods he employed to deduce elements of crime scenes and reach the conclusions he reached, that was only a guidepost for me. It is the way my brain functions, and the connections it makes, that enable me to see what is obvious to me, yet indistinct to others. In the same way some people have musical abilities or are artistic, and still others possess mathematical prowess, my talent and aptitude are in the realm of observation, deduction, and the solving of complicated mysteries, enigmas, and dilemmas. I have no other explanation."

Roland ambled up to their table. "How was the meal, lads?"

Scorbion wiped the last of it off his lips before replying. "Quite tasty, my good fellow. I will leave my gastronomic fate in your cook's hands at any time if this repast we just enjoyed was an indication of what I would be ingesting."

Billy agreed. "It was well done. Very savory."

Roland beamed. "That's what I was hopin' to hear you say. Are you havin' anythin' else tonight?"

When Scorbion said no, Roland told him what the tab was, and Scorbion paid it—over Billy's protestations that he should pay his fair amount—and then they both departed for their residences.

This story is based on characters first introduced in the award-winning mystery novel, *Pignon Scorbion & the Barbershop Detectives.*

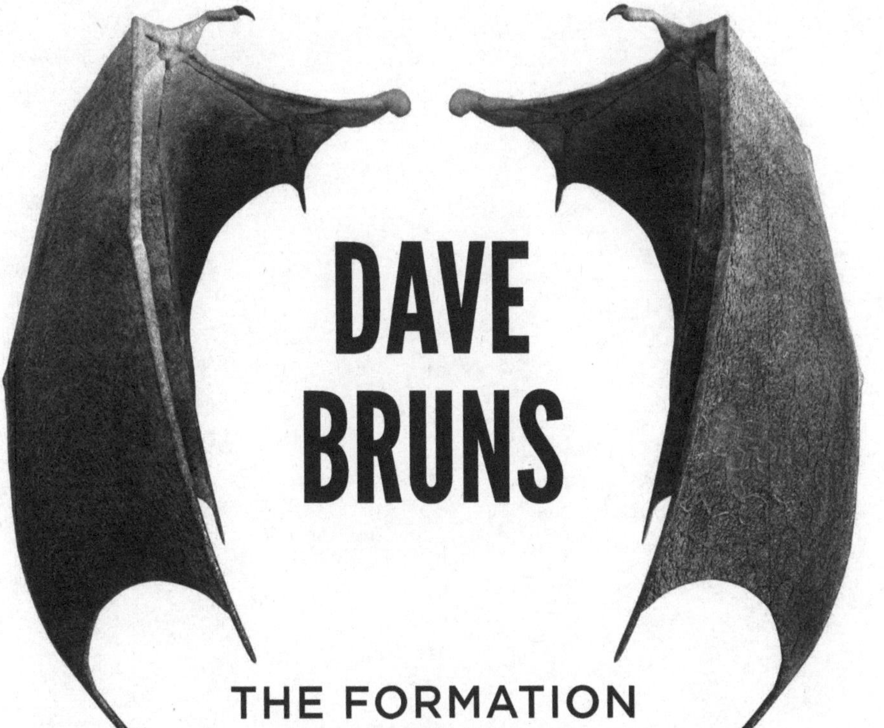

DAVE BRUNS

THE FORMATION OF THE PACK

"You hear 'em before you see 'em, that's for sure."

The old man looked like he was part of the southwest Texas desert—leathery skin, bald with cancerous lesions dotting his head. The diner had been there in the middle of nowhere for more years than Carl Boyd had been alive and the old man had run it from the start. The kind of place locals loved and tourists avoided like the plague.

"And they asked for me, by name?"

"Well, they asked for Tico before they asked for you, but I wasn't about to tell them anything about you, and I sure as hell wasn't going to tell them anything about Tico. I don't have no death wish."

"Any idea why they wanted to talk to me?"

"I figure they know that you know Tico. Get to him through you. I'm just a poor old man trying to get by out here. You? You got connections."

Carl stretched, yawned, then returned to his coffee. Perplexed. Carl's province was the sky. The Pack ruled the roads.

In New Mexico. Not here. Why was a New Mexico–based motorcycle gang looking for Tico? Well, Tico had lots of people looking for him, but most were too fearful of his reputation and the Desperadoes, his two bodyguards, to be very open about it. The Pack was notorious for their brutality and their heavy involvement in the Southwestern drug trade but their reach had always been limited to several chapters in New Mexico and a couple in Colorado. Hells Angels they weren't, but they were bad enough to get Carl's attention.

He knew only what he read in the news—the leader of the Pack was a guy named Revv, two Vs, like a Harley throttle being gunned, not one V like a minister. Nothing remotely holy about Revv. He'd served a twelve-year stretch in the New Mexico State Penitentiary for manslaughter after killing the leader of another club in a dispute over who got to show their colors in a roadhouse east of Albuquerque. He survived the 1980 riot there and took up where he left off upon his release, all the harder for the experience. In a year he built a drug empire around a series of meth labs in remote areas of New Mexico. Even based on the little Carl read, he knew he wanted nothing to do with the Pack or Revv. But then Carl wasn't much one for backing down and he didn't like having to look over his shoulder.

"Did this guy say he'd be coming around again?"

"Well, he said he'd be seeing you—maybe not here. Just thought you should know they was here and I wanted you to know I didn't tell them nothing. I don't need trouble with you." Carl had a reputation, too. Enhanced by rumors of his recent excursion into the Darién Gap. Rumors of blood and gold, antiquities and slaughter. The rumors didn't do the event justice.

"I'm around. You know how to reach me if you hear from these guys again. I'll talk to Tico, see if he knows what it's about. Do what you have to do—I don't want you getting hurt in this.

Just let me know what you know as soon as you can." Carl stood and stretched. He was not an imposing figure at five foot ten and 170, but it was all wiry muscle, and he projected a presence like a tightly coiled spring. *Revv might want to rethink messing with these boys*, thought the old man as Carl pushed through the door into the blazing Texas sun.

When Carl needed to think he let his mind take flight. Literally. In a Cherokee Six, his new plane, the first he bought and owned himself. Smuggling was profitable. Had its downsides, but the money made the risks tolerable. He wanted nothing more than to take flight right now, but as he stepped into his Jeep, he knew that beating the force of gravity was going to have to wait. The first call was a trip to his adobe to check on Nikki and let her know to be alert for the sound of twenty or thirty Harleys on the road half a mile distant. Tell her to keep the Charter Arms .38 handy. She'd used it before, but he hoped she wouldn't need it again. Then into Malagua to fill Tico in on the old man's story, see if he knew why the Pack might be interested in meeting him.

Tico had long ago abandoned the drug business. He ran a bar and a laundry in Malagua now, the bar serving beer and burgers, the laundry washing hundreds of thousands in cash for various illegal enterprises. Revv didn't sound like the kind of guy who would care about the Feds poking around in his finances. Strictly a cash business, the money stored around the desert, nothing to trace, no taxes to pay, no central business location to raid. Revv and the Pack lived on their bikes and never used banks, so there was no need to launder their revenue from the meth trade. Leaving Carl confused about their desire to find Tico.

Twenty minutes in the Jeep brought Carl to the dirt track leading to his tiny house. She would be there, maybe making lunch, maybe reading, maybe playing with the big mastiff mix Carl found in the desert and named Cherokee. He hated seeing her in danger but she knew and accepted the risks of living with him. It bothered him that this time he had no idea what the risk was or if there even was a risk.

The big dog knew the sound of the Jeep. Carl had rescued him from the life of a desert stray, fed him, and gave him water after the dog ran from his abusive owner. The dog returned the favor, saving Carl and Tico from an enemy from Tico's past. The dog ran into the small parking area to greet Carl. Nikki wasn't far behind. A tight hug, a long kiss. No, Carl wasn't going to put her in danger if he could help it.

"So how did the mysterious diner meeting go?"

"Hard to say. Sounds like trouble, though."

"Really? I'm shocked. It's always trouble with you, Carl. I just need to know what kind of trouble?"

"Not sure but looks like it involves Tico."

"Oh, it involves Tico. Now I'm really surprised." Totally deadpan. Like she said, it was always trouble and it was always Tico. "Good thing Tico's my favorite person in the world. Well, second favorite."

"Look, I'm not even sure it's trouble—could just be somebody who wants to do business."

Her mouth twisted into a smirk. "We both know better. You need to get into Malagua and give him the heads-up. Who's involved in this 'might not be trouble' trouble?"

"A guy named Revv. Two Vs. Heads up a motorcycle club in New Mexico."

"Yeah, right, a club. You mean gang, Carl. Just say it. I told you long ago I'm in with you on whatever you do, so let's get it done. Just tell me what I can do."

"Right now just keep the .38 nearby and keep an eye on Cherokee. Don't think these guys know where I live, but it pays to be ready. Like the diner man said—you'll hear 'em before you see 'em. If you do see them, take Cherokee and head out in the desert. I'll see how Tico wants to handle it and get back as soon as I can."

"This puzzles me, Carl. I have dealt with drug gangs, arms dealers, and any number of bad actors. But never any with known connections to motorcycle gangs. Of course, I know of the Pack, but only what I hear through my sources." Tico had hoisted his small frame onto a barstool, swiveling away from the bar and his open detective novel to face Carl. There was nothing intimidating about his physical presence, but Carl knew the stories and had seen him in action in Mexico and Texas. Underestimating Tico was a dangerous proposition. His two bodyguards, the Desperadoes to Carl, hovered nearby. Carl had never learned their real names, just knew they had fearsome and well-deserved reputations and intense loyalty to Tico.

"Has me stumped, too, Tico. But let's approach it from a different angle. You don't have any dealings with bikers but you do with marijuana dealers and gunrunners. Any of them have ties in New Mexico or southern Colorado?"

"I see where you are going with this, Carl. There is merit to that approach, and immediately, a man comes to mind. Brian Stallworth. I have worked with Mr. Stallworth for only a short time. I recently cut connections over a dispute about the percentage of my cut from his ill-gotten gains. He agreed to 20 percent, then later learned that some others only pay fifteen. He was angry. I explained the biblical story from Mathew 20." Not a biblical scholar, Carl looked confused. Tico explained.

"A man hires workers to harvest a crop. Some work a full day, some work less, but all are paid the same. Those who worked longer complained, but they had agreed to the wage and got no sympathy from the landlord. Mr. Stallworth did not feel the analogy pertained to him. Nevertheless, I took the agreed-upon 20 percent. He told me that I had not heard the last of him. Perhaps he is outsourcing his intended vengeance?"

"Well, we could always ask Revv. How about I talk to Harold, the diner man, and set up a meet? At this point, he just sees me as a pathway to you. I can sound him out, see what's up?"

"I appreciate that you would do that for me, Carl. Please be careful though. I would not like to explain to Nikki that I put you in any danger. You would be a challenging adversary but Nikki . . . Nikki would terrify me." Smiling the little smile that was the last smile a lot of men had seen.

Revv adjusted the shaded goggles on his face and stared into the desert. He sat astride his Harley Shovelhead, focused on the diner a quarter mile distant. Waves of heat distorted the image but he could make out the green Jeep Wrangler in what passed for a parking lot. The vehicle he was told to look for. Behind him, twenty more Harleys burbled the trademark "potato" sound of an idling engine. A scruffy group for sure, tattooed and bearded, cutoff jean or leather jackets with the club emblem, a wolf riding a flaming bike, stitched on the backs.

"OK, looks like our man," Revv said, turning to his vice-president, Grime. "Take five guys around back, pick five to stay here and five to cover the other end of the road. You and me, Lobo, Wildman, Weed, and Bob attend the meet. If there's anybody in the diner, they go out before we start. I want this guy alone."

Grime turned and shouted directions to the group, bikes peeling off as he did, headed to their assignments. The noise drowned most of Grime's orders but the crew knew their jobs. No need for a lot of communication. *Like a well-oiled machine*, thought Revv. Good to know he could count on them. Revv's rule: Finish the job for the client. The meth trade was profitable, and he wasn't sure that getting into this new line of work was the best idea, but it was a condition of working with Brian Stallworth, and Stallworth ran one of the biggest drug wholesale operations in the Southwest. So do what needed to be done up here, then back to the familiar home turf of New Mexico. *Finish the job.* And this was step one. Revv kick-started the Shovelhead and eased onto the road to the diner.

Carl heard them coming before he saw them. The roar of twenty Harleys at full throttle was deafening. The entire group circled the dusty parking area a couple times, raising a cloud that made it difficult to know how many bikes were out there. The noise abated some as most of the bikes split off and moved away from the diner. When the cloud settled, six men sat on their bikes facing the front door. The point was to intimidate Carl, but Carl had flown weed for Diego Fuentes in Monterrey, rifles for FARC in Colombia, and had fought the Pathet Lao in Southeast Asia. He didn't intimidate easily. He sat patiently on a barstool, watching the six while Harold, the diner owner, crouched behind the bar cradling a sawed-off Remington. Carl had to give him credit. Scared or not, he had picked a side and was prepared to go to war. Carl didn't figure that was going to be an issue, and he wished Harold would go back and hide in the freezer. He didn't want anything to happen to the old man.

The riders were stepping off their bikes, two of them backing toward the door, checking for an ambush or making sure their buddies were in place—maybe both, Carl thought. The tall, clean-shaven one in the center paid no attention. Carl figured him for Revv. Like Tico with the Desperadoes, he had no fear because his lieutenants had it under control. Carl sighed and moved away from Harold and the bar, picking up his Shiner Bock and striding to a booth near the big picture window that fronted the diner.

—

Revv was a bit surprised. Guy didn't look like much. Not even six foot, but Revv had learned in prison that size didn't always count for much. The New Mexico State Pen riot saw some big guys die at the hands of a little guy with a blowtorch and the malice to use it. Wouldn't pay to underestimate this guy. Revv had heard stories—plane crashes, gunfights, jungle warfare—this Boyd guy had seen it all and was sitting here calmly sipping a beer. Boyd raised a hand and swept it across the empty dining room. "Just us. Have a seat, boys." The place did look empty and Boyd wasn't obviously armed. Revv signaled Grime to stand at the door while two other bikers walked into the kitchen. Carl wasn't sure where Harold had gone, but the bikers hadn't seen him.

"Nobody here, Revv." One of the kitchen bikers reported back, and then he disappeared toward the back door. Carl was impressed. An almost military operation. Revv and the other two bikers took seats facing Carl. Revv was upright, attentive, and aware. The other two lounged back, convinced that no threat existed.

"You're Boyd." Not a question, so Carl didn't answer. He just met Revv's eyes, holding his gaze until the biker chieftain looked away.

"You wanted to meet. We've met. You know I'm Boyd, I know you're Revv. Anything else, or can I finish my beer in peace?"

"Tico." The name hung between them. Carl continued to look into Revv's eyes, waiting. "Your friend. I want to meet him. Not in town, not where there are cops. I got business with him."

"Lots of people have business with Tico." They had talked and sketched out the rudiments of a plan, but it was left to Carl to improvise. Tico would adjust. "And I do business with Tico, but 'friend'? I don't know about that. If you want to meet him, why are you talking to me? Tico has a bar in Malagua. He's easy to find."

"Like I said, not in town, no cops. He's got people there I'd rather not deal with. You're going to convince him to meet me. Out here. In the desert. Business will be brief. I just have a message for him. Once he gets the message, we're out of here. But I always finish my business. So, here, out in the desert, or in town where there's lots of innocents if things go south. Your choice."

"I can get the word to Tico but he doesn't work for me, and I don't work for him. I don't mind acting as an intermediary but I expect something for my trouble. I'd say $2,500 should do it. I don't get him to the meet, you don't pay."

Revv didn't hesitate. "$2,500? No problem. You'll earn it." *Too easy*, thought Carl. *He has no plan to pay me. That means he has other plans.* Carl was pretty sure those plans included Carl and Tico's bones bleaching in the Chihuahuan Desert. So, no simple message from a business partner. Now Carl just needed to confirm who wanted the "message" sent.

"This message. I need to know no one gets hurt here. You want to put on a show for Tico, convince him what could happen if he doesn't hear the message, fine. But carrying out a threat here causes me problems because I'm the one who set up the meet. I'd like an assurance from your guy that he hasn't hired you to take out a rival on my turf."

"My guy? None of your business who my guy is. Let's just say he's not someone to trifle with, and in my neck of the woods, his name alone is enough to get his messages across. He's the biggest and has the deepest pockets so he gets what he wants. I speak for him, and I'm telling you, nobody gets hurt unless Tico forces our hand."

Carl had what he needed. Biggest guy in New Mexico and he did business with Tico. The only possibility was Stallworth. Revv should have just shut up but Carl figured guys like Revv like to hear themselves talk.

—

"On the topic of messages, there'll be one here tomorrow, same time. I'll try to set Tico up. If he agrees to come, Harold, the owner, will have the word on when and where. Any problems at the diner and the deal is definitely off. And Harold gets a hundred dollars for his trouble."

"I can live with that. Don't even think of backing out of this thing, though. I finish my jobs. As long as there's a paying client, he gets his money's worth."

—

Carl knew about rules and respected those who lived by them.

But Revv's history didn't support the notion that he was a man of his word. Carl guessed he'd have an opportunity to find out. Revv was standing now, an almost imperceptible movement of his head drawing the other five bikers to him, two stepping outside and scoping the landscape before giving Revv and Grime the thumbs-up. In minutes, the parking lot filled with bikers gunning their engines. Carl wasn't really impressed. He'd seen a lot of tougher guys, guys who terrified people merely by walking through a door. Guys like Jorge in Colombia. Guys like Tico. But the bikers were still a formidable group and they didn't plan to leave any witnesses. Twenty-one guys on bikes against Carl and Tico. The Desperadoes got the numbers closer to balanced but Carl could see that he needed something to tip the scale. And he had an idea.

That went better than expected, thought Revv. But in that little part of his brain that focused on survival, some neurons were firing. Warnings. Boyd's easy acquiescence didn't fit with the man's reputation. No threats had been necessary, no bargaining, just a straight cash deal. Boyd was supposed to be a straight shooter, loyal to his friends. Revv wasn't buying Boyd's act and he was convinced that the job wasn't going to be easy despite the small army he commanded. A lot of things could go wrong, and the Pack better be ready for anything. He turned toward Grime. "Fire 'em up, we're out of here!"

"I think this could work, Carl." Tico was a little surprised that Carl had thought the plan through so thoroughly. He was a bit of a hothead whose standard MO was to charge headlong into action and overcome adversaries by sheer will. This plan was simple but as effective as one could be when the odds were twenty-one to four. "Please relay the message to Harold, giving him the time and place. I will speak with my men."

"You sure they'll be OK with this? The numbers are way skewed against us."

"I can only assume that's not a serious question, Carl. They will be there and I will be there. But we will be counting on you. You hold the key to this operation."

Carl's excitement had tempered by the time he left Tico's. The initial rush of adrenaline, the "Hey, this could work" moment, had passed and he was faced with the reality that his small group would be facing a pack of twenty-one bikers who had proven both vicious and competent. Of course, those two adjectives could apply to Tico and his Desperadoes as well, and Carl had certainly had his moments. The only thing not in question was that the standoff would be ugly. For one side or the other. But Carl figured he had an edge. If everyone else was on board, the odds just got a little better.

They met at the diner. Carl, Nikki, Tico, and the Desperadoes. Tico spoke first.

"Carl has developed a plan. The fact that Carl planned something instead of rushing in without thought and shooting people should be celebrated, but that will have to wait." A faint smile from Tico and laughter from the group. "Carl will explain. It is a good plan, but we must remember that no matter how good the plan, we are outnumbered twenty-one to four."

"Make that five." This from Harold who had pulled the old

Remington 12 gauge out from under the bar. "I'm not going to let these lowlifes ruin my business and push me around without a fight."

"Your courage is admirable, Harold, but you are perhaps too old and inexperienced to engage in this sort of enterprise."

"I'll tell you what, Tico. You're no spring chicken yourself, and I fought in Burma with Merrill and his Marauders. Guess that counts as some pretty damn good experience! I've killed a slew of men, and if it comes down to it, I can kill some more."

"Very well," Tico, a little surprised at the man's passion. "Welcome to our little tribe, sir. That makes it twenty-one to five."

"Six." Nikki spoke for the first time. "I'm not sure when I went bad, but you all have had a profoundly negative influence on me, and I want you to know how much I appreciate it."

"That is definitely not happening, Nikki." Carl and Tico replied in unison.

"Try and stop me, Carl. You know you can't. My mind is made up. Put me in the least danger if you want, but I shot a man before, and I think I can help. So shut up and move on."

Carl started to raise another protest but Tico was already talking.

"Fine. If things go well, Nikki should be safe. All of us should be safe. So now we are at twenty-one to six." A low growl from under Carl's chair broke the line of conversation. Cherokee was voicing his opinion.

"Guess that's seven," laughed Nikki.

Revv gazed up at the sun, unrelenting in its brilliance and heat. The Pack was camped in the desert, more from a desire to not attract attention than to save on camping fees. But the heat was brutal. *Not sure I'm cut out for this anymore.* Twelve years of his life gone over gang colors. His fortieth birthday was in the rearview, and his body was starting to feel the accumulated effects of hard drinking, hard fighting, and hard riding. No way to back out of this one, though. He had a client and money was paid. As long as he had a client and the client's money, he finished the job. A stupid rule in retrospect, but one he wasn't prepared to back away from.

He looked over at Grime. Grime would love to be in charge. Young, dumb, and full of cum, just like Revv when he was twenty-five. He'd learn the hard way, just like Revv. If he lived long enough.

"Grime! Get Bob and Magnum. You got to visit that old man!" Grime was a step slow, his face a little twisted toward a smirk. Not really insubordinate, just letting Revv and the rest know he wasn't going to ask, "How high?" when Revv said, "Jump." *Yeah, he'd take over given half a chance. And maybe I'll let him. After the job. After I finish my business.*

Two hours later Grime pulled alongside Revv, shouting over the noise of the bikes.

"Boyd was as good as his word. The old man had the directions. Only thing is, he says Boyd is going to be there. Wants his money and wants to make sure the old man gets his."

Revv was feeling less and less motivated. Boyd seemed like a guy you could ride with. A guy who would skirt the law but would always have your back. He wished Boyd wasn't going to be there, hated that he'd have to leave no witnesses. He had counted on Tico having some backup, but not enough, and not Boyd. Got to be done, though. He took the scribbled directions from Grime and studied them for a minute. Looked like a dirt road into a narrow box canyon. Revv figured he'd show up late, forcing Tico's back against the wall, leaving him no way out. Send a couple guys ahead to scope out an ambush. No way was

Tico showing up with twenty men. So he either was accepting his fate or he had a plan. Didn't matter. Revv was OK with playing the numbers game. He looked over his shoulder. Twenty of New Mexico's toughest bikers waiting for his word. He gave it and the crew fired up the engines and moved out in formation.

It looked surreal. Beyond imagining. Maybe the opening of a Fellini movie, the backdrop for the opening credits. This little guy in a neatly pressed suit, dark blue tie with a powder blue diagonal stripe, and Italian shoes standing in the middle of a deserted dirt road in the middle of nowhere.

They came to a stop a hundred yards away, feet down, eyes moving side to side, surveying the scene. Grime spoke first. "Looks like he's already dressed for the funeral." Revv wasn't so sure. It was more like a power suit for a business meeting where the guy in the suit held the power.

"So where's Boyd? The old guy said Boyd would be here. I don't see anyone."

Grime took another look around. "Could be up in those rocks down there. Maybe got a rifle?"

"Yeah, those rocks concern me, but they can't hide more than a handful of guys. Ride on back and tell the rest to be ready. I've gotta give this message personally. Part of the deal."

Grime hit the throttle, turned, and sped back to where the Pack was waiting. Revv moved in the opposite direction. Toward the man in the road.

Everyone was there. Everyone but Carl. Tico had survived worse, but he believed that a great calendar existed somewhere, and on one day, his name was entered in a neat hand. Perhaps the name had moved from page to page, the date had changed, had dark lines struck through it. But one day the name would remain. He had done what he could to ensure that today would not be the day his name was called. He watched calmly as the tall man on the motorcycle approached.

"You are Señor Revv, I suppose?"

"That's right. Got a message for you."

"I understood that was the case. And this message is from Mr. Stallworth?"

"Right again. Guess you know what the message is going to be, huh? Mr. Stallworth doesn't like the way you do business. Thinks other people he does business with won't respect him if he doesn't address the issue." Revv looked back over his shoulder before he continued. "That's the Pack back there. Blooded, every one of 'em. They do what I say. We'll end this here. Today."

"If I may speak?" Tico sounded almost deferential. Then the menace entered his voice. "If you are able to return to Mr. Stallworth, please tell him that I am not enamored with the way he conducts his business, either. He made an agreement but did not honor it. Honor in business dealings is very important to me."

"Yeah? Important to me, too. As long as I've got a paying client, I finish the job. Me and the Pack."

"Well, Señor Revv, we all have a pack. Some are like yours, large and loud. Others are small and efficient. But we all have our pack."

Revv heard a sharp metallic sound from his right. A big Mexican guy had appeared above the road, folding out a tripod up on the rock wall. The tripod didn't concern Revv. The .308 M60 attached to it did. As did the AR15 in the hands of the other big Mexican guy now visible on his left. And the ancient shotgun wielded by the old man from the diner, now stepping out from behind a giant boulder. *Never would have thought he had it in him.* The woman who joined Harold just had a pistol, but she looked like she knew how to use it. *Five. Versus twenty-one. My guys are armed, too, but this looks like it is going to get ugly. Has to be done, though.* Revv spun his bike in a circle, waving his arms overhead. The Pack moved out in formation. *Like the 7th Cavalry,* thought Revv. He didn't have time to reflect on the irony of his 7th Cavalry comparison because another thought intervened. *Wait, where's Boyd?*

They heard him before they saw him. The roar of the bikes drowned out the whine of the Cherokee's Lycoming engine until the last second. The riders in the front had almost enough time to react, but the shock of the plane coming at them head-high from behind froze them long enough to prevent that. The guys in the back had no chance at all. Bikes spilled over the dirt road, some merely spinning out and dragging their riders in tight circles, others pitching their riders into a deep gully that ran alongside the road. One of the Pack did a spectacular end-over-end flip, culminating in a headfirst collision with a large projection of limestone. A few, less injured, rose to their feet but dropped again as a line of bullets from the M60 raised dust just in front of them.

Revv was the last to fall and he could see Carl's dead, cold stare as the little plane forced him down and off his bike. He lay still for a moment, assessing what had just happened. The Pack was done, that was certain. But the job wasn't. His big Colt Python, jarred from his hand when Carl and the Cherokee forced him from his bike, lay in the road just beyond his reach. Tico's little pack was moving among the bikers, assuring they were out of commission, but Tico himself stood like a small statue where he had remained throughout the brief battle.

He could still end this, finish the job. He stretched a long arm toward the pistol, only to stop short when he heard a snarl and saw a salivating mouth and inch-long canines. He didn't know where the dog came from, but it was obvious he was never going to reach the gun. The battle was over. Revv just hoped to survive, maybe win the war. As long as he had a client . . .

Brian Stallworth loved his big house, his Bentley, and all the trappings the drug trade afforded him. Not so sure he loved the new gardener, though. As he stepped onto the front porch, he saw the guy standing by the car, admiring it. Big Mexican guy, probably planning to steal it. The last gardener was good but unreliable. Quit without notice. Family emergency, he said. The guy seemed real nervous, so whatever it was that made him quit must have been bad. He recommended this new guy who seemed competent but was kind of scary-looking. Like those guys in the old Tony Anthony movies.

"Hey, don't you have work to do?"

"Yes, señor, I plan to trim the hedges by the road."

"Then do it!"

The man nodded, picked up a sickle, and wandered off down the long driveway. *The hedges by the road.* Good. That put him a long way from the house where Stallworth's latest conquest was sleeping off a night of debauchery. Stallworth would check his work later, but now he had business to attend to. A quick drive in the Bentley for a meeting with Revv in Albuquerque. Somehow, Revv and twenty—TWENTY—bikers botched the job on Tico. Stallworth was getting a little tired of

Revv's "As long as I've got a client, I get the job done" shtick. The job didn't get done and Revv had a nice down payment of Stallworth's money pocketed. Stallworth planned to tear Revv a new one, get some assurances and a time frame. There were other guys out there who could do the job and Stallworth wasn't sure Revv's heart was really in this. One more chance and that was it. Stallworth turned back to the house to grab his keys.

—

The biker and the gardener stood just outside the gate, the biker astride his Harley. "That's a beautiful car, huh?"

"1961 Bentley S2, Caribbean Blue. It's a classic."

Revv was impressed. The gardener knew his cars. "I feel kind of bad. About the car, not Stallworth."

"Yes. It hurts me, too, but some things must be done, messages sent."

They saw it before they heard it. A brilliant flash of light, but the roar and the shock wave followed so closely that the three were nearly simultaneous. Steel, leather, and rubber rained down on the carefully manicured yard.

There was a brief silence, something like mourning. For the car, not Stallworth.

Revv broke it. "Looks like you're out of a job. So what now?"

"I'll return to Malagua," the gardener said, smiling. "I work for a guy who owns a bar there. A friend and I have work as bouncers."

Another pause. Revv saw a hand tighten on the sickle the gardener held. "And what about you, Señor Revv? What will happen now?"

Revv stared down the road for a moment. "Dunno. Grime took most of the crew to Arizona and plans to start a new chapter. A few guys split, a couple are still in the hospital. I got a rule that if I have a client, I always finish the job, but"—he waved his hand toward the yard—"doesn't look like I got a client anymore."

The gardener nodded his head. "And Tico?"

"Tell your boss I got no issues. It was always just business and my business with him is done."

The grip on the sickle loosened. Revv went on. "Pretty much tired of this life anyway. You're young. You'll learn. Comes a time when you gotta move on. Me, I might take the bike east. Never seen the Atlantic or New York. I hear New Orleans is great. I been around since the formation of the Pack. I had twelve years in the slammer, ten in this life. Time for a change. But where? I don't know." He twisted the throttle and the big bike roared like a wounded animal. The biker smiled. "Right now, I'm all revved up with no place to go."

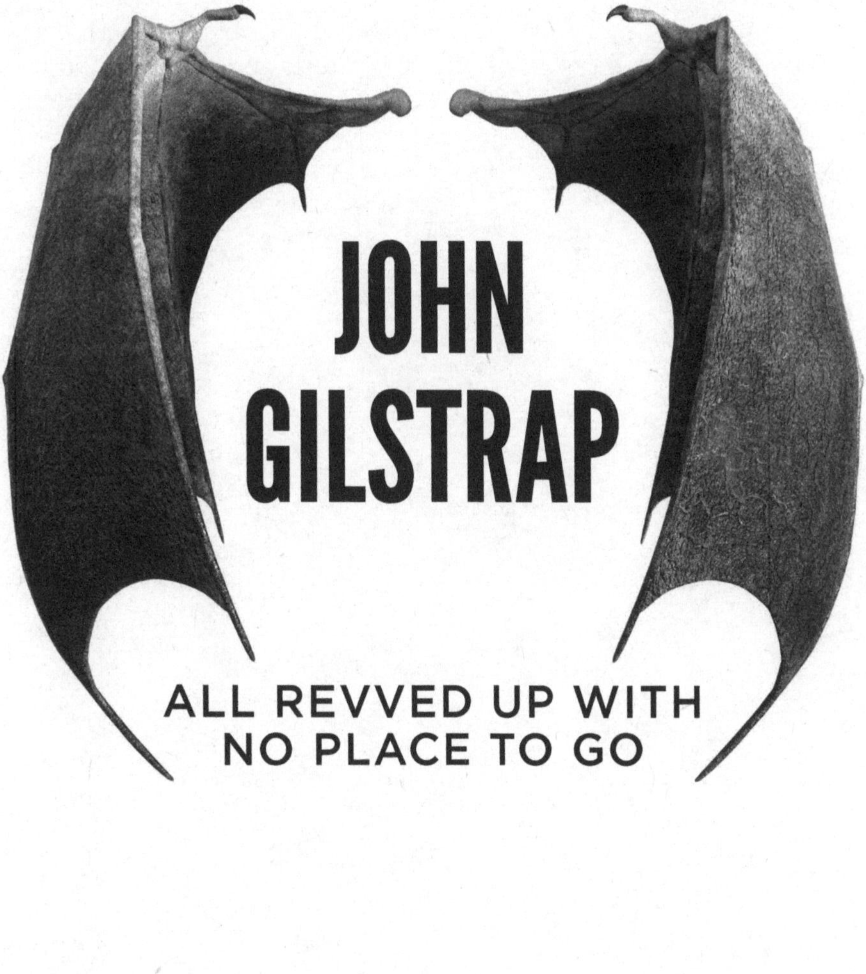

JOHN GILSTRAP

ALL REVVED UP WITH NO PLACE TO GO

"Dammit, Ace, slow down! You're going to kill us!"

"That's what seat belts and roll bars are for, Deb!" Ace hollered over the noise of the racing engine and rattling frame. "You said you wanted to go four-wheeling."

He'd done this fire road only twice before, and knew if she was panicking now, she was going to totally lose her shit in another mile when they started running parallel to the river. Roll bars didn't mean jack at the end of a fifty-foot fall off a rocky cliff.

"This isn't four-wheeling!" Deb shouted back. "This is suicide!"

"I know what I'm doing, babe, I promise. Enjoy the rush. Ain't nothing like it!"

His off-road Jeep Wrangler had been stripped to the frame, and he'd jacked the wheels up an extra six inches for additional clearance over rocks and roots. The suspension was as stiff as a horny teenager, so it took everything Ace had to keep his hands on the wheel and his feet on the pedals as they bounced and bounded down the dirt road cut. This hobby beat vehicles to death, triggering a constant stream of repair expenses, but the one area where Ace never cut corners was on the restraint system. His seat belts would be the envy of race car drivers and stunt pilots.

Airbags, well, not so much.

"Ace, you've proved your point!" Deb yelled. "I get it. You're good at this. Now, please, for my sake, please, please, *please* slow down!"

This was their third date, and he knew there wouldn't be a fourth. He'd totally misread the vibe she was throwing off. The day he first met her at the outfitter store, he had her pegged as a redneck adventure fiend, same as him. That flash he saw in her eyes when he said he did backwoods search and rescue for the fire service led him to believe that she might be his new bunkroom bunny.

The first date had been a standard dinner and movie thing, but she held her own splitting a pitcher of beer. On the second, they decided on a daytime adventure, which turned out to be an eight-hour hike along the New River Gorge, half of it in pouring rain, and she seemed to love it.

How was this power ride through the West Virginia woods not an extension of the same kind of fun? And goddammit, he wasn't even going all that—

He saw the hazard a half second before he hit it, and it registered as some kind of hole—either a deep depression in the ground or a wide space between erupted hardwood roots—and he hit it hard. First impact hammered the front tire, wrenching the steering wheel out of his grasp, and launching an impact wave from his tailbone through the top of his head.

After the impact, they took air. Ace didn't know what the hell happened next. The world spun both vertically and horizontally as the laws of physics thrashed him behind his seat belts.

"Fold your arms!" he yelled to Deb. "Don't let them get

outside the frame." Roll bars saved lives, but they also made for excellent amputation devices.

Ace hugged his elbows tightly to his chest as they rolled. Something flashed behind his eyes as his head slammed into the padded roll bar. He heard yelling. He thought it was Deb, but it might have been him. Hard to tell.

It seemed as if they would never stop tumbling and rolling and spinning, but when they did, the world was silent—no sound at all. It was also out of focus and devoid of color. Ace was dimly aware that something was wrong, but he couldn't quite—

—

". . . dare die on me, you son of a bitch. Now *wake up*!"

Ace didn't know that he'd been sleeping. Last thing he knew, he was bouncing down a fire road with . . . Why the hell was he hanging upside down? And who the hell was shouting at him?

"I'm awake!" he yelled. "Jesus, stop! I'm awake." When he turned his head to the right to get a look at the source of the bitchery, the movement launched a kaleidoscope of broken glass swirling through his brain. Sudden movements were not his friend.

His new girlfriend, Deb, looked stupid hanging upside down, with her long hair streaming straight out and puddling along the dirt beyond the spot where a headliner would be in any other car.

"Are you hurt?" he asked.

"I told you to slow down!"

True but unhelpful, he thought. "Are you *hurt*?"

"I've got bruises on top of bruises. What the hell were you thinking?"

"Okay, let me ask it this way," Ace tried again. "Are you *injured*?"

"No, but not because of you."

He guessed that meant she was okay. He took inventory of his own systems. He'd clearly lost consciousness. "How long was I out?" he asked.

"How would I know that?"

"Oh, for God's sake. How long have you been hanging upside down?"

"I don't know. Ten minutes maybe?"

He shot her another look, and this one didn't hurt as bad. "Ten minutes! Did you get knocked out, too?"

"Not that I know of."

"Then why—" He stopped himself. He realized it didn't matter why Deb didn't merely work the latches on her seat belts and get herself back to a stable position. She didn't do that, and the why of it really didn't matter.

It was his turn to do that very thing. Raising (lowering?) his left hand against the ground, he used his right to lift the flap on the clasp at the level of his belt buckle. At the speed of gravity, his shoulders dropped into the cradles formed by the shoulder straps, which stopped his momentum just enough to shoot his right hand to the ground next to his left. From there, a short push-up and a shrug got him free of the restraints, and he was able to slide out of the vehicle and help Deb extricate herself.

The act of moving and performing served as enough of a triage for him to know that he wasn't seriously injured. As for Deb, he didn't see any visible sign of damage. He took particular care to cradle her head as the belts let go so that the ground and her brainpan wouldn't have too awful an argument.

Judging from the way Deb was able to crawl free of the wreckage, she was also anatomically sound.

"Sorry about this," Ace said. There. Why not get out ahead of it? "It's not what I was planning."

Deb's cheeks reddened as she clearly considered launching another tirade, but to her credit, she controlled herself.

"Structurally, the Jeep looks in pretty good shape," Deb observed. "Any chance we can just roll it over and be on our way?"

Ace had contemplated the same thing until he stood to his full height and got a closer look at the undercarriage. "Unfortunately, no. Look there." He pointed with his forefinger. "The front axle snapped in two."

"And from the way you say that, I assume that's a fatal injury?"

Ace scoffed, "No, it's curable. But not without a tow truck and parts I don't have with me right now."

"Okay, let's call a tow truck," Deb said, pulling her phone from the pocket of her jeans. "We can use my Triple A card." Her smile disappeared an instant after she looked at her screen. "Zero bars."

No surprise there, Ace thought. "Welcome to the wild and wonderful Mountain State. Cell coverage sucks. You can drive for forty-five minutes and not have a signal."

"What about GPS?"

Ace walked around to the passenger side and stooped to gain access to the glove box. "Satellite navigation is less of a concern," he said. He pulled out an old-school compass and a folding USGS map. "As much as I'm in the backcountry, I'd be a moron not to have an analog backup." He reached back into the box and retrieved the Ruger Max-9 pistol that always resided there. When he stood, he put the map and compass in his pocket and clipped the holstered pistol to his belt, under his shirt.

Deb's features had folded into a deep scowl. "What are you planning to do?"

"We're going to hike out of here."

"Like hell we are."

"What's the alternative?"

"Seriously?" Deb gave him a look that read, *What kind of idiot are you?* "When you get lost in the woods, you're supposed to stay put so people can find you."

"We're not lost," Ace said. "I know exactly where we are. And exactly where we are is a long damn way from any place that can help us."

"People will come looking for us," Deb said.

"Who knows we're here?" Ace asked. "You didn't know because I didn't tell you, and I didn't tell anyone because, well, it didn't occur to me to tell anyone. Staying here is *not* the thing to do."

Deb crossed her arms and leaned against the upside-down grill. "You go ahead then. I'm staying here."

"Yeah, right, like I'm gonna do that," Ace said with a dramatic roll of his eyes. He checked his watch. "Look, it's almost one now and it's already getting chilly. It's supposed to go into the forties tonight. We don't want to be up here in the middle of nowhere when that happens."

"It gets dark around seven," Deb said. "Can we get back to civilization by then if we walk?"

"No, but we can get closer to it."

"But we'll still be in the middle of nowhere," she pressed. "What difference does it make which nowhere we're in the middle of?"

Ace felt his temper beginning to fray. "Are you being deliberately bitchy?"

"Bold talk for the macho jackass that nearly got us killed."

Deb wanted to fight and maybe he deserved it, but fighting now wouldn't help. They were in serious deep shit here. If they stayed on the fire road in either direction, they'd intersect a state road four miles behind them and four and a quarter ahead of them, but from either choice, the nearest house that he was aware of was still miles farther down the road.

"I don't think you understand," Ace said. "We are literally on the road to nowhere. There's no place to go from here. If the world's not on fire, or you're not willing to trespass like I am, we can wait here for days and never be seen. We need to move."

"Yes, you do!"

They both jumped at the sound of the basso voice that boomed at them from up on the road.

"Holy shit!" Ace exclaimed. "You scared the shit out of me." As he laughed at his embarrassment, he scanned the trees for a view of the person he was talking to. "Where are you?"

"Are either of you injured?" the man asked.

"No," Ace said. "Just a little bruised and humiliated."

"Does the lady have a voice?"

"Of course," Ace said. "She's—"

"I've got this," Deb said. "I'm Deb Farmer. This is Mike Spade—"

"People call me Ace."

"He's not the off-road driving guru he thought he was," Deb finished. She led the way climbing up the steep bank back up to the road.

Ace stayed close behind, his hand extended, ready to catch her if she fell backward. It took a good two minutes to get back up to the paved surface and finally come face-to-face with the man with the voice. Not as big as he sounded, the guy stood about six feet tall, and he wore hunter camo, complete with face paint and a floppy camouflage hat. He carried one long rifle with a scope on a sling that hung vertically down his front, along with another rifle Ace couldn't quite see slung by a strap over his shoulder in the back. A pistol of some kind was strapped to his chest in a holster.

"You're out here hunting?" Deb asked.

"I am."

"What's in season?" Ace asked. It was too early for deer, and the weaponry wasn't right for turkeys.

"The spoiled redheaded trespasser," the man deadpanned through flat features.

Ace tried to ignore the chill that raced down his back and forced a laugh. "I know, right?" he said. "But you've got to cook those real slow if you don't want them tough and gamy."

"Oh, I don't cook 'em," the man said. "I just shoot 'em and leave their carcasses for the wild hogs." His face didn't change, the scowl didn't soften.

"I didn't catch your name," Ace said.

"I didn't offer it to you. But you're Ace and Deb, right?"

"Doesn't seem fair that we don't know yours, too," Deb said.

"Life just sucks sometimes," the man said. "But since you're pretty, I'll tell you that it's Niles. Niles Decker."

"Pleased to meet you," Ace said. He made his smile bigger—the one that always charmed people.

"Oh, I don't think you are," Decker said. "Or, if you are, you shouldn't be. I guaran-goddamn-tee you won't be for long."

Ace was done with the creepy bullshit. "Okay, so I'm getting the vibe that you're not here to help us. I was going to ask you for a ride, or to use your phone, but—"

"I'm going to kill you, Ace," Decker said. "You and Deb both. Just like I killed the last two sets of shitheads that came through here treating my property like a raceway. A man buys a piece of property, he wants a little privacy, you know?"

That chill down Ace's back had infested his whole body. He was suddenly very aware of the pistol on his hip. Problem was,

Decker was loaded for war, and Ace's Ruger wasn't even chambered. By the time he drew the weapon and racked the slide—

"You're just joking, right?" Deb asked. Her voice quivered.

"I kinda wish I was," Decker said. "I take no pleasure in killing you folks, I tell you that, but some things just gotta be done. I'll take your phones."

The shift in topic startled Ace. "What? Why?"

Decker made a show of shifting his grip on his rifle. "Do you really think this is a good time to be asking questions? The last groups I made get naked to go on their run through the woods. At least I'm not doing that with you. Well, not yet. Unless you ask more stupid questions." When he smiled, Decker's teeth gleamed unnaturally bright white.

In unison, Deb and Ace slipped their phones out of their pockets and held them out as they approached.

"No, no, stay where you are," Decker said. "You can just toss them to me. Not at me, mind you, but to me. Let them fall to the ground at my feet."

They both did as they were told.

"You any good with that peashooter on your belt?" Decker asked.

"I'm okay," Ace said.

Deb stomped her foot. "Ace!"

"Don't be mad at him," Decker said. "He done the right thing. He didn't say he was a marksman, didn't say he could shoot birds on the wing out of the sky. Said he was *okay*. I want somebody to be at least that good if he's gonna be carrying a firearm in public."

Ace knew the order to disarm was coming, but he didn't want to reach for the pistol until he was told to.

"I want you to keep that," Decker said. "Gives you more of a sporting chance."

"To do what?" Deb asked.

"To survive and get out of here alive," Decker said.

Just like that, in an instant, things crystallized in Ace's mind. "You're going to *hunt* us?"

Decker clapped his hands once and tapped his forefinger in the air. "Bingo. Give that handsome young man a gold star. Where've you been? Got cotton in your ears?"

Deb took a reflexive step back. "Why would you do that?"

"Why do you trespass on other people's property? Why are crows black and cardinals red? The world is filled with perplexing questions, isn't it?"

Okay, this guy was crazy. That was Ace's first data point, and crazy meant unreliable. Crazy meant liar. It also meant murderer. The Ruger on his hip seemed to be calling his name.

"Go ahead and try it, Ace," Decker said through a wide smile. "I know what you're thinking because I'd be thinking the same thing. This rifle here is a Remington Seven Hundred, chambered in three hundred Win Mag. Don't know if you understand guns, but with this, I can reach out and blow a hole through you at three thousand yards. If you think you can clear your holster and get off a shot before I do the same, I guarantee we'll never be this close again."

Ace's heart hammered hard enough to bruise itself against his breastbone. They say the eyes are the windows to a man's soul, and Decker's eyes were obsidian black and set hard. This man meant every word he said.

"I-I'll make you a deal," Ace stammered.

"Ace!" Deb was horrified.

"Oh, w-w-will you now?" Decker mocked. "I can't wait to hear."

"We'll do it like cowboys," Ace said. As he spoke the words, he couldn't believe he was speaking them. "You put down the rifle, and we'll go pistol to pistol. It'll be a fairer fight."

Decker threw back his head and laughed. It was a hearty, throaty thing, genuinely amused. "A fairer fight? Fair fights are for idiots." He laughed again. "No, I'll keep my advantages, thank you very much. And for what it's worth, that peashooter at least gives you a chance. Your clothing and your shoes at least give you a chance. All of that's more than I gave the assholes who died before you."

For a long time—it felt like a minute, but that wasn't possible, was it?—they all stood still and stared at each other.

Deb broke the silence. "So . . . How does this work?"

"How does it *work*? You mean, what are the rules?"

Deb's head moved in a kind of spastic nod. "Yeah."

"You're funny," Decker said. "Okay, you want rules, I'll give you rules. Here they are. Pay close attention now because while they're not complicated, they're very important. You ready?"

Ace added his nod to Deb's.

"All right. You pick a direction and run toward it. Run fast and tell yourself you have a chance of living till morning. If I see you, I'll kill you. Muzzle velocity of almost thirty-two hundred feet per second. Whichever one of you I hit won't have any idea you've been killed. But Christ almighty, it'll scare the shit outta the other one."

"How big a head start do we get?" Ace asked.

"I don't know. A minute? An hour? Ten minutes? Ten seconds? I haven't made up my mind yet. But if I's you, I'd be running by now."

Ace reached for Deb's hand, but she pulled away. They took a step back. Another. Another.

Decker lunged from the waist up. "Shoo!"

That was it. Ace spun on his heel and took off at a dead

run, heading straight down the road for the first fifty, maybe hundred yards, before cutting to the left and charging into the woods. Fifty steps in, a vine caught his right ankle, causing him to pirouette into the trunk of a thick hardwood. He didn't quite hit the ground, but it was close. As he recovered his balance, Deb blew past him, slaloming between the trees and heading progressively deeper into the forest.

"You're an asshole," she called over her shoulder as the forest swallowed her.

Pushing himself off from the tree, he started to follow, then stopped himself. This Decker asshole wanted them to panic. He *needed* them to panic. That was part of his sick psycho game.

It was okay to be scared shitless—which was great, because that's squarely the space Ace was occupying now—but panic brought bad decisions.

Come on, he told himself. *This is your wheelhouse.* Whether searching for a lost hiker or fighting a forest fire, it was impossible to overstate the importance of always knowing where you were. You couldn't just run randomly through the forest and hold any hope of ever being found—or of ever finding civilization. He settled himself with a deep breath, dared a glance behind him around the tree, and then pulled the map from his pocket and opened it.

He should have done this two or three hundred yards ago. Woulda coulda shoulda.

He needed to settle down. His trembling hands made it difficult to separate the edges of the map and spread it out flat.

"Where am I?" he whispered. "Where am I? Where am I?"

He needed to find the main road they'd turned off of—Route 1732—and, from there, find the church building with the graveyard. The fire road would be four-tenths of a mile north of that spot.

A US Geological Survey map is different from your average road map. These maps didn't care about roads as much as they cared about geological features such as elevations and rivers and streams. Buildings were marked by tiny squares, and elevations by contour lines—the closer together the lines, the steeper the slope. Ace had been reading these things his whole life, but it still took thirty seconds or more to orient his vision and his brain to interpret the markings into useful data.

"There you are," he whispered. He put his finger on the intersection he was looking for and then traced the fire trail to the point where it started to parallel the cliff that dropped down to the river. Then he backed up what felt like the right distance to the approximate spot where they'd wrecked. From there, he gave his best guess of the route he'd run so far, used a stick to poke a hole in the map, and declared it to be his current location. Precision navigation this was not, but being in the ballpark was better than being clueless.

If he could keep the river on his right, he'd be continually heading nominally west, and sooner or later that would have to intersect with Route 7229, a north–south route that would eventually lead to something that looked like civilization. He refolded the map in a way that the face showed his location, and stuffed it back into his pocket. He pointed his compass west and started walking.

What the hell was he supposed to do about Deb? An hour or more into this walk, that question still nagged at him.

This was new territory. Where did chivalry begin and end? She'd called him an asshole, for crying out loud, before running off to whatever she thought she was running off to. Since she'd made her choice, did he owe it to her to find her and get her to safety? Wouldn't that be part of the macho mindset that so pissed her off before? She'd made her choice *despite* knowing that he was armed and skilled in woodland navigation.

Maybe it was a blessing that they'd split. If they stuck together, they'd make an easier target. They'd make more noise and be easier to track. Plus, if past was precedent, Deb would whine about every decision Ace made, injecting unnecessary doubt into his own mind.

Plus, Deb would undoubtedly have a better chance of survival if she ran into Decker and Ace wasn't with her. None of this was her fault. Maybe she'd talk sense into Decker and earn some mercy from him. It was probably a long shot, but it was something. A better chance than she'd have if she was caught in Ace's company.

It had been too long anyway. They'd been moving separately for at least ninety minutes now. God only knew where she'd run to—or if she was still running. He could spend valuable time putting space between him and Decker, or he could spend that time chasing her down with near-zero chance of success.

"Sorry, Deb," he said softly. "You're on your own."

When hiking like this, distance and time are measured in strides. Ace guesstimated that each step he took spanned three feet, which would be six feet traveled every time his right foot touched the ground. Ten touches, sixty feet. One hundred touches, six hundred feet. He did the math in his head. When his right foot touched the ground 880 times—round it up to 900—he'd have gone a mile.

Holy shit, that's a lot of steps.

On flat ground, he knew he could average four miles per hour, but the complications of walking through the forest while off the trails would cut that back to maybe two, two and a half, max. Because of all the rocks and deadfalls, he'd break his legs—or his neck—if he walked with his nose buried in his compass. The trick was to sight in a landmark—a unique-looking tree or bush that sat due west of where he was and then walk to the landmark. From there, he would take aim at a new object and do the same thing. Over and over and over again.

People get lost in the woods because they naturally walk in circles. Without a visual reference to target, our dominant leg overpowers our weaker leg, pushing us a tiny bit to the weak side with every step.

He knew a thousand little survival details like this but none of them applied to keeping him from getting shot. He couldn't shake that crawly feeling that crosshairs were centered somewhere on his body for a kill shot.

What could he do about that? Decker made a big deal about his rifle being deadly at a million miles, but what good was the range if he couldn't see the target? All these trees had to give him ample cover, right? Of course. That's what he was betting on, anyway.

He picked up his pace. The more distance he put between himself and Decker's arsenal, the better his chances of survival.

His thoughts drifted back to Deb. There was no way that this could end well for her. How hopelessly lost was she by now? Was she even alive still?

If he survived and she didn't, how was that going to make him look? What were people going to think of him? What were they going to say about him?

Were people going to say he was a coward? He could almost see it in his head, finally stumbling into a place where he could get help, the police arriving, and with them, the reporters. What was he going to say when they inevitably got to the question, "What happened to Debra Farmer?"

He could always tell them that they got separated. That was generic enough. People always—

What was that?

He slid to a stop and listened. He could swear he'd heard a voice, but now all he could hear was his own heaving breath. He inhaled and held it.

Now, all he could hear was his pounding heart.

Maybe it was nothing.

No, nothing was what he *wanted* it to be.

"Ace!"

Very far away, but that time he definitely heard it.

"Ace, where are you?"

Shit. Why was she yelling like that? What was she thinking? That was tantamount to raising a flag and announcing, "Here I am! Shoot me! Shoot me!"

"Ace! I'm lost! I think I broke my ankle! Help!"

At least that's what he thought she said. So, so far away. Ace closed his eyes, clenched his fists, and stomped at the ground. "God*dammit*," he spat.

Well, he couldn't very well leave her now, could he? What if she *survived*? A scene formed in his mind like a nightmare. There he was, freshly rescued, lamenting having gotten separated, only to have Deb show up a day or two later to tell the press how she called and called for help only to have him ignore her cries.

He could claim to have never heard her, but people wouldn't believe him. Social media would tear him apart.

"Ace! Please! If you can hear me, let me know! I need help!"

The sound was coming from his left—from the south, though the woods were famous for masking the direction of sounds. For sure, the one thing he *wasn't* going to do was shout out in reply. He was crazy enough to be listening to her. He wasn't going to prove abject insanity by announcing his position.

He started walking that way. He'd keep walking due south until he started hearing the voice from a different direction, and then he'd shift to go that way. As long as he didn't double back to go east. That would mean undoing the work he'd done so far.

Once he found Deb—if Decker hadn't already shot her by the time he found her—as long as they continued to walk due west, they would still intersect Route 7229. He wouldn't know where on the road they were, but it would take them sooner or later to someplace useful.

"Please don't leave me out here! Please help me!"

"Please shut the hell up," he grumbled.

No, he thought, she needed to keep shouting. If she didn't shout, then he'd never be able to locate her.

On the other hand, if she did stop, he'd have a plausible reason not to have to deal with her. If she'd truly broken her ankle—or even seriously injured it—that was going to slow them down a *lot*. They'd never get out of the woods before nightfall, and for all he knew, Decker had high-tech night vision that he could use to track them.

Or heat-seeking technology on a drone. That thought made Ace's stomach hurt. He'd seen it in a movie. People are hotter than trees and foliage, so heat-seeking radar, or whatever it's called, can see right through a canopy of leaves to find people and target them.

"Oh, God, Ace, please help me! Don't let me die out here! Let me know you can hear me!"

Ace placed his feet carefully, trying his best not to step on sticks, but this time of year, it was damn near impossible not to make noise when you moved through the woods. He was definitely getting closer. The sound of Deb's voice was becoming louder, the tone clearer.

Where the hell was Decker? Why wasn't he taking his shot at Deb while she was making such a ruckus?

Maybe the killer was in the same position as Ace, zoning in on the sound—

Ace jerked to a stop and dropped down to one knee. Up ahead, maybe twenty yards away, a face was staring at him.

"Jesus!" He said it louder than he wanted to.

Hands trembling, he remembered the Ruger on his hip, and he drew it, cursing himself that he still hadn't racked the slide to chamber a bullet. He dropped the compass onto the mulchy forest floor and worked the slide to fix the problem. Another noise that was too loud, but his instructor on the range had made a big deal out of the fact that if you don't let the spring close hard, you run the risk of the bullet not seating properly. This was not the time for a misfire.

For all the noise, though, the face didn't move, didn't react at all.

"Ace! Please come find me!"

With both hands on the pistol, his finger hovering over the trigger guard, Ace rose to a squat and moved ever so slowly toward the guy looking at him. He'd closed the distance by half when he saw that the face was barely even a face anymore, and the man was really only half a man, a torso. His eyes were gone, the flesh of his cheeks reduced mostly to just tendons and connective tissue. And the torso had been reduced to little more than bone. The skin and viscera were all gone, presumably consumed by predators. Now, a cloud of flies, and churning layers of bugs were taking care of the last bits.

Ace's stomach churned at the sight. He looked away. That must be what was left of one of the other people Decker said he had killed.

"Ace! I'm over here! Please!"

Holstering his pistol, Ace started to move back toward the sound of Deb's cries, then stopped.

The compass. He needed his compass. Where had he dropped it? It was back where he'd first seen the remains of the dead guy. But where was that?

"Shit." Everything out here looked the same. He was so freaked out by the sight of the dead guy that he didn't pay attention to anything else.

He retraced his steps to where he thought he'd been when he first saw it, but the ground cover was thick. He stooped to his hands and knees and ran his palms over the ground, but he still couldn't find anything.

"Ace! Please, Ace! Help me!"

"*Dammit!*" He cringed at the sound of his voice. He was being stupid now. He needed to calm himself down.

If the compass was lost, it was lost. He'd have to adapt. There'd be a way. He didn't yet know what it was, but there'd be a way.

Time to press on.

As the shouting continued and became clearer, Ace became progressively more bothered that Deb was still alive. Not that he wanted her dead, but it didn't make sense that Decker hadn't yet fulfilled his demented promise.

Five minutes later, he knew he was *very* close and he slowed his approach to a rate of less than one step per second, each time taking extreme care to place his foot silently.

"Ace! Please!"

That time, Deb's voice was so perfectly clear that she could have been just a few yards away. He froze.

Something wasn't right. The woods had changed in a fundamental way. He saw more light. The trees had thinned, and he realized that he'd been walking with far less effort for quite some time. Since he'd been following the sound of Deb's cries, the terrain had flattened out. Beyond the thinning trees lay an open field, and an open field was a death trap.

"I don't want to die here! Please! I'm hurt!"

Deb's cries were coming from the field, from beyond the trees. This wasn't right at all.

Standing absolutely still now, though he didn't know why, he moved only his head to take in his surroundings. A buzzing sound drew his attention to more naked remains, this man's guts likewise consumed by critters, but at least he was in one piece.

This clearing must be part of the game.

"Ace! Please!"

Oh, so slowly, Ace lowered himself to his knees and crawled closer to the edge of the tree line, taking care to stay back in the shadows. And there she was. Deb was tied to a post that had been driven into the ground. It was hard to tell the height of the post because she was sitting, but Ace guessed it to be four feet, and Deb looked to be thoroughly trussed, with her arms pinioned behind the pole and her waist and neck both cinched to it.

"You bitch," he whispered. She'd allowed herself to be turned into bait, and now she was trying to draw him out to be shot. He imagined a promise of survival in it for her if it worked. He also imagined there was a ticking clock. If Ace didn't show up within X amount of time, Decker would blow off her head and go about chasing Ace down separately.

Even though he didn't know Decker, it felt like something Decker would do.

But Ace wasn't going to play.

So, now what? As Deb continued to call out for him, he forced himself to tune her out and think through his options.

What did he know? Beyond the obvious, Decker had to be close, right? Sure, there was the bullshit about the three-thousand-yard shot, but he wasn't going to do this from a half mile away. And if he was going to make the shot, he had to have a clear view. That only made sense. He wasn't going to go through this elaborate setup and not have a clear view of his target.

And a clear view meant high ground.

Ace sat back and folded his legs under him as he pulled his map out of his pocket again. He oriented himself to the hole he'd made however many hours ago and imagined the rough distances he had walked. He knew for a fact that he'd gone due west for about two hours, so he traced a five-mile westward track, and then he tracked due south for another quarter mile. He marked that spot with another hole and then searched the map for flat terrain and a clearing.

The contour lines made it easy. There was only one patch on the map within the margin of error for his calculations that showed the wide separations he was looking for, and sure enough, there in the middle was an area devoid of trees. And on the western margin of the clearing, where the forest thickened again, the terrain rose sharply.

Where the hell was the western margin? Maybe he should have spent more time searching for the damn compass.

Time for old-fashioned methods—a trick his pop-pop had taught him on a long-ago camping trip. The post to which Deb was tied cast a shadow that he could see. The shadow terminated at a spot on the grass about five inches to the left of an erupted rock. He made a note of the spot in his mind and went about the business of staying invisible as Deb's cries became progressively more desperate. From her tone, he was convinced now that her life was on a countdown clock tied to him walking into this trap.

After what felt like ten minutes, Ace looked back at the

shadow cast by the post. The end of the shadow had moved farther to the left of the first spot. An imaginary line between those two points defined east and west, with the first point marking west. From Ace's viewpoint right now, that put the likely sniper's ridge ahead and to his right.

Now what? That was a lot of real estate.

"Ace! Please!" Deb had started to cry. Her clock must be ticking down to zero.

Now that Ace knew where to look, he started scanning the trees for some indication of where—

A bright white flash scared the shit out of him. He winced and waited for the impact of the bullet, but nothing happened. Not even the sound of a gunshot.

He hadn't realized he'd closed his eyes till he opened them again, and then he saw it again. Just a brief flash a few degrees off the horizon in the trees about 150 yards ahead of him. Almost like a flare of reflected—

It was Decker's rifle scope. It had to be! Holy shit! Holy holy shit shit!

Ace drew his pistol again because it seemed like the right thing to do, but come on. He couldn't make a shot like that. *Nobody* could make a shot like that. He couldn't even see the guy, for God's sake.

Ace had to get closer. He started advancing through the woods, closing the distance, sending out the magic invisibility vibes he used to employ during hide-and-seek games as a little boy. And no, they didn't work for shit back then, either, but there was no harm in trying.

He was a moron for doing this. He was certain to die in the process, but what were his options? He couldn't sit back there at the tree line and watch Deb get blown apart and then wait his turn. The smart move would have been to stick with his first plan and save his own ass. Ignore the screams, get the hell out of here, and go on to have a happy life. Hell, with Decker hanging out here waiting, Ace could have walked unmolested all the way to Ohio.

Ace tried to think like a sniper. In his mind, he saw Decker hunkered down in his lair, concentrating on the moment when his next target would bolt out of the woods and he could put a bullet through his brain. He figured that all of Decker's energy would be focused ahead on the field. That's why Ace had to come at him from a direction he wouldn't be looking at.

Maybe he could snipe the sniper.

The terrain had gotten way steeper in the last twenty or thirty strides, making it harder to walk quietly. His feet wanted to slip after every step.

"Ace! Please help me!" Deb could barely get the words out through her sobs now.

He needed to hurry, but at this distance, hurrying would give his position away. Him getting killed wouldn't help Deb. And it sure as shit wouldn't help Ace.

Off to his left, maybe fifty feet away, something moved in the bushes.

Ace froze. It could have been a deer, he supposed, or a breeze. But he knew it was Decker. Except it could have been his imagination. His Ruger Max-9 held twelve nine-millimeter bullets, which should be plenty to kill Decker at this range, but it wouldn't make a mark on his imagination. Still, he thumbed the safety off.

It moved again. Not his imagination.

Decker was settling his big Remington rifle into a tripod and pressing the buttstock into his shoulder.

"Aw, Debbie," he called out. "I'm sorry, honey. We can't say we didn't try our—"

Ace assumed the best stance he could, spreading his feet apart on the steep slope, his right higher than his left, the pistol grasped in both hands. He rested the front sight on the spot below Decker's left shoulder and he pressed the trigger.

The Ruger barked in Ace's hand at the same instant that Decker's .300 Win Mag split the universe with its ear-shattering report.

Ace fired again and ran forward.

He fired again and again and again. He didn't know how many times. Fewer than twelve, because the slide never locked back. He didn't shoot it dry.

Decker had dropped out of sight. He had to be dead, right? Or at least severely wounded. Even a terrible marksman would have hit him at least a couple of times with that many shots fired.

Ace closed the distance to about ten feet and stopped. It was time to approach slowly. The instant he saw anyone—any*thing*—that looked like Decker he was going to shoot him again. He'd seen this movie too many times, where the bad guy you knew was dead suddenly came back to life. Ace was going to put a bullet through Decker's head. He was going to kill him, wake him up, and kill him again.

The lair revealed itself a little at a time over the course of two seconds. First, he saw the clearing and a rifle propped up against a tree. It was an assault rifle, like the ones everybody talked about on the news. Then he saw a squatty folding chair, like one you'd use at the beach. This one was pink and green and black. A couple of orange candy wrappers. Reecey Cups?

But no Decker.

"Shit." Ace let his legs fold under him as he dropped to the ground and covered his head, waiting for the shot that would kill him.

Nothing.

"Ace! Kill him! Jesus, Ace!"

Nothing made sense now. He scrambled to his hands and knees, crawled through the shield of creepers and sticker bushes, and collided with the folding chair.

"Ace! Oh, my God, Ace!"

Decker had left his sniper's position and was stumbling across the field toward Deb, who was struggling in vain against her ropes. Ace had hit him, all right. The whole left side of Decker's body shimmered with blood. From this distance—twenty, twenty-five yards—Ace thought he could see blood pumping from a neck wound, and the killer listed heavily to his left.

Ace raised his pistol for the kill shot, but Decker was staggering too wildly not to risk hitting Deb. He glanced over at the black rifle, but he saw that the bolt was open—the bullets exposed—and he saw the switches and buttons he didn't know how to operate.

"Screw it."

Ace took off after Decker at a run. The killer wasn't moving fast, but a twenty-five-second head start was still a lot of distance to make up.

Ace dug in hard with each stride and pumped his arms hard. He wanted to be really damn close before he took his kill shot.

Ace didn't see the pistol in Decker's right hand until only fifteen feet separated them, and the killer whirled around with it extended at arm's length.

Reflexively, Ace threw himself backward as the pistol fired. He hit the ground hard, launching a flash of light behind his eyes, but if he was hit, the pain hadn't found him yet. He knew another bullet was coming. The first target he saw was Decker's knee and he shot it.

Decker fired again as he fell, and this time Ace felt something hot hammer his jaw.

The killer's face was a mask of agony as Ace watched it impact the grass. He might have been screaming, but Ace couldn't hear it. He couldn't hear anything.

In his silence, he fired his final five bullets into Decker's face, stopping only when the slide locked back.

If the sonofabitch wasn't dead by then, well, to hell with it.

Ace rolled to his back and looked at the sky. He wanted to check his jaw for damage, but his hands felt too heavy. Somebody had drained all of the color out of the world. The clouds actually seemed . . .

"Ace!"

"I got nothin'," he tried to say, but his mouth didn't want to work. His face felt five sizes too big. "If he's not dead yet, I'm out of bullets."

Somebody had re-inked the sky and the trees. He gently lifted his right hand to explore his jaw and found a trench carved out of his flesh. It felt like the width of a finger, and it hurt like shit, but it didn't seem to be bleeding too badly. And hey! He could lift his hand now.

"Oh, thank God you're alive. I thought you'd killed each other."

Ace didn't want to move. He worried that moving was going to launch lightning bolts, but to be honest, he couldn't think of an alternative.

He rolled gently to his left side, then pressed himself to a sitting position. Yeah, Decker was most definitely dead. Dead times five. Brains dangled out of cracks in his face. Ace looked away and crawled on all fours over to where Deb sat trussed to her stake.

"Oh, my God," she said when she got a good look at him. "You look terrible. Were you shot?"

"A little bit," Ace said. His words slurred through his swollen jaws. From what he could tell, all his teeth were still there. "You, on the other hand, don't have a bruise on you. I thought you had a bad ankle."

Deb stared back at him, clearly at a loss for words.

"What, did you just voluntarily sit down and let him tie you up?" They sat face-to-face, separated by only a few feet, he with his ankles folded under his calves, she with her feet sticking straight out.

"He had a gun," Deb said. "What else was I going to do? Now, would you untie me, please?"

Ace dabbed at his wound again, testing the nerve endings. Without stitches, that was going to leave one ugly scar. "Right before I saved your life by killing Decker, he was about to say something. He said you and him did your best. What did he mean by that?"

"Seriously, Ace? We're going to sit out here and have a conversation? Please untie—"

"Did you at least try to bargain for me *not* to get killed? Or did you just jump at the deal right away?"

Something changed behind Deb's eyes, as if she'd been caught in the act of doing something bad. Over the course of ten seconds, the look changed to one of defiance. "What, you expect me to apologize for wanting to live? Like you wouldn't have done the same thing? Like you weren't going to just walk out of here and leave me to die?"

Under the circumstances, it seemed stupid to mention the fact that he'd risked his life specifically to come back to save her sorry ass. Yes, she had a point that he'd previously decided to move on without her, but that was because she'd run off without *him*. After calling him an asshole, thank you very much. He didn't owe her an answer. Plus, not using his mouth saved him some pain, too.

When he again rolled to his side to get on his hands and knees and then to his feet to stand, it took way more effort than he wanted it to.

"Where are you going?" Deb asked. Her voice carried an edge of panic.

He limped over to Decker's body and patted down his pockets. He found a Ford key in the left front pocket of his trousers, and in the inside pocket of his hunting jacket, he found the Holy Grail—a satellite phone. "Now we're talking."

"Are you going to untie me now, Ace?"

"I was wondering how he got all his equipment down here so fast," Ace said. "He's got like a whole little campsite up there. A chair, more weapons, some food. He didn't impress me as someone who would want to hump all that stuff down in a backpack, so I figured he must have a vehicle here somewhere." He dangled the key by its fob so Deb could see it. "And I was right."

"So, we can just drive out of here?"

He walked around to where Deb could have the clearest view of him. He put the key in his left front pocket, the sat phone in his back right pocket, and from his right front pocket, he withdrew his six-inch clip-on folding blade. He snapped it open with a flourish and gestured at Deb with the point as if it were his finger.

"It really hurts my feelings that you were setting me up to be shot down like that," he said. "I mean, I know you didn't like me all that much—in fact, you were kind of pissed at me—but Jesus, that seems harsh. You couldn't even have known for certain that he wouldn't have killed you anyway. That means that you were willing to lure me to my death just on the outside chance that you might live. You can see how that's hurtful, right?"

"W-what are you planning to do?" There was the look of fear he'd been trolling for.

"Are you afraid I'm going to leave you here?"

Deb started to cry.

He gave the knife a little wiggle in the air. "Think I might kill you like you would have had me killed?"

"P-please don't."

"I would never," Ace said. "You think so little of me."

He walked behind Deb and her stake, where she held her hands out, ready to be cut free.

"So, here's my story," Ace said as he circled back around to the front and made a show of folding the blade closed. "Before all this happened, I lent you my knife." He placed it on the ground, adjacent to her left hip. "After we got separated in the woods, I ran the hell out of here. I don't know what happened here, but apparently, you somehow got the knife out of your pocket."

"Please don't do this."

"It's right there, Deb. You just have to figure out a way to get a hold of it." He started walking back toward the sniper's lair and the truck that he knew had to be nearby somewhere. He'd keep pushing the alarm button on the fob till it went off.

"Ace! Come back! Please don't do this."

"I'm not sure what predators are out here, but they're big-time meat eaters," Ace said without looking back. "If you make a lot of noise, maybe they'll just munch on Decker. For the next day or two, anyway."

"Ace!"

He hadn't walked five hundred steps when his third press of the alarm button on the key fob woke up the horn that led him straight to the Ford Excursion that would get him out of there.

DON BRUNS

TWO OUT OF THREE AIN'T BAD

Obviously, it hadn't played out as planned. There were two bloodied, crumpled bodies on the floor of Bodine's Jewelers on Royal Street in the French Quarter. A uniformed security guard named John Lewis, and a man in a gray New Orleans Saints hoodie, sledgehammer still in hand. Sticky red liquid pooled on the tiled floor.

The whole caper, crime, con, and smash and grab had resulted in wholesale carnage. Two blood-spattered jewelry cases and the cream-colored floor, featuring red-stained grout that would always be a reminder of that hot afternoon on June 12.

Two clerks and a customer were detained. They were walking detectives through the store, explaining how it all came down and then came apart.

"The two of them just walked in, hoodies and COVID masks on their faces," Jesse James said. "It wasn't ten seconds before one swung the hammer. Bang, crash."

"I'd been looking at a ring in that case not more than a

minute before," Brenda Kahn pointed to the smashed glass. "The hammer hit that case and that shattering sound was deafening."

"Mr. Lewis," Jesse shuddered as she looked at the bodies, "our guard, he was here as a deterrent. You know? He was our security, and we felt pretty safe with him in place. His job was just to warn someone who might try to pocket a locket or palm a diamond ring. Yes, he wore a gun, but I never saw him pull it in the seven years I've been here." She shuddered. "Oh, my God. The poor man . . ."

"The other man," Detective Quentin Archer spoke to the second clerk, "the one who ran? Did you get a good look at him?"

Damon Short shook his head. "Honestly, Detective, it all happened so fast. I was in the back room, and I ran out when the glass shattered. Lewis pulled his gun, and the man with the sledgehammer spun around and swung it at him. Lewis's gun went off the second the hammer crushed his skull."

Archer glanced back at the corpses as the forensic team took pictures and blood samples. Too late to make any difference. The damage had been done. A bullet through the heart and a crushed skull. His job was to find the other culprit.

"How much inventory does Bodine's carry?" Finding the second thief didn't constitute evidence, but he was curious. How much could the two thieves carry out?

"I don't own the place. I don't know, but we were told that last year, we sold over seven million dollars' worth of jewelry. Gross. If that helps." Short looked at the bejeweled rings and gold and silver bracelets in the broken case and on the floor. Archer focused on James, the blonde young lady with dangling gold earrings and a blue-stoned pendant necklace that hung deep into her ample, tanned cleavage. "And what happened to the other masked man?"

"He ran," she said. "I was focused on the hammer and Mr. Lewis, but I saw him turn and run."

Archer nodded and glanced at the robbery detective, Conor Hennessy.

"Conor?"

The man studied the bloodied floor.

"We'll need to see camera footage immediately."

"Uh," Damon Short looked at the ceiling. A camera was mounted squarely above the shattered case. "I just spoke to Mr. Bodine. He's in Kentucky at the moment. We had no knowledge of this, but he says the video system broke down two days ago and the repair crew isn't due in until Friday."

"Convenient." Archer shook his head. "For the robbers."

"Jesus, Quentin. This is an S and G operation. Smash and grab. Got to be. They've hit jewelry stores all over New Orleans. But there have never been any killings. The crew are in and out in two or three minutes. This security guy . . . if he'd just let it play out, he . . ."

"Not what he was being paid to do," Archer said. "Let it play out? He was here to stop a robbery."

"Has anyone done a smash and grab since you've worked here?"

Jesse shook her head, tears on her cheeks.

He'd heard of the alleged gang. The S and G gang showed up everywhere, at any time, and concentrated on a select group of jewelry establishments, often hitting the same ones two times a year. It appeared they'd never robbed Bodine's. Smash and grab. Netting one hundred to four hundred thousand dollars per heist. No gun, so no armed robbery. Except now. A sledgehammer as a weapon. And a dead security guard. Oh, the hammer-swinging thief was dead, a fatal bullet through the heart, but the other party, whoever tagged along on this smash, that person could be . . . would be charged with accessory to murder. It was now time to make someone pay. The job now was to find the cohort, someone who possibly spearheaded the heist. The guy or girl who hit the road when things turned south.

"Gloves, so there are no fingerprints on anything." Archer pointed at the robber's body. "Forensics will fingerprint him, and we'll try to match his photo. The kill shot was in the chest, so the face is recognizable."

"I don't go out on many homicide cases, Q. The robbery division deals with stolen cars, tourists who get their cell phones or purses ripped off . . ." Hennessy shook his head. "I've been on maybe two smash and grabs in the last year. Never ended in a death."

Archer looked at the assembled. "Okay, no one saw the other guy's face, so we have no idea what he looked like." No one spoke. "Who owns this place?" Archer looked at Jesse James.

"Mr. Bodine." She watched as two uniformed medics lifted the bodies into black bags.

"So it's still a family business? Still the same name?"

"It is," she said.

"I would have thought it might have changed hands. The store has been here for . . ."

"Forty-five years," she said.

"Really?"

"Third generation." She held up three fingers. "This is the Quarter, Detective. The Brennan family restaurants, the Vaucresson family café, the Meyers' hat store, the Rubensteins' clothing store . . . New Orleans is filled with legacy family businesses. Adler's jewelers up on Canal started here in the Quarter, over one hundred years ago. Still owned by the Adler family. Now that's the Tiffany & Co. of New Orleans. One hundred years. There's a ton of family history here in the Easy."

"Bodine's first name?"

"Jason. Jason Bodine." She paused. "Not only does he own

the store, he's the president of NOJA, the New Orleans Jewelers Association. Since I've been here, seven years now, Jason has been in charge. We've seen our ups and downs . . . COVID and everything after that, but Jason has been strong throughout."

Archer surveyed the carnage, seeing the scattered jewelry on the tiled floor.

"Did he take anything? The other robber? The guy who survived?"

James followed his gaze.

"I don't know," she said. "There was the smash, the gunshot, and screaming." She paused awkwardly. "The guy who ran, he may have scooped up something, but I didn't see it."

"There was absolutely no time," Damon Short said. "He stood by the door, kind of like a lookout. He wasn't really even close to the pieces."

"Maybe some of them scattered toward the door?"

Short shrugged his shoulders.

"We'll need to see an inventory list," Hennessy said. "As soon as possible. We need to know what items may show up at pawn shops or on the internet. Okay?"

"We happen to have a detailed list of inventory. Mr. Bodine has a schematic of every jewelry case, every day," James said. "I'll check it against what's here." She shook her head in disgust, surveying the jewelry strewn on the floor. "We can wash the pieces covered with blood, right?"

"Forensics has blood samples," Archer said. "Do what you have to do. But we need to know if all inventory is accounted for." Unsuspecting people were going to buy rings and bracelets that had been tainted by dead men's blood? And then the detective thought about the blood diamonds mined in Sierra Leone that were sold to finance terrorism and wars in South Africa. And murders in the gold rush town of La Pampa, Peru, where miners are killed on a regular basis for that precious metal. So what's a little blood on some New Orleans bling? Archer closed his eyes for a second. He knew far too much about violent crime.

She shuddered. "And we'll get that list to you, hopefully by tonight," James said.

"We'll need to talk to Jason Bodine," Hennessy said. "You said he's not in town?"

"He's out of state but very much aware of what's happened. We've been in touch," she said.

"So you have his cell number?"

Of course, they did.

"We may have to work this together," Archer said, nodding to his partner. "We know it's a murder case. It's probably a robbery case regardless of whether anything was stolen."

Hennessy nodded. "Apparently, it all happened so fast. Hard to believe that the other suspect had time to pick up any pieces."

But when the inventory list was posted three hours later, three rings were missing. They were valuable, precious mounted stones, with a value calculated to be sixty to eighty thousand dollars.

And Archer and Hennessy sipped coffee at Cafe Envie on Decatur Street, both checking their phones for updates.

"It's hard to believe this guy, whoever he is, had the time and presence of mind to reach down between these two dead bodies and pick up three specific rings."

"Remember, Q," Hennessy cautioned, "eyewitnesses don't always have total recall. Apparently, there was some pretty violent stuff going on. I can't imagine the shock of seeing two guys killed in a split second."

"And no video? Here's a company with an armed guard and they have an inoperable video system? It just seems a little strange. Security seems to be paramount and then it's not."

"The first case they destroyed, Q, was a case containing estate jewelry."

"And that has significance regarding . . . ?" Archer said.

Hennessy frowned. "You may not know this, Q, but as a robbery detective, I can tell you that estate jewelry is often highly overrated."

"Meaning?"

"A jeweler can sell new items at exorbitant prices. Markups are astronomical. But when you advertise estate jewelry, with a sometimes-manufactured history, the sky is the fucking limit."

"Manufactured history?"

"Okay." Hennessy took a swallow of his black coffee. "A jewelry store owner buys items at an auction. Or from someone off the street. Pennies on the dollar. He then calls it estate jewelry."

"Explain *estate.*"

"Some dead person leaves jewelry to be auctioned off. Or some down-on-his-luck kid sells his mom's emerald earrings to a store. A cat burglar sells his evening take to a fence. The fence sells it to a pawn shop and the pawn shop sells it to a 'legitimate' jewelry store. Simply put, estate means *used*. It's as simple as that. Kind of like a car, Q, when you drive it off the lot, it immediately loses value. It's now a *used* car. But in the jewelry business, you can't say *used* jewelry. Sounds cheap and tawdry. You can't give your wife a tennis bracelet and say, 'It's used.' That's not going to fly. You say, 'It belonged to Princess Diana's sister,' then it becomes estate jewelry. So, the jeweler uses the word *estate.* It's a word to add value to the item. Lots of value. It could be a five-hundred-dollar engagement ring from some lady who lives in a trailer in Desire." He tapped his fingers on the tabletop. "You don't get much lower than that, but when they call it an estate item, well, the value goes up."

Archer knew Desire. High crime rate, and over one hundred

murders in the Desire and Lafitte area last year, mostly in the housing projects.

"The jeweler can be honest, telling a prospective buyer that the ring was the property of an indigent, an all-but-homeless person who needed money to buy food. Or they can make up a story. European aristocrat who smuggled the ring, hidden in a jar of olive oil. Or rumored to be part of a haul from a high-end West Coast heist." He paused, taking another swallow. "Whatever. He spins his story and sells some ring he paid $150 for, for $700. Talk about a markup."

"So the smash-and-grab gang starts with a case that has estate jewelry?"

"Good bet. When the jeweler makes his insurance claim, he's going to declare the high-end jewelry, starting with his estate pieces. The thief can then use that as a base to sell the pieces he lifted."

"So while we're looking for the crooks, the crooks are sometimes running the store."

"Hey, I'm not condemning all retailers," Connor said, "but yeah, there are criminals at all levels of the retail business."

"Up to eighty grand in value. And somehow, our thief, in a matter of seconds, walks out with these three rings?"

"We'll get to the bottom of this, Q. I solve the robbery, you get the accessory to murder."

"No video. No leads."

"Except for a repeat pattern. Same MO. Only now . . ."

"There's a murder. Someone crushed the skull of a beloved security guard and we're going to find the son of a bitch who orchestrated the heist. I think we're going to be fast friends when this is through."

The French Quarter's Cat's Meow fronted a small courtyard, with a very small former slave cottage at the far end. Archer rented the six-hundred-square-foot domicile, paying more than he could really afford, but he loved the neighborhood.

The Meow, the Quarter's most storied karaoke bar, kept the noise going until the wee hours of the morning, but with a couple of shots of Knob Creek bourbon, earplugs, and a sound machine, Archer could usually catch a night's sleep. Usually.

And just when he was about to drift off that night, his phone buzzed. He didn't hear it, with the foam in his ears, but he felt it. A little groggy from the shots, he answered.

"Quentin, it's Solange Cordray."

The young female voodoo practitioner. In the short time he'd been in the Crescent City, they'd formed a tenuous relationship, neither trusting the other one hundred percent, but solving half a dozen murder cases.

"I'm sorry to bother you this late . . ."

1:00 a.m.

"Quentin, I'm truly sorry, but you're involved in a homicide investigation that . . ."

"It's kind of what I do."

"Yesterday. A security guard was bludgeoned to death."

"And the murderer was shot." Archer was pretty sure the mainstream media hadn't run with it yet, but social media probably knew the story before it happened.

"I know. And there were three rings stolen. Or at least missing. Am I right?"

How she knew that, he had no idea. The robbery, the death of two men—that was certainly on the web by now. But his team had deliberately kept the information about the stolen items from being released. Solange Cordray never failed to surprise him. Voodoo vibes, maybe. Good connections were more probable.

Yes, he was skeptical. It might be magic, it might just be the people that you knew.

Big Easy voodoo queen Marie Laveau, a historic figure in the New Orleans legacy of iconic characters, had owned a hair salon in 1830 that catered to high-society ladies. The gossip that emanated from that business was rumored to have fed her side hustle. Reading fortunes, casting spells, the knowledge of tawdry affairs, illegal business dealings, and conjuring up voodoo spirits to intercede in people's lives.

Solange Cordray had helped him solve several murder cases. Archer always questioned the voodoo influence. But, a case closed was a case closed. If she was connected, or if she had supernatural powers . . . the end result was what he was after.

"How you know that, I haven't a clue. However, let's assume you are correct. Three rings were stolen."

"Quentin, I feel certain I'm correct. They were poison rings."

Archer paused. "Poison?"

"Old poison rings. Passed down through generations. Families. Let's meet. I'll show you."

"Name the place."

"Twelfth Night Coffee on Rampart Street. Seven in the morning."

Walking distance. A long walk, but anywhere in the Quarter was doable.

He drifted in and out of a dreamless sleep and was groggy when he finally got out of bed at 6:00 a.m.

At 7:00 a.m. sharp, they met.

She was seated at a small table in front of a mural of Joan of Arc, drinking a frozen hazelnut latte. Breakfast in the Quarter. Archer took the chair across from her and smiled. She was beautiful. Glowing, her coal-black hair pulled back, highlighting the high cheekbones and sparkling green eyes. They'd worked several cases together and the detective realized how much he missed her. If there was a chance that something more might happen . . .

"Black, chicory and coffee mix, right?"

"Nothing as exotic as what you are drinking."

"And here's your coffee, sir."

Surprised when she served him, he nodded to the waitress.

"I ordered for you. I hope that was all right?"

"Great," he said.

"Joan of Arc," Solange pointed to the wall-sized mural. "Twelfth Night is the twelfth night of Christmas, January 6. Also, Joan's birthday. And, it's the first night of Carnival."

"You're a native," he said, "and I'm relatively new here. I do know a little about Joan. A nineteen-year-old teen who led the French against the British? Isn't this painting a little like the gold statue in Place de France in the Quarter?"

Solange laughed. "Joanie on the pony," she said. "The French people sent that statue to us back in the fifties."

"History lesson received. No tests, please."

"There will be none. However, Quentin, there is some history you need to know. It's regarding this." She opened her hand, and a ring fell on the tabletop.

An intricately scrolled gold ring, topped by a small octagonal gold box. In the center, a sparkling green stone.

She let it rest on the surface, the din of conversation filling the space. The tinkle of a bell sounded when the door opened, alerting them the place was filling up with an early morning crowd.

Finally, she said, "It's a perfect Colombian emerald, Detective. No bleeding, never treated with oil, and a deep green consistency."

He had no idea what she was talking about.

"And the value of the gold and gem is probably close to one hundred thousand dollars."

Sitting there, right in front of him, a very expensive stone. A lot more than he would make in a year.

"But, the value could be much higher due to this surprise," she said. "Watch."

Picking up the ring, she flipped the gem with her thumb, and it opened on what appeared to be a very tiny hinge.

"What the . . ."

"There's a small cavity under the emerald."

He took a sip of coffee and shook his head.

"To what purpose?"

"It's a small vessel. You can fill it with cyanide salts, ashes or ground bones of a saint, herbs, weeds, spices . . ."

"Again, to what purpose?" He was intrigued, to say the least.

"Whatever purpose you need. For casting spells, for spies and assassins who want to poison someone, for keeping the spirit of a dead one alive . . . whatever purpose, Quentin."

He picked up the ring and gazed at the shallow cavity.

"And the history of *this* ring?"

"This specific one is my mother's ring. Handed down over generations."

Again, Archer thought. Family was everything in New Orleans.

Her mother, Clotille Trouville, had been a famous voodoo queen in New Orleans. Not so much anymore. She spent her days at a dementia center down by the Mississippi, and only occasionally recognized her daughter, who volunteered at the home.

"I'm trying to make sense of this. Please, help me."

"I'm not being difficult, Detective. I'm trying to make a point."

"That is?"

"The ring you're holding contained cyanide salt many years ago."

He put the ring back on the table.

"Pretty deadly drug."

"Vitamin B12 is a great antidote if you ever need it."

"Slim chance."

"There is energy in this ring. When I touch it, I feel it. In the early 1700s, one of my ancestors was accused of witchcraft because she supposedly cast a spell. A spell that caused a rival voodoo practitioner to become ill and bedridden. Deathly sick. Voodoo religion is rooted in faith, of course, and like most religions, in violence. Rather than face a burning at the stake or something worse, my great-great-aunt swallowed the cyanide she kept in the ring. Cardiac arrest, respiratory paralysis—legend has it she was dead within a minute. Apparently, she always thought she might get caught."

And Archer remembered his history classes at Renaissance High in Detroit. Joan of Arc was burned at the stake. Apparently, the French warrior didn't wear a poison ring.

"Solange," he spread his hands, "what are you trying to tell me?"

"Your thief stole three *poison* rings."

"It was a split-second robbery. According to eyewitnesses, the jewelry case was shattered, the two victims were killed in a flash, and the third party was out the door in seconds. No time to pick up scattered jewelry and absolutely no time to discriminate what was a poison ring or even a valuable diamond or emerald. My understanding is that the entire incident took less than twenty seconds. So how the hell did the surviving robber, now an accessory to murder, lift three specific rings during all that chaos? Three poison rings?"

"I have no idea, but I can tell you what the ramifications may be."

"Please, do so." He gripped his porcelain cup of coffee.

"Someone has those rings in their possession. I saw a mention of the homicide online, and it came to me in a dream last night. I can't explain how or why. You are a skeptic. You often dismiss me because you don't understand. You can't argue that, Quentin." The fiery young lady reached across the table and grasped his hand. "We've worked together before. When Baron Samedi speaks, when one of the spirits talks, I listen. He's the god of death and he watches over cemeteries, over dead people, and I am certain he spoke to me. He wants me to be involved, to find who is responsible for the murders."

Archer shook his head as she released her grip, and he sipped his bitter coffee.

"I appreciate your interest, and I don't dismiss you. But, out of the blue, in the middle of the night, you have this revelation? A voodoo spirit named Baron? Not to sound ungrateful, but I would think you have more pressing issues of your own to worry about. Your mother being most important."

She stared into his eyes, and Archer looked away, embarrassed. Here was this vulnerable girl, sharing intimate secrets with him, and he was mocking her. He took another swig of coffee and there was an awkward silence between them.

"Tell me about it, Detective. Tell me. Damn. Damn." The voodoo lady spread her hands on the table and gave Archer an icy look. "I have clients who depend on my spells, prayers, my gris-gris bags, clairvoyance, and advice. I have Ma at Water's Edge Care Center. I carry the weight of a failed marriage, an ex-husband who wore me on his arm like a mulatto trophy wife while he had dalliances with . . . I don't know how many high-society women are in this city. I don't want more on my plate. Believe me, I pray every day, every single night that I may be delivered from divergences." She took a deep, ragged breath. "The gods, they don't give anyone a pass. Or at least they don't give any to me. When they feel I can intercede, I don't have a choice. Okay?"

"Loud and clear," Quentin said, mustering all the sincerity he possessed. "I understand pressure." A wife who was murdered, a family of cops in Detroit who disowned him when he uncovered their drug dealing. Archer was no stranger to pressure.

"Quentin, I do not want this responsibility. It is forced on me. I don't expect you or anyone else to understand. Please. I will give you what I know and you can deal with that."

"Let me have it. I'm sorry you're under this stress. I'm truly sorry for my frustration." Not a spiritual man, not a person of faith, he didn't understand. But if she felt a calling, he was willing to see where it led.

"The spirits, for a reason that's beyond me, are trying to right some wrongs. They want to give you who is truly responsible for the death of the security guard. Give a serious history to the rings. To most, these poison rings are an expensive novelty. You can buy cheap metal and plastic replicas at souvenir shops all over New Orleans for a few dollars. But to a more informed group of devotees, those *real* rings, the ones that are missing, have energy. I'm certain it radiates off those jewels. They may have carried ashes of saints, remains of loved ones, even . . ." She paused.

"Poison?"

She pushed her unfinished latte across the table.

"Let me put this in perspective. My understanding, until now, is that these robberies have been dangerous, costly, and violent. But not deadly."

"And your point is?"

"This changes everything. Kid gloves are off. Murder is now on the table and the stakes are much higher."

"And what does that mean? How do you think that changes things?"

"I don't think that, Quentin. I know that. Everyone involved, you included, is on the firing line. Someone who is accused of killing another person . . . someone associated with that death . . . they really have nothing to lose, do they?"

"Well, there are degrees of . . ."

"I believe that there will be another killing. To protect one of the guilty parties, and then it can spiral. Please, be very careful. And warn anyone associated with this crime that their lives may be in danger."

"I appreciate the insight, but . . ."

"One more thing, Detective. There are numbers I've been given. I have no idea what they mean, but they are supposedly an integral part of the equation."

"Numbers?"

"Fifty-six and thirty-six."

"What does . . ."

"I don't know." She threw her hands up. "I can't interpret everything that I am given, but I believe they are important to your case. It adds up to ninety-two, if that helps. Just look out for those numbers."

He gave her a grim smile.

"It just gets stranger, doesn't it?"

"I have to go." Solange stood, picked up the emerald poison ring, nodding to Archer, as the portrait of Joan of Arc, mounted on her horse, watched with a piercing stare as the voodoo lady walked out of the shop.

—

"Hennessy, it's Archer."

"Q, what's happening?"

"We've got to interview Jason Bodine."

"Of course. It was his store, I mean . . ."

"Find him. Book him for a sit-down. It's imperative."

"Funny you should say that. Just got a call an hour ago, and Bodine is back in town. I think he'll be in the store at opening. 10:00 a.m."

"You know . . . I'm sure you are aware that in the past I've dealt with a voodoo practitioner . . ."

"Everyone on the force knows, Quentin. You've broken some cases with her help and we respect that. It's a little strange, and we don't necessarily understand it, but . . ."

"Yeah, neither do I. But she has a theory about the missing rings."

"I'm listening."

"She was visited by . . ." Archer hesitated. "Doesn't matter. She feels certain the rings will lead to the killer. The rings, if they really are what Solange believes, are poison rings."

"Poison? Jesus, Q. Sounds serious. Tell me more."

And Archer did, until his partner had all the information that he had. Which wasn't much.

Archer walked back to his cottage, got into his car, and headed down to Canal for his visit to the homicide bureau. He barely noticed the dark Black man who watched him, smoking a long cigar and wearing a black suit with a tall top hat. There were a lot of scary characters in New Orleans.

Bodine was a short, stout, bald man with fringes of white hair over his ears. His office was in a back room, behind the nine jewelry cases in his showroom. A stale room possibly smelling of ancient cigar smoke that had permeated the walls, and filled with filing cabinets and bank boxes stuffed full of paper. In the rear corner, behind the man's battered metal desk, stood an iron Mosler safe. A wooden-bladed fan mounted to the ceiling spun lazily, barely stirring the humid air.

"It's a sad, sad thing, Detectives." The man remained seated in a cracked vinyl rolling chair. Nervously, he rolled a little left, a little right, and back and forth. "Poor John Lewis. Like a father to me. He was here when my father ran the store. And all he was doing was . . ." The man coughed, seemed to choke for a moment, and tried to regain his composure.

Hennessy, standing in front of the desk, nodded. There were no other chairs in the crowded room.

"Did you have any recent disgruntled employees? Have you fired anyone recently? Can you think of a reason you might have been targeted?"

"I'm sure you know, there's a gang of smash-and-grab crooks who . . ." Left, right, back and forth.

"We're well aware and we're taking a more aggressive look at the stores that have been targeted. Yours hasn't been a victim until now, am I correct?"

Bodine wiped a bead of sweat from his forehead.

"We have not. Thank God. We were very lucky. Friends of mine . . ."

"You are president of an association?" Archer asked.

"NOJA, the New Orleans Jewelers Association. Yes."

"So you have a business relationship with some of your competitors," Archer said. "I looked into some of the other similar robberies. No deaths to my knowledge."

"No," Bodine shook his head. "There have been some serious

losses due to theft, but . . ." He shuddered. "No deaths. And insurance has covered most of the losses."

"The association, what purpose does it serve?"

"We look out for each other. If a customer has a specific request that one store can't fulfill, we canvas the members to see if they have a similar piece. We make suggestions and use our buying power as a group. Like, some of us use the same insurance company and they give us a discount. We have a marketing committee that promotes our member stores. Tourism brochures, online ads. And, we research the latest anti-theft gear. Camera systems, tracking devices . . ."

Hennessy nodded. "So have you and the organization had conversations about the robberies? The smash and grabs?"

"Of course," Bodine said. "We talk about it all the time. You can check. A number of our stores have been hit. So, this year we contracted with a new company to put in a state-of-the-art camera system in most member locations. Inside cameras track customers to an outside camera with an image sensor. Even when it's dark, these 4K cameras have infrared LEDs and we can see what direction the robbers go when they leave the store." He looked back and forth at the two detectives. "We can even zoom in to get a clean close-up."

Archer nodded. Wear a hoodie and a COVID mask and even with a zoom, it was hard to identify faces. But a digital camera picked up other things. Mannerisms, shoe size, maybe a tattoo on someone's hand, a distinctive watch on their wrist. But there was no video available this time around.

"I mean, nothing's foolproof," the jeweler said. "And Jesus, jewelry stores have the most valuable inventory of any retail establishment, Detectives. Diamonds, rubies, emeralds, gold, and silver. We are ripe for robbery. Ripe." He rolled to the left. "It's always on our minds. Every day." He spread his hands on the desk. "Do you know that jewelry theft in the United States is over one hundred million dollars a year?"

Archer recalled a notorious bank robber from the thirties and forties. When authorities asked him why he only robbed banks, Willie Sutton famously said, "Because that's where the money is." Apparently, the money was also in the jewelry stores.

"How many stores in your organization, Mr. Bodine? The . . ."

"NOJA. And there are thirty-two," he responded. "New Orleans has easily a hundred and fifty stores that sell gems. We've got twelve prominent stores here in the Quarter alone."

The room apparently lacked air-conditioning. Archer wiped his brow, sweat beginning to run down his face.

"Mr. Bodine. Do you have the new security system installed?"

"No. No one has it yet. Installation will happen later this year. I mean, right now our current system is down. We have an incident like this and these clowns, the company that sold us this piece of shit, can't spare a repair crew for a week. One reason we are switching."

Archer glanced up at the office ceiling camera.

"Do you review your system on a regular basis?"

"Mm, not sure what you mean."

"You've never been robbed. So why would you review your video?"

"No, I don't. Not all the time. Not . . ."

"I'm sorry, sir. I just wondered how you knew the system was down if you seldom check it."

"The last time I did check the feed, I noticed it wasn't working. That's all I can tell you."

"Is it possible someone cut it off? Are there safeguards?"

"Look, Detective Archer, I'm not the technician. When they finally show up, I'll be happy to put them in touch with you."

Archer noticed the frustration in the man's voice. Hell, he'd lost an employee, a family friend. It was a frustrating time.

"Do you have any thoughts about who runs this robbery gang? Or, are these incidents possibly unrelated? Some independent operators? Any ideas?"

"No. I don't. It just pisses me off with all the technology we've invested in identifying the criminals, our system broke down just before the break-in."

"Have you been in touch with your current video company? The ones you're not pleased with?"

"Of course. I'm considering taking them to court."

"Mr. Bodine, your inventory is short by three rings. That's all your staff reported."

"I've seen the chart."

"It is our belief, without video obviously, that the entire robbery and murder took place in under twenty seconds."

"Talking to my staff, that sounds about right."

"And those three rings were, what I understand, called poison rings. Am I right?" Archer studied the man's eyes.

"No question, Detective. They are on the inventory sheet. Three rings with a rich history. Estate jewelry. Worth a lot of money."

"In twenty seconds, amid all the chaos, could you, Mr. Bodine, find three specific poison rings, pocket them, and vacate the premises? Could anyone?"

"I would find it very difficult to navigate with the . . . I've seen the photographs," he paused, "with the blood, the bodies, the broken glass."

"And yet they're gone." Archer took a breath. "Mr. Bodine, I know you weren't here, but keep an ear to the ground. If your employees or any customers remember anything at all, please call us immediately. We want to find anyone who had anything to do with John Lewis's murder."

"Top of my list, Detective. Top of my list."

"The Mosler safe," Hennessy pointed to the ornate iron box. "How old?"

"Been in my family since before the store, and the store's been around for three generations. Belonged to my great-grandfather. It's probably one hundred years old. At least."

"Great condition," Hennessy said. "My father had a Mosler. As a jeweler, you probably know, Mosler has a reputation when it comes to precious metals."

"I do," Bodine responded. "Cincinnati company. They built the vault at Fort Knox, Kentucky, where the government stores all of its gold." He gestured to the safe. "I had it restored several years ago, before COVID. You know, like everybody, COVID took a huge bite out of our business." The man rolled back his chair and stood up. "Thanks for your hard work, gentlemen. I want everyone involved to be held accountable. John Lewis was family. Family, Detective. In New Orleans, family is sacred."

"We've got the dead man's ID." Archer talked to Hennessy on his cell, driving his car back to the Quarter. He'd been in the office, the bullpen for homicide detectives, not more than twenty minutes ago, working late on three other cases. Staff shortages were a bitch. The identification had just been texted to him as he was driving home.

"And?"

"Arrests, aggravated assault, shoplifting. The usual stuff."

"Associates?"

"I'll run it when I get home. Guy's name is Elijah Whitaker.

Tomorrow let's split up the stores that have been hit in the last six months. Get some firsthand reports from the victims."

"I've already run a list, Q. Eight stores have reported being hit. All in the NOJA group. Tomorrow sounds like a plan."

Archer took a right on Canal. Traffic was light, and with any luck, he'd be in his cottage in twenty minutes.

The girl was on his mind. Attractive, sexy, smart, wily . . . but the baggage between them was heavy. And there was their working relationship to consider.

Still, maybe he was ready for a new connection, the wound of his murdered wife still somewhat fresh. Possibly a romantic encounter, a sexual fling might take his mind off the situation. A little vacation from his nightly demons, his frightening dreams. Apparently, Solange Cordray had those too.

Elijah Whitaker was definitely on the web. He was no saint, and no one who might be missed, excluding immediate family. Archer wasn't sure even family would miss this loser. He'd been charged with countless misdemeanors, a number of felonies, done time, time after time, and yet this guy kept going to the streets. Well, not anymore. He checked his known associates. A list of at least six known felons he'd been associated with. One of them may have been the accessory. One of those names might be guilty of accessory to murder. But there was a load of work trying to tie one of these suspects to the actual crime. Tomorrow, he'd interview employees and owners of stores that had been robbed. He'd try to find similarities that might tie things together, lead to a ringleader, lead to a murder suspect, lead to a conviction. Tomorrow.

Archer put his Glock 22 under the pillow, took a double shot of bourbon, pushed the plugs into his ears, and laid down on his back. He tried to let the demons go. Find a happy spot, a childhood dream. Focus on a quiet place in his mind, where he could be alone with no distractions. And he dreamed about walking, arm in arm with his deceased wife, laughing and kissing on a sunlit beach, waking early in the morning with a smile on his face and an ache in his heart. Life went on.

"The owner isn't in this morning, but I may be able to help." The man in a dark suit and burgundy tie examined Archer's badge. "I'm Arthur Levin, store manager. What questions do you have?"

Quarter Jewelers had been hit just three months ago. Insurance claims totaled $212,000. Public record.

"I know you people have been through the interrogation before, but did you see any faces? Did you notice a wardrobe? Did you . . ."

"Detective Archer," the older man with wispy hair said, "I was on the floor. I saw it all. Scared the bejesus out of me. No. I didn't see faces. Hoodies, COVID masks, and gray sweatpants . . . there was nothing to see."

"What do you remember about the invasion?"

"Damned security cameras were acting up."

"Acting up?"

"The network wasn't connecting. They were apparently down when the robbery took place."

"Oh . . . really? Kind of convenient for the robbers, don't you think?"

"My understanding is that we're getting a new system in the next couple of months."

"And the inventory . . ."

"We reported it to the Jewelers' Security Alliance. It's a national association. They give it to the FBI and they keep an eye out for the pieces. I don't know exactly how it works, but there are notices sent to pawn shops, other jewelers in the area . . ."

"Where do you think the jewelry ends up?"

Levin shook his head. "I'm pretty sure the pieces haven't shown up yet. My guess? South America. Colombia, Peru, Ecuador."

"As far from the crime scene as possible."

"The FBI has an entire division devoted to those countries. The South American Theft Group something or other. Apparently, some of the smash and grabbers around the country are South Americans. It's kind of like the mafia used to be here in the States."

"Mr. Levin, two more questions. How do you report the loss to your insurance agency, and how soon do you get paid?"

"The owner, Rita James, makes up the list. Submits it to our insurance company and the security alliance. She determines the value, and I think we get a check within four weeks. I'm sure the insurance company keeps working the case, but they pay out so we'll always have working capital."

After the third interview, he called Hennessy.

"Conor, there's one thing that is consistent."

"Bum camera systems."

"Apparently no one on our side has figured that every store hit had a faulty system."

"An inside job?"

"What is our slogan in the investigating business? There are no coincidences."

"The average take in five of the cases is around $250,000. If the take on all eight stores is the same, that's close to two million dollars."

"Except," Archer said, "at Bodine's."

"They smashed but didn't have time to grab."

Archer felt the buzz, looked at the screen on his phone, and said, "Hold on, Conor. I've got another call."

Punching the hold and answer icon, he said, "Solange?"

"Quentin, I want to visit the jewelry store. As soon as possible."

"I don't understand."

"Neither do I. But it's important you are with me. I believe there is energy there that may be beneficial to your case."

"How soon can you be there?"

"You know where my shop is. Ten minutes, twenty tops."

"I'm working out of the cottage so that's no problem. Again with the energy?"

"Everything living or inert has energy. Gives off an aura. Good energy, bad energy, if people spent more time being sensitive to that field of force, the world could be a different place."

"Sometimes you . . ."

"It's not voodoo, Quentin. There's gravitational energy, chemical, inert, light, magnetic . . . even Einstein proved $E=mc^2$. An inert mass has energy. Just meet me. I have a strong feeling."

He switched to Hennessy. "Conor, I'm meeting the voodoo connection at Bodine's in ten. Any chance . . ."

"Not in ten minutes. I could be there in half an hour?"

"Make the trip. Hopefully, I'll see you there."

Archer beat her to the store, and was greeted by the well-endowed clerk, Jesse James.

"Detective Archer," she gave him a wide smile. "So good to see you. Under more pleasant circumstances."

Archer nodded, his eyes surveying the repaired jewelry case.

The glass had been replaced, and the damaged metal frame had been straightened or replaced.

"Ms. James," he indicated the camera above them. "How often does the camera system malfunction? On average?"

She looked up. "I have no idea. We never—I never—have any interaction with our security systems."

"Does Jason Bodine review the footage on a daily basis? Once a week? Do you have any idea?"

"Detective Archer, I open up in the morning, and Damon usually closes. Mr. Bodine stops in for a couple of hours some days and I really don't know if he reviews the video." Shaking her head, she said, "If nothing has happened in the store, I see no reason he would take the time to view an eight-hour video. He's never here for more than a few hours." She smiled. "Don't get me wrong, Mr. B is a great boss, but he doesn't really spend a lot of time here."

"How about John Lewis? Did your security officer review the video? Did he ever complain about the cameras malfunctioning?"

She shook her head. "I think, if the cameras were not working properly, Mr. Bodine would have said something. I never heard him complain until the theft."

"As you pointed out, maybe because you never needed the camera. You've never been held up. Isn't that right?"

"Not in the seven years I've been here. And I've never heard of a theft before that."

"And yet, Jason Bodine said the cameras were breaking down on a regular basis and the company couldn't send a repair crew."

"Detective, I know nothing about our security system. After seven years here, I probably should, but my job is selling goods and services. Please, take it up with Mr. Bodine."

"Quentin, I'm sorry I'm late." Solange walked in the door,

eyes darting around the room and finally resting on Jesse James, the tanned thirtysomething woman wearing a low-cut, tight-knit dress.

"Solange, this is Jesse James, one of the clerks here at Bodine's."

"Great name," she answered. "The famous thief."

"Solange is an adjunct to the force. She . . ." he hesitated, "she approaches our cases from a different perspective."

The store phone rang, and Jesse looked back at the register.

"I'm sorry, but I do have a store to run." She quickly walked to the phone.

"I was wrong. I am so sorry, Quentin. I was certain I would immediately feel the energy but . . ."

"Take your time. They're not going to kick us out. They want to find who was responsible for John Lewis's death."

"Elijah Whitaker. Technically. With a sledgehammer blow to the head. However, the person who set this hit up . . . that's who we should be looking for. And believe me, Quentin, someone set this up."

"So this energy you thought you could sense? It's not here?"

Solange walked up to the case of estate jewelry.

"This was the case?"

"The only one Whitaker had time to smash."

"There was something here."

"Three rings."

"Yes, yes. I know. And there's a trace of a force."

"You really feel this?"

She looked up as the door opened and Hennessy walked in.

"Solange, this is Detective Conor Hennessy, robbery division."

"I was telling Quentin," she said, "I thought, I dreamed I would find energy in the store that might lead to the person responsible for setting up this robbery."

"And?"

"I sense it's not here. Not in this room. Not in this store. I was sure . . ."

Hennessy nodded, looking at the repaired case and then studying the floor.

"They've bleached the grout, Q. Only a faint trace of blood, and there was a lot of it."

"Detectives, I'm sorry," Solange said. "I didn't mean to waste your time. I truly thought I . . ."

"There's a back room. An office," Hennessy said. "Maybe we can see if your energy is there?" There was a tone of amusement in his voice.

"Jesse," Archer approached the counter, "we'd like just a moment in Jason's office."

"We don't often go back there. I mean, it's his office, but if you need to see it . . ."

The three of them walked into the room with its faint cigar odor and stifling heat. The ceiling fan slowly spun round and round but didn't seem to move the stale air.

"This is probably the way this office space has been for over forty-five years," Archer said. "Maybe, if this space is the hub of the business, you could find . . ."

"Good call, Detective." Solange looked at Hennessy, smiled, and pointed to the Mosler safe.

"What?" Archer asked.

"Energy. Something in that safe wants out. Now."

Hennessy glanced at Archer, and the detective shrugged his shoulders.

"What do you think we'd find?"

"I don't know but I feel it. Quentin, it's coursing through my body. I can't understand how you don't feel it."

Hennessy again looked at Archer and shook his head.

"Can you get into the safe?" she asked.

"No. We have no reason, no warrant."

Solange turned and walked out the office door back into the store. The detectives followed. Jesse was busy with a young couple. Several diamond rings were displayed on a purple velvet cloth as she described their size, clarity, and price.

"Solange," Archer called out as she exited the store.

"Quentin, I've given you every bit of information I have. The rest is up to you."

As she turned, a coffee-colored Mercedes S-Class sedan pulled up to the curb. Archer gave an admiring glance, then turned back to Solange.

"Oh, my God," she said, frozen as she looked at the car. "The license plate. Quentin, the plate."

Archer and Hennessy both studied the plate as Jason Bodine stepped out of the automobile.

56 36 COM

"Detectives?" Bodine looked quizzically at the duo.

"Some follow-up questions for Jesse," Archer mumbled. "We have what we need. Thanks."

The man nodded and walked into his store. Over his shoulder, he said, "Hope you are close to who was behind this."

"The safe," she said as she stepped closer to the car. "Combination fifty-six, thirty-six, and *one more number*. A vanity plate to remind him of the first two numbers."

"Q, a word?" Hennessy grabbed Archer by the shoulder and pulled him to the side. "I respect your relationship, Quentin, and please don't take this the wrong way. The lady is a knockout, very attractive, possibly very smart, but she is batshit crazy."

Archer let out a long breath. "Yeah. I know. I'm not disagreeing with you, Conor. But on regular occasions, she's been known to be right. Crazy or not."

"I deal in facts. Good detecting. Standard police procedures. In this short time, I've got to tell you, I'm not on board with any of her crap. Call me if you find the energy, Q." Hennessy walked away.

"Quentin, I won't apologize for what I feel. How can I?"

"The plates? The safe combination?"

And Bodine came striding out of the store.

"Detective." He nodded, stepped into the Mercedes, and pulled away.

"Give me one more opportunity. Let's go back to the safe."

"Solange, this has gone far enough. We can't just . . ."

The girl walked into the store, and as Archer followed, she walked up to Jesse.

"We would like one more short visit to the office. I think it might help solve the crime."

Jesse looked at Archer, who shrugged his shoulders.

"Okay. Mr. Bodine just left so . . ."

"And in the estate jewelry case . . . I observed a gold pair of dice with diamond markers. Could you let me see them?"

The two of them walked back into the office and Solange studied the sturdy safe.

"Fifty-six, thirty-six, and there should be a third number."

Archer dialed Hennessy.

"I've got the energy, Conor. You know Mosler safes. Do you know how the combination works?"

"My father had a Mosler in his furniture store in Holly Springs, Mississippi. Four turns to the left, three to the right, two to the left, and then turn right until you hear the click."

"Got it."

"And, Q? If that crazy lady actually solves this case, I owe you an apology."

"You owe *her* an apology. And a drink."

"Got it."

"Solange, it's possible that we've got two of the numbers. Where do we find the third?"

The girl stepped to Bodine's desk, stared at the gold cubes in her hand, and tossed them on the metal surface. Snake eyes. Never losing her concentration, she scooped up the dice, warmed them in her small hand, and threw them again. A five and a two. Nodding, she looked at Archer.

"Twenty-seven. It must be twenty-seven."

Not a religious man, he prayed she was right. The possibility, the probability being so improbable . . .

She'd nailed it. The door swung open on newly oiled hinges, the pouch tucked into a corner on the second shelf of the safe. Three beautiful poison rings. One mounted with a sparkling red ruby, one with a two-karat diamond, and the other with a topaz topping.

"Two of these once carried sacred remains of an oungan and a manbo."

"A what?"

"A female and male voodoo practitioner. Probably several hundred years ago. Maybe ashes, maybe crushed bone. Someone carried their remains for spells, for inspiration, for ceremonies. The energy emanates from those two rings."

"You continue to amaze me. I am so thankful you came to me with this."

"Now, you need to find a way to legally open this safe, and prove that Jason Bodine was behind the robbery and the murder."

"Conor," he was smiling when the robbery detective picked up his phone, "we found the rings. My guess, we interview the eight other stores that were robbed, and we find that the owners were filing claims with their insurance companies, paying off the smash-and-grab gang, and selling the jewelry to the black market. Pocketing the insurance money *and* the black market sales. Eight stores. Someone is going to crack, and we solve eight robberies and a murder."

And they did. Two owners immediately admitted to being part of an insurance fraud, with leniency for turning on ringleader Jason Bodine. Archer got the warrant, and when Bodine pleaded ignorance as to the combination, the detective showed him how to open the massive safe. Conor Hennessy was along for the opening and unveiling of the rings.

"I don't believe it, Q."

"And I don't either, but she continues to amaze."

"Bodine took the rings several days before the heist. He could have covered it up if the two guys had grabbed dozens of pieces, but it turns out they didn't grab anything, yet three rings went missing."

"He would have filed for a lot more money, but the two deaths put a crimp in his plan." Hennessy nodded.

"Still, he filed for the three rings and probably was going to sell those out of state or out of country. You can have your cake and eat it too," Archer said.

"We just follow up leads. That's what we do," Hennessy said. "And she's a lead."

"A substantial lead."

In the rain and mist of a New Orleans afternoon, the two walked out of the store, followed by officers taking Bodine out in cuffs. Arms over their heads, protecting themselves from the downpour, Archer and Hennessy briefly noticed the man in the black long coat and stovepipe hat smoking the long cigar. He stood under an awning in the shadows, staring intently as the two detectives got into their cars and drove away.

The Black man tapped his cigar ash on the sidewalk and disappeared into a hazy fog.

C. J. KUDLACZ

PARADISE BY THE DASHBOARD LIGHT

Ten miles to Canada and Jacob Mills had an empty gas tank, a flat tire, and his stepfather's body in the trunk. The proximity to the border couldn't even be counted as a positive; his mother's mobile home sat sagging on its cinder blocks just east of Caribou, a mere eight miles from freedom as the crow flew. Roads only complicated the process. Roads, mechanical difficulties, and bodies. Corpses, if one dispensed with the pleasantries, as was increasingly his habit.

It was also about to snow.

"Damn it!" He indulged himself, burning a few precious seconds and kicking the crap out of the car as if it wasn't beat to hell already. His heavy work boots barely altered the scarred rear panel, but the exertion helped just a hair. It relieved a bit of tension, hoping Clint could feel it, hear it, wherever the hell the rest of him was, as his body cooled in the trunk.

Corpse. Whatever.

"C'mon. Think." He blew out a slow breath, pulse pounding in his ears. Swallowed against the rising vomit. Probably a concussion, dressed up with adrenaline. One mile down, ten to go.

Pop the trunk, 24601. I'll hand you the jack, pussy, get 'er done. His stepfather's mocking whine bounced crazily through his brain, battering the throbbing welt at the base of Jake's skull.

A farm truck slowed as it passed by, horn blasting a query through the scraping November wind. He looked up and met John Beaulier's concerned gaze with an instinctive wave, pushing him along down the road. He couldn't manage a conversation, couldn't be stopped, not now. He waved again. All good here, John, thanks.

The truck slowed further.

"Christ." Jake dove into the car and turned the key, a blast of Led Zeppelin and the growl of the 305 joining his final attempt at a casual wave, finally satisfying Beaulier that no assistance or advice was needed this time. The truck rattled away, the old man doing a fair job splitting the difference between cranking up his window and staying on the road.

The trunk was off-limits, even assuming his mother had a spare tire in there to keep Clint company, which was highly unlikely, given her dedicated neglect for everything else in her life. At least the Monte Carlo had rear-wheel drive—if he kept it slow and got lucky with the road, he might not destroy the flat front tire driving the half mile to Citgo and might be able to get it to hold air. The impending snow was another issue entirely.

A stunningly stupid car for New England, let alone northern Maine. "A classic," Mom insisted, even as it steadily deteriorated, mirroring their existence. A lovingly restored relic of his dad's, talisman of sunnier Kentucky days and warmer lives before he'd gone and gotten himself killed. Blown up in Afghanistan trying to help a local boy trapped under a cart, if one believed what the stone-faced army man told them, dead eyes and tight jaw set against the slowly dissipating lie of a Smoky Mountain summer morning.

It didn't matter what one believed, whether Dad died trying to save some kid or not. He had a son back home who needed him, whose life was forever ruined without him. Fuck that kid.

Mom had thanked the soldiers, made Jake a giant pile of bologna sandwiches, and then drank the house empty. Dried out and packed the Monte Carlo the following week and drove them straight through to Aroostook County, where her people came from. Introduced her nine-year-old son to the grandfather he'd never met, held Jake tight at night as they held a weeklong crying competition, then started drinking again.

Near as Jake could tell, she hadn't stopped since. Unless one counted breaks for pills.

Hazards flashing, he limped the car down the highway, keeping it slow and straight, praying for no potholes or twilight wildlife. Not that he'd be able to nail a moose at fifteen miles an hour if he tried, unless it was a particularly stupid one. The traffic was thin. The farm community was buckling down for shorter days. A few cars roared past him, the occasional horn. A truckload of middle fingers from some varsity baseball tools who recognized his lumbering wreck of a vehicle. Wolf pack bravery, situational safety in speed and numbers. They wouldn't dare do that to his face.

One minute to the gas station under normal conditions. One-sixth the speed, six minutes seemed like twenty. Semi-rural blight inched along behind the windshield. Nothing to punch, nowhere to run, just a slow, agonizing roll. The wheel shimmying under his torn knuckles, every bump the imagined deathblow for the tire and his odds of escape. Too many obstacles, even if he got past this one.

"Goddamn it, Mom." Why couldn't she have gotten it right

this once? Why couldn't she have decided to fight two years ago, before the hole had gotten too deep? Jake shook his head gently, clearing the fog a little. It had happened so fast. A shot to the ribs to get Clint off of her, another one to the fucker's yellow teeth. The smooth wood of the bat humming in his hands like justice. Then flying backward off the front step, a blackout impact to the back of his head. Some piece of crap or another, lying in the yard.

"*Take the Chevy, Jakey. I need you to go to your grandpa. Don't stop, don't open the trunk.*" Lifting him into consciousness, rope fragments in one fist. Pressing the keys to the wrong car into his hand, her eyes less red than usual. Bright, seeing him for a change. She had blood all over her shirt. His, hers, Clint's. The ties that bind. Sun hadn't moved much, but it felt like he'd been out for years. Her eyes confused him, sharp and green like when he was little, when Dad would play drums with his band and she would dance and laugh with him way past bedtime. Clear and sad, like when she cleaned up for county court to say goodbye before they shipped him Down East, before Clint.

Some plan. Send your juvenile delinquent to visit Grandpa in Saint-Leonard. Grandpa, who had washed his hands of them both years ago. In an overpowered rear-wheel beater into a blizzard because a corpse-sized tarp is more conspicuous tied up in the open back of a pickup. Closed trunks are more likely to make it across the border. Less chance of a limb rattling loose in the back of the truck to wave at the Mounties. Also, even less gas in the pickup. "*Sorry. Had to pay the bills,*" she'd said. "*Should be enough gas in the Chevy.*"

"The bills," he muttered, the lights of the Citgo finally inching into view. What bills was she paying? Hadn't been electricity in the trailer for two months. Water was probably next. Jake had been playing chicken with his stepfather, saving up what he made at the garage, sneaking cash to Mom when he could. Aware that everyone and their brother was waiting for him to start stealing for her again, that Clint would gleefully hand him over to the sheriff and be rid of him. Clint probably would have ponied up for propane once winter took hold for real. They'd never know, now. Goddamn bills.

Jake eased the car to a stop next to the air pump and climbed out. Two dollars, not even air was free anymore. He fished through his pockets and the cup holders for quarters but no luck. With a shrug and a sigh, he resigned himself to going inside. Bad enough that he was probably on camera, if the weathered box above the door was even functioning. Now he'd have to have an interaction.

Might as well get gas while he was at it. Normal enough activity at a gas station. "Ten dollars on four, please," he mumbled, handing the clerk his last ragged twenty. "And some quarters for air."

"Better get that sled home right quick, Jake." Benny Williams grinned at him with all five teeth. "Big storm comin'."

"Yeah."

"Anything else?" Idly rummaging through the till, one bleary eye on Jake. Jake always bore watching.

Jake looked around at the shelves. *Loaf of bread, 24601?* Shut up, Clint. Stay dead.

He hadn't eaten since breakfast and worked straight through lunch so he could get out early and dodge the weather. He'd learned about irony in English class. Behold, a practical lesson.

"No thanks," he said, collecting his change. He paused on the way out the door. "Pack of Camels?"

"Well, that depends," said Benny. "Your birthday still in April?"

Jake left with a shrug, Benny's raspy know-it-all cackle

pushing him out into the cold with his last ten dollars. Goddamn small town. Goddamn bills.

The snow had started. Goddamn weather.

He jacked eight quarters into the air pump. Spun the valve stem off the flat and attached the hose, firing off a half-hearted prayer to a god who'd only ever shown him malice.

Please.

The pump rattled angrily as he waited, ice pellets and snow blowing against the side of his face, chasing the chill down his spine as the tire slowly inflated. Paused slightly as the pump shuddered, redoubling its efforts with a staccato buzz. Inflated again.

Then held.

Jake stopped holding his breath and blew out an incredulous sigh. Step one down. He hung up the hose and put the valve cap back on, then moved the car slowly, superstitiously, to pump four. Started to pump the three or so gallons that would be enough to get him to Canada, if he got that far. Whistling snow mixed with the gas fumes, eddying around him like one of those uncorked perfume bottles in the old cartoons. Tempting him, beckoning to the border, its promise of freedom. Or prison.

Staring at the front tire, willing it to hold, he never heard her coming.

"Hi, Jake."

The gas pump snapped off, startling her. Covering for him.

"Summer? What are you doing?" He didn't have time. Couldn't lose focus. Not now.

"Your mom called. Said you were leaving."

"What?" *Mom did what?* He couldn't hide his confusion and flailed. "How did you . . ."

"Nan drove me." She hitched a thumb over her shoulder at the weathered Jeep Cherokee idling near the convenience store.

Transitioned to pulling windswept hair away from her dark brown eyes. "She's worried about the weather."

He nodded, worried about a lot of things. He put the nozzle away and twisted the gas cap back on, his mind spinning in neutral.

"I tried to call you," she said.

Shit. He glanced into the car and patted his coat pockets. "I must have. Shit, I left it at home." He rubbed the back of his neck, wincing as he grazed the bruise.

"Hey. What's going on?"

"Nothing." How stupid he sounded. How stupid Mom was, calling Summer. Adding her busybody grandmother to the witness list. Who'd show up next, Father Cote? He had to get moving.

"Your mom said maybe. Maybe, I'd want to say goodbye. I don't."

"Summer—"

"Ja-ake," she cut him off, two singsong syllables, then shrugged and leaned against the trunk. He tensed and opened his mouth in brief panic before snapping it shut. Tried to be cool. Clint stayed dead. "You can tell me, if you want. Anything, always."

He couldn't hide from her, couldn't come up with any good answers. They were just out of time. "I know. I just. Need to beat the storm, I'm sorry."

"You're not coming back." Half a question.

"I . . . I don't know." Half an answer. One way or another, no.

She wrinkled her nose, lips pursed. Blinking back tears. He'd never seen her cry. "It's not your fault, you know." She tugged at the cuffs of her sweater, worried to threads. Unseasonably dressed, immune to the cold as always. *What's in a name*, she'd always joked, after they discovered the line in freshman English. She was the warmest person he knew on many levels.

He couldn't reply.

"Your mom. Dad. All of it."

"I've done plenty." Fighting, stealing. Murder, maybe. At least an accomplice. As the unbelievable weight of it crushed in, framed against his oldest friendship, he almost reached out. Habit. But it was too much to ask, to horrify her with what she was leaning against. Get clear of her, let her go. She had a future, college. Away from here, and him.

She nodded with a tiny sniff, setting her jaw. "It's not my fault, either."

"Never said it was." Confused.

"Jake—" a honk from the Cherokee. Nan was done waiting, the storm gathering strength.

"We should get going. I'll call you." If he could.

"You don't even have your phone."

"I'll get a new one."

"You won't."

"I'll try." He couldn't lie to her. Should have tried.

Eyes blazing, Summer gathered a protest when another blast of the horn cut her off. "Fine," she said. She reached out, handing him a package wrapped in foil—still warm. "Nan thought you might be hungry. Be safe." Her hand brushed his, and his resolve wobbled, pulled toward her touch, her grandmother's devastating small kindness.

She saved him again, whirling away and stalking back to the Jeep. Her door slammed as they pulled away into the night, Nan offering a hesitant little wave, Summer staring away from him as they faded into the darkness. In another world, he would have grabbed her hand and stopped her. Taken her away with him right then. They'd cross the border and go west. All the way to BC. Vancouver, somewhere by the ocean. Lay low for a year until they were both eighteen and go wherever they wanted. Move to Kentucky, open a garage, and pay the bills. He'd learn to like whiskey. Play music and raise a kid and never, ever leave him.

He shook it off and put the car in motion, drums pulsing, Dad riding shotgun and singing along with Robert Plant. Fishtailing in the snowy parking lot, he pulled it back a bit as he rolled east on 89. Ten minutes to Limestone and the border not far beyond that, but only if he didn't end up sideways in a ditch. The snow was letting up some, but the temperature was dropping rapidly. The road was slick as he crawled past the speedway and the hulking darkness that used to be Loring Air Force Base. Back when Mom had been his age. Back when the town had been something, she liked to say.

Hadn't ever been anything to him. It wasn't the town's fault. He'd never had a chance, had never given it a chance. You either loved your home here, or you were stuck. Dedicated teachers and a scarce few friends could only do so much, especially after he'd been sent away. After Clint took over. It wasn't anyone's fault. His parents were buried in a closed box near Fort Campbell, and they weren't coming back. He was on his own. Something resembling relief simmered in the back of his mind, insidious and premature.

As if in reminder, a Limestone Police cruiser's flashing lights awaited him at the intersection of Foster and Main. Not for him. Precaution, he was pretty sure. A reminder for everyone to take it easy on the first big snow of the year. He wasn't the only game in town, but it was easy to feel everyone's eyes on him, on the leaden infinite silence weighing down the rear of his vehicle. He white-knuckled his way through the intersection, following the small line of more sensible 4x4s on their way back home after work. He forced himself to wave at the officer as he passed.

Two miles to the border. Thirty miles per hour, four minutes. The rear end broke loose for a second, and he slowed it down to twenty. Five minutes. Weather trying to decide between snow and freezing rain. The music way too fast for the occasion, he punched past a few tracks and settled for the absurd optimism of "Going to California." What he wouldn't give for that big jet plane.

He tried to do more math, tried to remember how many times he'd been asked to open his trunk at the border. More or less, to or from Canada? Divided by how many times he'd crossed it, off to Edmundston for class drinking trips. Different portage, did that matter? Divided further, maybe. Maybe the officer would be less willing to leave his warm shack in this weather.

Maybe. Four minutes.

The math kept his brain from exploding, but it didn't matter. Mom had made her move and forced his. Finally trying to throw his stepfather out of the house, no matter how hopeless her effort was. Two years of dependence. Shattered leg, pills and booze, lost jobs, unpaid bills. It didn't matter, he told himself. Didn't matter who had killed Clint, just that he was gone. Would have been nice if he'd been hit by a potato truck while crossing the street, but the world didn't work that way.

Three minutes.

Either he'd make it through, free in Canada and free of Mom, or he'd be in prison. Real prison, this time. Either way, she'd be covered. He had the body, the motive, the record. They'd both be free, in a sense. No longer desperately clinging to each other while the world slowly drowned them, they'd each be forced to sink or swim on their own.

Two.

He'd miss Summer. Why couldn't he at least tell her that? Maybe she'd write him again, send books, like when he'd gone away last time. Big brave criminal thoughts aside, he was still just seventeen. Exhausted, wrung out, dog tired of how unfair everything was. Every day, for everyone.

The police car was looking for him this time. He blinked away tears, suddenly noticing the blue and red strobes keeping pace just behind him. Reflexively, he checked his speed—he'd let it run down to fifteen while he indulged his self-pity.

"Shit." Not a speeding ticket, then.

Give it up, 24601. Tell 'em your ma did it.

"Shut up."

Lose him, then. Just a mile to go, quit crying, and man up.

"Shut up, shut up, shut up!" he screamed at the trunk, pounding the steering wheel.

His heart sank as a jolt of adrenaline set his body further on edge. Stupid, stupid. Why had he waved? No teen ever waves at a cop, especially a teen with a record. Jake eased over to the side, trying to avoid the worst of the snow. Plows wouldn't be through for a while. At least he didn't have to worry about getting buried in a slush pile. He popped the glove box, dug the wallet from his pocket, and turned off the music. Window down as the wintry mix knifed in, hands on ten and two. Noticed his skinned knuckles and dropped his hands into his lap, waiting to see who was behind the approaching flashlight.

There were only two cops in Limestone, so it was a coin flip as to exactly how this could go wrong. Robby Jondreau was an idiot, but a mean one. Four years graduated, captain and team bully when Jake was a freshman on the varsity baseball team. Before things (and Jake) went south. Like many a local star athlete, Robby had peaked at the regional championship. Suffered a minor injury in a major faceplant at the state tournament and still blamed it for the loss of a pro career that would have never been. The good ones moved on or moved away. Found jobs, families, and ways to be fulfilled. Robby just spent most shifts flexing his badge and talking glory days. He'd either settle for giving Jake shit about not playing ball anymore or try to impound his "white trash car" for being unsafe.

The coin landed tails, Pete Fortin dropping his light out of Jake's face.

"Evening, Jake."

"Chief."

"Rough night for hot-rodding," Fortin mused.

Jake nodded and tried to reply as the words stuck in his throat. Jondreau would have gone one way or the other as his whims dictated. Interim Chief Pete Fortin was a real cop, and would make decisions based on observation and experience. Did he know already? Had somebody seen Mom, bloody and battered, loading the tarp into the trunk? Had Summer's grandmother sold him out? Seemed unlikely after her gift of food, but the old lady loved to talk.

He's looking for me, Little J. Clint sounded positively gleeful. *I owe him fifty bucks. Had to pay the bills.*

Jake shook his head. Fortin had also been in the Army Reserve with Clint and grew up with him. Probably why things were never going to change. Until Mom had changed them.

"Okay, Jake?"

"Sir?"

"I said, everything okay?"

"Uh. Yes, sir."

"Your hazards are on. More car trouble?"

Idiot. He'd never turned them off after stopping at the gas station, distracted by Summer, Dad's music too loud to hear the signal click-click-clicking.

"Ah, damn." Be cool, Jake. "No. Sorry. Yes, I mean, earlier. Flat tire, but I fixed it. Slow leak, I think." He stopped babbling and tried to smile, but his face stayed frozen. Probably just as well. He fumbled a hand over the button to shut the blinkers off. The sound continued, his heartbeat taking over, ticking in his ears like in the Poe story Ms. Conlogue had them dissect in class. What a stupid criminal, he had thought, he could have gotten away with it. Now, not so sure. Could Fortin hear his heart? See his pulse in the darkness? Smell him sweating, twenty degrees outside?

Was that a noise, in the trunk? He coughed to cover it. Just in case.

"Headed out of town?" The chief flicked his flashlight toward the front, then the rear, checking the tires. Then the back seat. Back to Jake.

"Trying." He meant the weather, but it came out like attitude. Stick to the facts! "Sorry. Weather came faster than we thought. Grandpa's laid up, gonna help him dig out after it's over." A sudden inspiration, this excuse.

Fortin's eyes narrowed. "Laid up, how?"

Keep it simple. "His back, I guess. Bad timing. I should get there okay, though."

Please.

The chief nodded. "Saw him in town last week. Seemed okay."

Jake nodded back. "Yes, sir."

"How's your mom doing?" As if he didn't know.

Unusually sober. Bloody. "She's okay." Don't blink. "Clint can help while I'm gone."

Fortin snorted. "Not unless there's a six-pack buried in the snow."

Could he laugh at that? He tried to smile instead but found limited success as hatred for Clint clashed with contempt for a cop who would do nothing about him—two anguished specters rolling in a ball of rage toward the deathly silence of the trunk.

Jurisdiction be damned, Fortin knew better, for all his professional politeness. Jake almost preferred Clint's constant jibes and name-calling. 24601. Dumb sonofabitch had fallen asleep watching HBO and woken up to a scene from *Les Misérables*. Thought it was hilarious, tagging his delinquent stepson with the number.

Be cool.

"Well," Fortin said, giving him another long cop look.

Calm.

"You should get moving, crossing closes at six."

"Yes, sir."

Quiet.

Fortin started to move away, then turned back.

"You want a ride out there? We can have Williams come tow this heap back to town."

Heart hammering, Jake paused, hoping it looked like he was thinking about his options.

"Thanks, Chief. But it's not far, I'll go slow. Not sure how long I'll be gone."

Fortin considered it, the snowflakes moving in slow motion through his light.

"Okay." The vise around Jake's chest loosened an inch. "You really should get rid of this thing. Can't drive it but half the year anyway."

"Yes, sir." Kentucky summer, flying through the hills with the windows down, Soundgarden or Zeppelin or Rush, sitting up front like a big boy. Dad's big hand pressing him back, patting the drumbeat into his chest. "Maybe."

"Take it slow, Jake."

"I will. Thanks."

He watched the rearview until Fortin disappeared into the snow. Tried a few deep breaths to clear his buzzing head, hands shaking, teeth chattering. Waited some more, until the cruiser's headlights swung a slow U-turn and headed back toward Limestone. Until his hands were under control again. Then he fired up the engine, cranking the volume as he skidded cautiously back onto the road, half a mile to the border. *When the levee breaks, mama, you got to move.*

The odds kept getting lower, but he was committed at this point. When Clint turned up missing, Jacob Mills would be person of interest number one, and he'd be easy to track. Williams would remember him from the gas station. Summer's Nan, even Summer herself. Now the damn Limestone Police. Canada might not be far enough, and New Brunswick sure wouldn't be. Maybe Grandpa would give him some money so he could keep moving. Maybe he should dump the car and start hitching. Plenty of places up north to vanish, if he was careful. Walk the earth, some Arctic Kerouac bullshit.

First things first. He slowed down as the snow picked up the pace, the wind whipping the flakes nearly horizontal as he approached the Limestone–Gillespie Portage at an easy idle. He dimmed his headlights and rolled the window down, coming to a stop next to the station.

"Evening," he said to the border officer.

"Hello. All the windows, please." Heavyset and red-faced, the official held his hand out the station window.

"Right, sorry." He rolled down the rest of the windows. Despite the overhead cover, the snow started to take up residence inside the car as Jake handed over his passport.

"Bringing anything with you?"

"No, sir."

"Bringing anything back?"

"No."

"Business?" He raised bushy eyebrows at Jake.

"Going to see my grandfather."

"Where to?"

"Saint-Leonard."

"Saint-Leonard? This weather. Why not cross at Van Buren? Much better, the roads."

With all the obstacles on his way here, Jake hadn't considered that question. He couldn't just say this was the fastest way out of the country, could he? He tried not to look surprised, brain moving through slush to churn out an answer.

"I had work. In Limestone."

The officer nodded. "What's in the package?" He pointed to Nan's gift, sitting in the passenger seat.

Shit. Get it together, rookie. "Oh. Sorry, forgot." Jake unwrapped the foil. "Bread. Uh, pumpkin. From a friend. That's okay, right?" A little note fell out, Summer's jagged cursive:

As soon as you can
for as long as you can
I would very much love to be done
missing you.

His hands wouldn't stop shaking.

"Yes, okay." The officer eyed him again. "Anything else forgotten?"

"No, sir."

Time stopped as the man's narrow eyes searched his face. Should he smile? Don't move. Look him in the eye, Jake. Be cool.

Then it was over.

"Engine off, please." The customs officer stepped away from the window, pulling on gloves as he stepped outside next to the car. "Windows up, okay, keep warm. Can you open the trunk?"

Doomed. Jake shook his head no. Turned off the ignition

and removed the keys. Forced the words out, Clint's laughter rattling crazily through his bruised skull. "No. You'll need the key."

"Okay, then." The officer waited a moment, then tapped the roof of the car. "Okay?"

"Yes. Sorry." Jake woodenly handed over the keys. His last hope vanished into a gloved hand.

Cryin' won't help you, prayin' won't do you no good. Ain't that the song, 24601?

"Shut up," he whispered.

The officer fumbled with the trunk, working the key into the lock.

Get out, run for it. Fat bastard will never catch you.

"Shut. Up." Jake looked in the rearview, hardly recognizing himself. Eyes bloodshot and sunken. Guilty. It almost felt like relief. Surrender. No more bills. No more running.

The trunk lid swung up into view.

No, cryin' won't help you.

Jake closed his eyes. Saw his mother's, green and clear. Then Summer, all warmth and quiet smiling mystery. Sorry, ladies. Sorry, Dad. Did my best.

The customs man said something French into his radio.

Prayin' won't do you no good.

The trunk thumped down, a cell door slamming shut.

Jake opened his eyes, staring straight ahead into the swirling snow, gripping the wheel so tightly that his forearms ached. Holding on to Dad's car. Evidence. Would they bring it back to Mom, after?

A jingle of keys as his nemesis reappeared in his window.

"Okay."

Okay? Clint kept laughing, laughing.

"Mr. Mills?"

He forced himself to look up. The officer looked irritated, impatiently holding out Jake's passport and keys.

"Cold out here. You are all set."

Jake's voice had abandoned him. He nodded, hands numb, and managed not to fumble the exchange.

"Closing time, drive slow. Kilometers now, eh?" The big man chuckled to himself, retreating to the warmth of his station.

Reality tilted, the world turning offset and strange. Detached, he watched himself turn the keys in the ignition and watched the Monte Carlo pass through the border, snowbound headlights slicing through the night. Watched another minute, tires crunching through the muffled winter silence, rolling underneath the highway overpass. Finally sliding to a stop at a T-intersection, snow swirling a halo around the little church just down the road, lit up for the night. St. Peter's. *Saint Pierre, priez pour nous.* An owl sailed silently overhead from a nearby streetlight, quieter than the snow. He stared until it dissolved into the night.

He lost track for a moment, cold and snow-blind, then found himself standing in front of the trunk. He turned the key, and opened his eyes. Clint's tarp-wrapped body flashed out of the darkness, then vanished.

The trunk was empty. No spare tire or jack. No jumper cables. No corpse.

Just a pair of cardboard boxes. Dad's music in one. CDs and vinyl, a few unplayable cassettes. The other was full of books that Summer had sent him while he was away. His constant companions. Jake's knees buckled and he grabbed the car for support as the tension blew out of him, dizzy confusion rolling through in its wake.

"Mom. What did you do?"

Then he was parked again, the fraught, blizzardy half hour

to his grandpa's house swallowed in a fugue of concussion and question. Chasing fragments. Mom's quiet insults, escalating. Clint, almost too drunk to stand but always game to break someone. Blows traded, the bat flying from his hands as blackness crashed through his spine. Dull flashes, muddy conversation. Blue tarp, yellow twine. A trunk slamming. Mom's clear green eyes, scared but focused.

"*Go to your grandpa, Jakey.*"

The old man was on the porch of the primitive cabin gathering firewood as Jake pulled up, a heavy flannel shirt over denim. Three years gone, he could still feel the soft scratch against his cheek, rough wool, and cherry pipe tobacco. Grandma had passed midway through Jake's detention and Grandpa had moved back to the woods, having given up on Maine. On his lost daughter and ruined grandson. *The world breaks everyone*, Hemingway had written in one of the books in the trunk. And everyone breaks differently.

"Jacob. Come in and get warm." He couldn't tell if Grandpa had been expecting him, and the old man never said. A question Jake would turn over and over in his mind for the rest of his life.

The next morning broke calm and clear, eight inches or so covering the world as a different storm followed him up from the border. Jake was elbow deep in machine parts trying to coax Grandpa's decrepit snowblower into working shape when a somber Pete Fortin pulled up the drive, an RCMP patrolman in tow.

He listened numbly to what the police had come to say, appropriately shocked for inappropriate reasons. Mom was missing. The trailer had burned, sometime around midnight. Looked like Clint had been drunker than usual, smoking in bed or something, but it was suspicious. Mom had been in rough shape and made a scene as a bloodied and angry Clint dragged her out of the

Par & Grill and off into the cold around 9:00 p.m. Local police had been overwhelmed with accidents in the weather, nobody thought another domestic at the trailer was a pressing priority until the whole place burned down with Clint inside. His truck was gone, and so was Mom, and had Jake heard from her?

He had not, nor would he. Winter was particularly brutal that year, setting records for snowfall and low temperatures. It was a couple of months before a snowmobiler found the pickup half submerged in the icy Aroostook. There was nothing inside but traces of blood, and the passenger door was wide open. Two miles to the nearest gas station, way too far for a malnourished shell of a woman with one good leg to make it in a whiteout. They figured that she had made a wrong turn, drowned, or died of exposure, the final desperate act of a woman running from the wreck she'd made of her life. Jake wasn't so sure. She had left no trail, certainly nothing like the one he had made on his way to Canada. The obstacles set by his mother's failures and bad decisions. Her inexplicable phone call to Summer. It was hard to believe that she had set him up to be clear of Clint's death and placed witnesses in his path that night on his way to safety.

But. He'd seen her eyes, so fierce and clear, remembering who she used to be.

Orphaned for good, he stayed in Saint-Leonard with his grandfather. Never returned to Maine, with his last border crossing still fresh in mind, and Grandpa worried that the police would scoop him up for harder questions the minute Jake set foot in the States. His journey to Canada was a baptism into some surreal alternate life. Summer visited a few times despite her parents, sneaking rides with one friend or another. He got a new phone and they talked most nights, her bright voice easing his loneliness even as it carried her inevitably away from him. Her college acceptances were rolling in, schools he had to look up later in places well beyond his reach. Ithaca, Carnegie Mellon, Virginia. Wait-listed at NYU. Art, maybe med school. Creating, healing. Better worlds than this, with better people than him. How he wished he could watch her shine.

He finished high school three months early by correspondence in the snowbound cabin. He learned about the woods and land from Grandpa, helping out with the heavy lifting. The daily rhythm of snow and shovel and axe calmed his anxious mind. Cautiously, slowly, they rebuilt their relationship around sharing the hard work of getting through the winter. They grew stronger in their broken places.

The package arrived a few days before his eighteenth birthday. No return address, Portland postmark. Jake poured a cup of coffee and stepped out into the chilly spring morning, scaring up a trio of deer foraging near the driveway. Two does and a small male with baby antlers. The envelope held three bills from the old trailer in Caribou. Electric and water, both final notices past due. The third was a life insurance policy for Lauren Mills, started the month Jake was born. Paid through December of last year, right before everything changed.

Two hundred thousand dollars.

He sat on the porch as his forgotten coffee cooled, the crisp April sunshine an ephemeral whisper of warmer times ahead. Fragile, but inevitable. Watching the woods, he found that the young buck had lingered behind and was gazing back at him, nose in the air, snow clinging to its fuzzy antlers. They passed some time together in the late winter stillness, considering their next moves. The deer eventually tossed its head with a steam-frosted snort, turning away and gingerly picking its way through the underbrush. Jake watched his neighbor vanish into the frosted trees and sat quietly, staring at the forest. Trying and failing not to hope, clutching Mom's last paid bill.

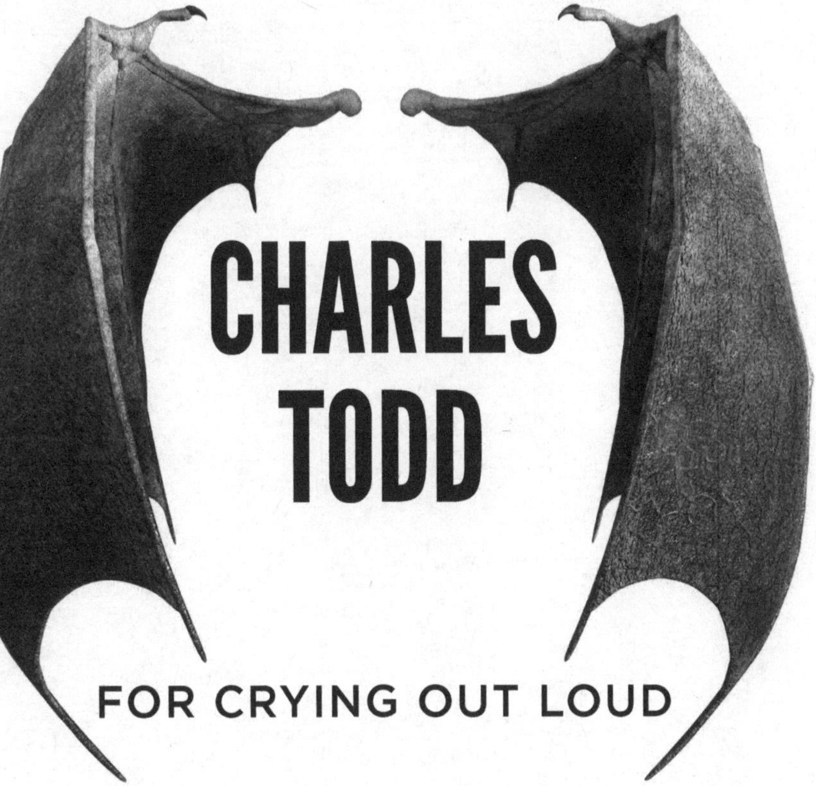

CHARLES TODD

FOR CRYING OUT LOUD

THE WESTERN FRONT, BELGIUM, SEPTEMBER 1915

Lieutenant Laurence Hughes is my name, now. I had been just Laurence before the army. My York and Lancaster Regiment was all excited to be headed to the front. Having graduated from Victoria University of Manchester with an engineering degree, I could have joined a prestigious engineers battalion. Instead, I joined the York and Lanc along with the other young recruits from Oldham, in Lancashire. Kitchener's pointing finger with the words Your Country Needs You on the recruiting poster was all we needed. We signed up in September of '14 and since arriving in France in January of '15, we had been held in reserve.

Now was our chance to go with our 2nd Battalion of the 83rd Brigade and take it to the Hun. This was the first major offensive for the Brits, and we were going to beat those Hun back to Berlin! We all called it the Big Push. From our vantage point on the road, we could see the digging of the trenches and the spreading of barbwire. I was not afraid of that, nor were my men in C Platoon. The whole regiment, under the command of Major Bayley, knew we would be the point of the spear to teach those Germans a lesson they would long remember.

Along with Sergeant William Evans, "Sergeant Willie" to all who knew him, I formed up the platoon with the regiment and marched to the entrance to the trenches. Like the rest of my lads, I had never been to France, much less Belgium. It had been a land of wonder, but now, as we approached the trenches, the land was scarred. The trees and fields were gone, replaced with a kill zone called no-man's-land. Soon we were in the trenches and kept our heads down. Peering over the top was deadly. Snipers were waiting for a mistake.

Now my whole world was mud, boards, and sandbags. I braced myself on a sandbag and realized they were not sand at all. The top bags were filled with straw and the lower ones with rock rubble. Suddenly, our world had closed in on us. As we approached our watch station, the mud was worse and dead bodies came into view. Half clothed and half eaten by the rats that scurried away with our approach, eyeless skulls watched our passing with an eerie grin. The smell was terrible. Grim as it was, my men remained in high spirits. Some said to the bodies as they passed, "We will get them for you, have no doubt."

At last, we arrived at our post. A blanket covered the hole in the trench wall that led into the officers' quarters. Captain Foley was finishing up some paperwork as we officers came in.

"Ah, we are all ready for you. Sorry about the digs. Best we could do in a rush. I am sure you all will make it like home soon." His grin was unconvincing as he stood when we entered. "A bit of paperwork Major, if you please." Major Bayley sat on a wood crate at the work shift desk.

"I hope they bring supplies soon. Alright, Captain, let's see your papers."

The captain spread the papers out for the major to review and sign. I went back out of the earthen cave to check on Sergeant Willie and the men.

The smell was not much better, but at least the late-September sun shone on my face. Willie had the men well in hand under the circumstances. The center aisle of the trench was clear for coming and going, and some of the men had begun setting up places to boil water. Rations would come later when their supplies made their way up to us. I saw the men lined up on either side, some in groups chatting and some just leaning against the wall. Going over the top would be a relief to everyone. They had been in the army for a year and were spoiling for a fight.

Over time, they settled in as well as possible. The supplies arrived and the men got accustomed to their surroundings as much as they could. Gone were the barracks and cots, replaced with exposure to the elements and sleeping where and when you could. The officers' quarters were only slightly better. There was a cook assigned to feeding the officers and a batman who mainly looked after the major. The regiment had made the best of it and soon would be teaching the Hun a lesson they richly deserved.

The first shell exploded in the middle of the night. It started and did not let up. Our artillery was softening the enemy up for us. I went out to the trench to check on the men. They were wide awake, as was I. Then it came.

The first few German shells fell short or over our trench. It was not long before they landed in our trench. We were all knocked down as bits of men splattered us. Shocked, our ears were ringing with the concussion of the shell. Suddenly, there in the darkness, our trench took on a whole new character. Almost as if it came to life and growled like an angry monster. Willie and I were not injured, so we took stock of the men. All of them seemed OK except one. Fred Jones, a private in my platoon, was dead. My first thought was that he would get up if we prodded him. We prodded him alright, only he rolled over, and half of his face was gone. I had no idea then that this would be the first of so many I would see blown to bits. Major Bayley brushed past me as he took stock of the losses. The battalion lost four men that night and we were horrified. We cleaned up as best we could and a group of men dug holes in the trench walls for the bodies. There was no other place to put them. To come out of the trench was certain death for us all. We were trapped in our small world of mud and death. By the time the bombardment was over, we had become numb to our situation. No place to go. No place to hide. No place, but this infernal hell.

It was under these circumstances that I began retreating into my own mind and memories of home. I had her letters wrapped in vellum in a leather wallet to keep them dry and safe in my trench coat. Thank God for Burberry!

Her name was Elsie Stonehouse, and she lived in Oldham, not far from where I lived. To me, she was the most wonderful woman in the world. I had known her since we were children and her parents as well. Elsie was a loving person. She was almost fierce in her devotion and I was lucky enough to be the recipient of her feelings. Her parents raised sheep, as many did. The land was not good for crops between York and Manchester, but the sheep managed. Now that industry was built up in Oldham, the town was the leading spinner of thread in the world. It was that industry that led to my studies in engineering. Elsie was always at my side and she made me whole. We had put off marriage until after I graduated from university, and now, until after the war was over.

Elsie had written frequently and I cherished her letters.

I was too intimidated to reply to this expression of love and her way with words. Elsie had a way of making me feel truly loved.

—

Major Bayley called us officers into our quarters. As we all gathered, the excitement was palpable. The Big Push was on!

"We have received our orders from the 5th Division as described by Brigadier Ravenshaw of our 83rd Brigade. Along with the French, we will advance across this flatland toward Arras and La Bassée." The major spread out a map of our area. "We will move out of our positions here." He pointed to a line on the map representing the trench line where we were stationed. "We are just north of the town of Loos here. The plan is that the bombardment will end in the early morning with an increase at about 0400 hours with a final extreme barrage at 0500 hours. Our chlorine gas will be released toward the German lines at that time."

We all made comments that it was about time the Hun got a taste of their evil medicine after their own attack at the Second Battle of Ypres!

"Make sure the men all have their P Helmets with them. This gas is nothing to get in your lungs. Inspect your lines well! According to the division, the fighting will last for several days, and we will have to take our great coats and rations until the cook stations get set up."

The major continued, "This is the key, gentlemen: Zero hour is 6:30 a.m. sharp. The whistles will blow and the men go over the top. No exceptions. Any man refusing to go will be shot. We have no time for cowards and second thoughts. Get those men over and into no-man's-land!"

"You will have your sidearm out, and once over the top, remember to pace your men. A soldier facing an enemy winded from running is no help to anyone!"

"Questions?" the major asked.

We were not interested in the big picture as much as the fight. Some questions were asked about overloading the men. A full pack is hard going. The major understood, but cautioned that it might be days before we would have shelter and hot food.

"Now, go steady your men. We are green and the artillery makes it hard to get ready. But we know our men and we will teach these Germans a lesson!" And with that, we were dismissed.

Sleep was gone now. We were all filled with adrenaline and excitement. Combined with the shelling over our heads, even the dead couldn't sleep. Sergeant Willie and I got the men ready. We took our time to make certain they knew how to put their P Helmets on for the gas and how to tuck them into their uniform blouses. The gas was nothing to play with. We checked each kit and then had them take their packs off and keep them dry under their rain capes. It took their minds off staring at their watches and waiting for zero hour. At 0500 hours, the massive artillery barrage was coming up, and the wait was making time drag on, one heartbeat at a time. We were all good mates and got along well. After the year that had passed, we were all trained together and all counted on our mates to get us through. Slowly, the final barrage stopped as dawn broke and the new shell holes came into view. Giant craters that had already begun to fill with mud amid the drizzle.

Major Bayley went up and down the lines. The word was

that the gas would go next at 0550. Dawn had broken, revealing the barbwire to be still intact. We all knew that meant the wire cutters had to be at the ready. Hard to fight and make way at the same time. The gas was released, and the wind took it across no-man's-land. We donned our P Helmets and checked our mates. With their faces covered, I couldn't tell who was whom. As soon as we went over the top, it would only get worse.

And then it was time. Zero hour. I blew my whistle along with the other officers, and Sergeant Willie led the way over the top. All the way along the line, as far as we could see, the men were leaving the trenches and heading out. The Big Push was on, and we were part of it. There was a rush of pride and determination among us all. Keeping an even pace, we advanced through passing clouds of gas that were blowing about knee height, making it hard to see our footing. Falling into a shell crater would not end well, much less would clawing and crawling out. We passed through our barbwire lines and entered the torn terrain between the lines. And then it happened.

The Huns opened up on us with their machine guns. Tom fell first and soon Peter and Alan. They turned and spun as the machine gun swept the field. We were hunched against the fire as if it were only rain. We tried to fire on the machine gunners, but to no avail. Stopping to fire made you a better target. Major Bayley was yelling for us to rush the machine gun that was in front of me and our men. We threw our grenades and began to run at the gun, cutting through the wire as we went. Some of the men had been caught on the wire and cut to pieces by the damn machine guns.

It felt hot when my leg was hit. I spun force, turning away from the line of fire and falling face forward into the mud. I rolled onto my back, my fingers searching for the place where I was hit. Suddenly one of my men had me by my coat and dragged me into a shell hole. I was screaming in agony, and yet even I could not hear my voice over the clamor of the fight.

It was James! He had dragged me into the crater. His face was covered and his voice muffled with his P Helmet, but I knew who he was. He was getting his kit out and soon he was putting a tourniquet around my thigh. I could feel the strength going out of me and as I looked down. The blood was everywhere. As James tightened the tourniquet around my leg, the bleeding slowed.

"We have to get ye back to the lines, sir," James yelled to me, his face at my ear.

I was shaking my head no. We had only just started, I could . . .

ROEHAMPTON HOUSE, LONDON, ENGLAND,

CONVERTED TO A VETERAN HOSPITAL TO TREAT AMPUTEES

JANUARY 1916

I have vague memories of the Regimental Aid Post, but the Casualty Clearing Station was seared into my memory. I remembered them cutting my uniform off at Regimental Aid and wondering where I was going to get new pants. The Casualty Clearing Station is where they strapped me to a table and a man in white covered with blood cut my leg and sawed the bone through. That is all I remembered. It was the worst pain I had ever felt!

I have some memories of the hospital and the stretcher ride to the ship. Every bump and sway hurt like the devil. Now I was in a real bed with nursing sisters and men all around me. We all were gaunt with pain and bandages all over our bodies. The nursing sisters whispered and the quiet was deafening!

Suddenly I panicked! My letters from Elsie! Where were they? I sat up and looked around me. Apparently, that caught the attention of a nursing sister who was bearing down in my direction like a dreadnought with a full head of steam!

"You need to rest now. There is no reason for alarm." She spoke in a hushed tone that still conveyed the sense that there was no arguing with her.

Suddenly, I realized how dry my throat was and how sore it was, too. "I was looking for my things. Did they make it with me?" I sounded horrible, and I was not sure she heard me.

"You rest easy, sir. Your things are right here," she replied, pointing to a cloth bag hanging from the foot of my bed. She was kind and gave me water to help my throat.

After drinking greedily, I told her, "My letters, I need them."

"Not right yet. They can wait."

"No, the letters from Elsie. I must have them."

She walked to the foot of my bed and opened the bag with my things.

"They are in a leather wallet," I offered.

After looking for a minute, she withdrew my wallet from the bag.

"That is it!" I was so excited that it seemed as if the whole ward was looking at me.

She smiled as she put her finger to her lips. "I will let you have these, but you must be quiet. You need some rest, as do these other men."

I took the wallet from her extended hands and pressed it to my chest. There was no way I could express what these letters meant to me.

She fluffed my pillows and propped up my head. "The doctor will be around to see you and take a look at your thigh."

My thigh? I was hit farther down than my thigh. I reached down to my right leg.

Gone. My leg was gone. I vaguely remembered the surgeon cutting and sawing, but he took my leg? Where was it?

The nursing sister saw my look of panic. "There now, you need to rest and heal."

Heal? I thought. *Heal what?* It was gone. All this work to save me was for nothing. I might as well be dead. Elsie! Was I going to ask her to walk down the aisle with a cripple in a barrow being wheeled by some nursing sisters?

"I know you are in shock again. You will be fine and they will fit you with a new leg. Now rest." She turned and walked away, back to her other duties and patients.

A new leg, a fake wooden leg to limp around on with a heavy cane, no less. Elsie would have nothing to do with me. I was astounded that this wonderful woman had fallen in love with me when I was whole. Now . . .

It took me three months to heal and get fitted with my prosthetic leg. I hated the damn thing. The padding did not help and my stump quickly became inflamed. I still had no idea what I was going to tell Elsie. Her letters kept me fighting to get well and try to look presentable for her.

I had not written to her since I was hurt. What was I going to say to her? How would I let her go? She deserved so much more. I had made up my mind that when I was released, I was going to Oldham to see my home. It had been empty since I left. My father had died right before the war, and my mother died when I was a child. As the only member of my family left, I had lived there alone. Then I would go to Elsie's parents' home and see her. I had no idea what I was going to say to her or how to say it.

MARCH 1916

The sun woke me up that morning and I worked hard to get dressed in my new uniform. I had brushed it well and polished the gleaming brass, getting ready to leave. I learned how to prepare the bandaging and padding for the stump. Then came the leg with the leather straps around my waist to hold it in place. I knew to tighten them as much as I could using the buckles to get them just right. The less it moved, the longer and farther I could go. The metal knee, as they called it, was just a hinge. It clicked in place when I was standing, and a lever let it fold when I wanted to sit down again. They had made me practice this all day for months as part of getting accustomed to my "new leg." It was a painful and heavy piece of lumber to me. Then the uniform pants. Getting the contraption into the pants leg was another chore. I remembered the first attempts at this and the exhaustion that kept me from wanting to try. If it was not for Elsie's letters, I would never have made it. How was I going to tell this wonderful woman that I was broken and would never be the man she loved so much?

At last, the pants were on and I struggled to stand. One of the nursing sisters came over to my bedside.

"Let me help you there," she said nicely.

"No, I must do this by myself. You can't come home and look after me. These other boys need you now," I said quietly.

"I know you want to do it alone, but one last bit of help before you go," she said, straightening my tie and then picking up my tunic and holding it for me to put on. I knew better than to argue. Finally, my shoes, leather belt, and shoulder strap. My sidearm holster was empty, but the flap covered that. I took up my peaked officer's cap and placed it on my head with a bit of an angle. Now I was dressed. The one thing that worried me most was my valise. I had practiced carrying it for weeks. My greatest fear was falling. The balance had to be right. My leg prosthesis was set straight and I carefully picked up my heavy valise and then the walking cane. Now I was off.

Getting out on the street was a struggle, but I made it. I nodded to the cab that was waiting on the curb. I set my valise in first and then maneuvered into the cab, pressing the hinge open so I could sit. I settled into my seat and tried to hide my exhaustion. All the practice in the hospital was nothing compared to the world out here.

"Euston railway station, if you please," I told the driver.

"Yes sir, on our way." The driver had watched my ungainly process getting in, but kept his comments to himself.

Soon, we arrived at the station and the bustling people frightened me. I knew I could manage, but again, the fear of falling was weighing on my shoulders. I leaned forward, paid the driver, and slowly got out. Once I had my stance and balance set, I began to work my way through the crowded station. I was looking for the London and North Western Railway train to Manchester. I went to the ticket window and, when it was my turn, I set my valise down and asked for a ticket to Manchester. I doubt the ticket agent saw me, but I was amazed to see the agent was a woman. She was terse but polite.

"Your train leaves Platform Two at 12:30."

I thanked her and tucked my ticket into the breast pocket of my tunic. With care, I took up my valise and made my way to the platform. With time and patience, I arrived at Platform Two and sat on a bench. I opened my hinge and set my leg properly. It had been a trial, but I was pleased to be where I could catch my train.

When my train pulled into the station, I worked my way to my feet and left my valise on the bench. The incoming passengers needed to exit the train, which gave me time to gather my wits. As I approached the car, a conductor took my valise.

"Let me give you a hand, sir. The gap can be tricky." His voice was gruff, but his face was kind.

With the conductor's help, I made it to my seat. While I appreciated the help, I hated the looks from the other passengers who stared and then looked away. It was that feeling again that I was not whole or a man anymore. No matter how I tried, I could not make my appearance belie my handicap. I had never worried about how I carried myself. I had the assurance of being a man who was educated and fit. Standing out in a crowd was not in my nature. That was gone now, replaced with scorn and pity. Elsie would see that too. What was I going to say to her?

The train pulled out of the station and I began to dread my arrival home. They all knew me as Laurence Hughes, not this broken half of a man. I gritted my teeth and stared out the windows. As we left London and began to cross the farmlands and villages, I was happy to be home. I longed to see the Pennines and the land of my youth. Elsie came immediately back to my mind. She had loved me like no other. I could not have dreamed of having a better fortune than her love. She was going to be devastated. If I had died, it would have hurt terribly, but with time it would pass and she could get on with her life. Now, I would be the constant reminder of what had been. I would have to leave. It was crystal clear to me now.

At last, we arrived at Manchester's London Road station. I kept in my seat, waiting for the other passengers to rush off. I wanted to take my time and there was no use getting in the way.

The same conductor came up and helped me off the train. I tried to thank him, but he was off as soon as I was on the platform.

I knew this place well, and made my way to the front to leave the station. Stepping out into the sunshine, it was good to be back in Northern England again. For a time, I thought I would never be going home. There was a time when I would have walked to Oldham from here, but those days were gone.

A hackney drew up to the front of the station. The horse and driver looked a bit old, but I did not have far to travel to Oldham. "Ye be needing a lift, sir?"

"Yes, Oldham, if you please," I replied.

Observing my difficulties, the driver got down and helped me and my valise into the hansom cab. I hated this more than anyone would ever know. He was being polite and kind. I should have been appreciative, but inside, I was angry that I required help.

The driver took his seat and tapped the horse with his reins. I was used to the cool air and it was a pleasure to be out of the hospital. I fondly watched the landmarks I knew so well on the road to Oldham. I gave the driver my address and he pulled up in front of my home. Again, he helped me down onto the street and fetched my valise for me. After paying and thanking the driver, I looked up at my old home. I had only been gone for a year and some months, and it looked none the worse for my absence. I carefully opened the gate and went up the walk. Everything took time now. After negotiating the front steps and the door, I was inside at last. I dropped my valise by the front door and went into the front room. I did not even bother to take the cloth off the chair. I sank gratefully into the cushions. I was tempted to take off my uniform and artificial leg. While it would have been a great comfort, I wanted to look as good as possible when I went to the Stonehouse home and faced Elsie.

I still had no idea what to tell her. Whatever I rehearsed

would fall apart when I caught a glimpse of her face. I rested in the chair for the better part of a half hour before I was able to get up and face the dreaded visit. I struggled to my feet and got everything together to take the short walk to the Stonehouse home.

The afternoon sun was losing its warmth and I could tell it would be a cool evening. Leaving my valise by the front door, I made my way out the door and down the steps. My leg was starting to ache and the rest of my body was growing ever more tired. I could have gone back inside and told myself this could wait, but I knew better. Slowly, I made my way to the street and turned in the direction of Elsie's home. It took all I could to make my way, but both the fear and excitement kept me going. At last, I reached the door to the Stonehouse home and knocked.

It was as if they had been waiting for me. The door flung open, and Elsie's mother, Winfred Stonehouse, stood with her mouth agape.

"Laurence, you are home!" she said with a smile. Then she took in my appearance and her expression changed. "You are pale as a sheet, come in!"

"I just got back and I had to come here straight away."

Then the situation changed. Using my heavy cane, I worked my way into the house.

"Laurence, you are hurt! Here, let me help you."

I shook my head. "I am okay. I am learning how to work this thing, and I need to do it on my own."

Winfred was a wonderful woman. I had nothing but admiration for her.

She still hovered over me and guided me to a chair with arms. I had learned that the only way I could get back up was in an armchair. I sat down and manipulated the hinge so my leg would fold.

"I just put a kettle on, let me get you some tea. Herbert, it is Laurence! Come down and see him," Winfred said in a loud voice as she disappeared into the kitchen.

Herbert Stonehouse came down the stairs and smiled when he saw me. "Don't bother to get up, son! It is good to see you."

I struggled to get to my feet in spite of his protesting. I always liked and admired Herbert. He was not wealthy, but then who was in Oldham? He made a good living raising sheep, and that was hard enough, due to the soil around these parts. Herbert was not only Elsie's father—he was good stock, hard-working, and honest.

"It is wonderful to see you both. Where is Elsie?"

Herbert's face darkened and he sat down heavily. "Things have been difficult here with the boys like you off to war. Elsie decided to pitch in and went to London to work. It brought in a little money and she wanted help."

"Where did she go to work?" I struggled to keep my voice from betraying my disappointment.

Just then, Winfred came out from the kitchen with a tray. "It is not much, with the rationing. Those German U-boats are trying to starve us."

"Those bloody Huns, think they can make us give up. Don't know how we Brits are, now do they?" Herbert grumbled.

"I don't want you making a fuss over me," I tried to explain.

"No, Laurence. We are delighted to see you and have something to celebrate," Winfred said as she set the tray on a table and began to pour the tea. I remember how you like your tea, with one lump of sugar."

I did not have the heart to tell her that in the trenches I had gotten used to lukewarm tea with nothing in it. "So, where did Elsie go to work?"

Winfred smiled. "She wanted to do her bit and help out. She really didn't have to, you know."

Herbert interrupted Winfred, "She went to London to work at the Stratford Works rail company. Her skill as a seamstress got her a job working on the coaches they make for the trains."

London! I had just been there, and if I had known she was so close . . . "Is she staying in London, then?"

Winfred handed me a cup of tea and began cutting a simple tea cake.

"Yes, she is sharing a flat just north of St. Paul's," Herbert said in a tone that told me there was something more.

"That is in the warehouse district," I said.

"They have some flats there. Simple but clean, and her flatmates seem upstanding." Winfred interjected.

"The issue is that we have not heard from her in some time. I borrowed a telephone and called Stratford Works. They said she was still on with them. We have started to worry, but we haven't been able to get to London with the sheep and all," Herbert explained.

"I will go to London and make certain she is alright." It was a statement that was without question. No matter what had to be done, I would find Elsie! I was not well-off, but my father had left me a small sum. Not that it mattered. I would go to London.

"We couldn't ask you to do that, Laurence, with your leg and all! You look exhausted from your trip here. You need to rest!" Winfred said kindly.

They had not asked me about my injuries or what had happened. I couldn't tell if they were being polite or if they had seen the wounded coming back home. I had seen them in the train stations on my way to Manchester. We did not speak to each other—just that knowing nod. So typically British; we don't complain about our lot in life.

"No, I will spend the night at the house and then head back to London on the morning train."

While Winfred fussed, I noticed Herbert's nod of approval. It was the least I could do, leg or no leg.

It was difficult getting dressed in the morning. Much as I became frustrated with the nursing sisters' help, I realized how much they did for me. Finally, I made it out to the street and was able to get a lift in a motorized taxi carriage back to the train station in Manchester. It was faster, but the hansom cab had been much easier on my leg.

As I arrived at Euston railway station back in London, I asked a porter where the station office was located. It was difficult making it up the few stairs to the office, but the woman at the reception desk was very helpful. I returned to the ticket office and purchased a ticket for the tube to Stratford station. With all of the changes the war had brought to the locomotive and rolling stock, I was not sure how long this would take and whether I could hold up to the amount of walking I was taking on.

There was one thing that kept me going. I truly loved Elsie and she was worth the pain. I kept touching the front of my tunic, knowing the contents of the letters she had sent.

How could I turn my back on Elsie without telling her that I was not whole any longer? She deserved better than that.

At long last, I arrived at the Stratford Works payroll office. The woman at the desk I had been directed to see was working hard, with piles of folders and forms spread over her desk. Without looking up, she knew someone was at her desk.

"Who are you looking for?"

"Elsie Stonehouse, she is a seamstress," I said in a voice meant to disguise my pain and fatigue.

Suddenly the bespectacled woman with a pencil in her hair looked up at me. After taking in my uniform and valise, she replied, "Have a seat young man."

I gratefully took a seat in the chair beside her desk.

"Elsie Stonehouse, you said, right?"

She took a moment to locate a folder in a stack on her desk.

"Yes, ma'am."

"I thought so. I am very sorry sir, but Elsie was killed in a Zeppelin raid on September 7, 1915."

"No, she was working here." My voice broke as I forced my words out.

"I am very sorry sir. She was on her way home, walking from Liverpool Street station to her home in Bishopsgate, just north of St. Paul's. The warehouses in that area were hit with incendiary bombs. She was among many who were caught in the fire. Again, I am so sorry. Was she related to you? Her form says she was unmarried."

I had turned cold. What happened to my Elsie? My mouth went dry and I could not speak. After a moment of fighting to regain some control, I asked, "Was her family notified?"

Looking back at the form, she said, "Yes, a notification was sent to Oldham in Lancashire." Looking back at me, she said, "The mail has been difficult with the war, you know."

I knew she was right. Too often there was no mail for days. "Where was she laid to rest?"

"You will have to check with the hospital, St Pancras South Infirmary. They handled the burn patients and can direct you to the proper authorities. You never said if you were family."

"A friend of the family," I replied, wondering what else to say.

"You will have to be strong for her family's sake. You are from Oldham, then?"

"Yes, I am. Her parents are wonderful people and this will

break their hearts." I began to work my leg and rise from the chair. "I thank you for your time and patience."

For the first time, she looked up at me and smiled. "You need to take care of yourself as well, young man."

I walked from the office back to the train station in a fog. My mind was empty. I couldn't feel anything, and everything I saw was distorted. I bumped into people and muttered benign excuses. It was all I could do to make it to the ticket window. I heard myself mumbling something to the agent before going to the platform. I had some time to sit before the next train that would take me to the infirmary.

Setting my valise down, I worked my hinge and sat on the bench. Everything was closing in on me all at once. It was not fatigue or my leg, it was my mind. I just sat there staring straight ahead, not seeing anything at all. Nothing. It all meant nothing.

Finally, my train came into the station and I stood, picking up my valise. Minding the gap, I managed to find a seat. Suddenly, looking down at the upholstered seat, I wondered if Elsie had worked on it.

But I was lost and she was gone. I had been so worried about my injuries and no longer being man enough to take care of her. I should have been there.

At last, St Pancras station came, and I managed to get off onto the station platform. I knew I would need all my strength now for the walk to the infirmary. St Pancras South Infirmary was three-fourths of a mile, but I did not care. I was still in the echo chamber of my empty mind. I knew where I was told to go and what I had to ask, and that was it.

With a final burst of energy, I made it up the front steps and into the hospital. What looked like a corpsman in a white uniform rushed over to me. For once, I did not protest or complain.

"You look terrible, sir. Let's get you a seat over here. Let me take that valise for you," he said, taking my arm.

"Thank you." I think that was what I was mumbling.

"Wait right here and I will get someone to take a look at you."

"No, I am here to find someone. Not for treatment."

"All the same to you, sir, but you just wait right here and I will get you some help." He rushed away before I could respond.

From my time in hospital, I knew there was little I could say to keep him from doing what he believed was needed.

Shortly, a nursing sister was at my side, taking my temperature and pulse. It was obvious she was not pleased.

"When were you released from hospital?"

"Yesterday," I replied.

"Yesterday?" she exclaimed. "Weren't you told to go home and rest!"

"Yes, Sister, I was, but I am here for news about a woman who might have been treated here before she died," I said, feeling guilty.

"Whatever brought you here, you must be seen to first." She motioned two orderlies over to my side. Get this man into a wheelchair and over to triage. "We are going to take your uniform off. We'll take good care of it, and your valise."

Before I could protest, she was gone. The orderlies were very gentle and helped me into the chair. Soon, I was in triage, surrounded by curtains, as the orderlies began taking off my uniform and removing my prosthesis. I knew it was not going to look good. Fortunately, the wounded leg was not infected, but it was inflamed. I did not care. I did not care about anything. I knew I had to face Elsie's parents. What was I going to tell them? I was upset with my loss of Elsie, but they would also be devastated, her mother and father.

After they got me on a cot, one of the orderlies told me a

doctor would be in soon. It was good to lay back and rest my leg. But my mind was still reeling. What was I going to do? I was trying to rest when a nursing sister brought me a glass of water.

"You are dehydrated. Drink this down, and later, I will fetch you a spot of tea."

"Sister, can you tell me one thing?" I asked, taking hold of her arm.

"Of course, if I am able. What do you need?" she replied, looking at my hand on her arm.

Sheepishly, I released her from my grasp. "I am trying to get word about Elsie Stonehouse. She was caught in the Zeppelin raid in early September of '15. Her employer told me to ask about her here."

She looked at me with kindness. "I will see what I can find out. Are you related to her?"

"We were both from Oldham in Lancashire and I told her parents I would find out what happened to her."

"If I do my best to find out for you, will you lay back and rest?" she said with a stern look.

"Yes, Sister, I promise."

"Good, you do that and a doctor will be in shortly," she said softly. "Drink that water." And then she turned and left.

The water was cool and soothing. I lay back with my head on the pillow.

I must have fallen asleep because it was darker in the room, and a man in a white coat was standing over me.

"Steady on now. I am just checking on you. I am Doctor Miller. You have been overdoing things recently, young man."

I raised up on my elbows as the doctor lifted the sheet to

look at my leg. Adjusting the lamp, he was making noises and shaking his head.

"Yes, you did a nice job on your stump here. It is inflamed and weeping some. I am going to put some salve on it and a bandage. You will rest here tonight and then you can probably go in the morning. But you must rest this leg and stop trying to walk so much on it. Do you understand?"

"Yes, sir. I had something important to do, and rest was not possible."

The doctor grimaced. "You have no choice now. Lost your leg at the front, Lieutenant?"

"A machine gun got me at Loos," I explained.

"Well, they did a good job fixing you up. Stop mucking up their hard work," the doctor said as he applied salve to my leg. "The nursing sisters will put clean bandages on this now that it has calmed a bit."

"Thank you, Doctor."

"You can thank me by taking better care of yourself. If you behave, we will let you go in the morning. You understand, young man?"

"Yes, sir. I will do that."

Nodding, the doctor finished his work and left the room. A nursing sister came to the cot and carefully bandaged my leg.

"An orderly will bring you in some soup and tea in a bit. You just rest for now," the sister said before leaving.

It was not long after she left that the orderly came with soup, tea, and bread. It was some of the best food I had eaten in a while. I realized that in all the events of the day, I had not eaten at all. After the tray was taken away, I must have gone right to sleep.

I started awake when the nursing sister came into the room. I had spent the night in so many strange places the last few days that it took a while to figure out where I was. She gave me a nice smile and told me an orderly would be along soon with tea and a bite to eat.

"Now, let me see to your leg," she said as she lifted my sheet. Carefully, she removed the bandages and wiped the stump with a cool, damp cloth. "It looks like it has improved nicely. The doctor will be along to take a look. You can't go around on this leg like you have been."

I mumbled my apologies as she left the bandages off and the sheet pulled back.

"The air will be good for it, at least until the doctor comes in. Let's set you up properly so you can have a bite to eat," she said, fluffing my pillows and getting me more upright. "Now you rest and the orderly will be in soon." And then she left.

I looked down at my leg, or what was left of it. The sister was right, it was no longer angry and red. The throbbing had stopped during the night. After a short time, the orderly arrived with breakfast. I hadn't realized how hungry I was. It did not take me long to eat the food and sip some hot tea.

"There he is."

I looked up, and it was the nursing sister who had met me in the hospital's entranceway.

"You are looking much better than you did yesterday. How are you feeling today?"

"I do feel better. Did you check for some information about Elsie for me?" I said as the dull ache came back to the front of my mind. It had not gone away, but I had been so tired last night.

"Yes, I did indeed. You said she was treated here?"

"Her employer was Stratford Works. They said she was

burned in the Zeppelin attack on her way home from Liverpool Street station to Bishopsgate, north of St. Paul's. They said she was treated here." I hesitated. "And died."

"No wonder you were in such a state when you came in. Elsie Stonehouse was brought here after the bombing in April of '15. It was very busy. We had many burn victims from the incendiaries that night. But Elsie is not dead at all."

"What?" I sat up. "They told me she had been killed when I asked at the pay office at Stratford Works," I said, trying not to get my hopes up.

"She is fine and we are getting ready to release her. She suffered terribly, but she managed to survive. Are you her Laurence by any chance?"

"Yes! I am. That is, I was before I lost my leg. I am sure she doesn't want me now that I am no longer whole."

"Don't be that way. Her thoughts of you kept her fighting through all the pain and recovery. You can't turn your back on her now!"

"Can I see her?"

"Let the doctor check you over and make sure you can leave first. If he says you are alright, the orderlies will get you dressed. You can go upstairs for a visit. But be aware she has been through a lot. Don't you dare upset her."

"I promise I won't."

"You lay back and rest until the doctor comes to check you over. And please stop doing so much. You must heal as well."

"I cannot tell you how much this means to me. May I ask your name, Sister?" I said, trying to control my urge to run out of the room to see Elsie.

"I am Sister Jean. Ask for me when they are ready for you to leave, and I will take you to see Elsie." Sister Jean turned and went on about her business.

It was not long after she left that the doctor came in to check on me.

"Let's see what we have here. This does look much better. Lieutenant, I know you want to rush around doing things, but you must take this one step at a time. When were you released?"

"I was released from Roehampton House the day before yesterday," I said, my voice trailing off.

"And where have you been since?"

"I took the train home to Oldham and saw Elsie's parents and they told me she was in London. The next morning, I took the train back to London to look for her," I replied sheepishly.

"There is little wonder you ended up in hospital. I am going to release you. Take this salve with you. You can't wear that prosthesis and go all over the place. It needs to air and have a chance to let the inflammation reduce. I do not want to see you again for this, Lieutenant."

"Yes, sir. I understand." I knew what I had done but there was no other way. Elsie and her parents needed me.

"The orderlies will help you get dressed. You will have to take that prosthesis off after a few hours every time you are on your feet for any length of time."

I thanked the doctor, and he went on his way. As soon as he was gone, two orderlies came in to help me get dressed. I was very careful with my uniform. I knew that I would be demobbed soon, and my uniform allowance would end. It was going to feel strange wearing regular clothes again.

As soon as I was dressed and put the salve in my valise, I carefully walked out of my room. I saw a nursing sister and asked for Sister Jean.

It was not long before Sister Jean came down the hall. "You look much better. Would you like to go see Elsie?"

"If you please," I said, the eagerness getting the better of me.

"Come with me, then."

Sister Jean led me to a staircase. "Take your time here. It is not very steep, but use your walking cane to help you."

I wanted to run up the stairs and see Elsie, but the sister was watching my every move and I doubt I could have made it much faster, anyhow.

At last, we reached the upstairs floor and Sister Jean led me to the door of a room. "Remember what I said, don't you dare upset her. She is recovering well and her burns are healing well. It is mainly her left arm and part of her left side. She will need attention when she is released."

"I understand, Sister. You have my word."

Sister Jean opened the door.

I stood in the open doorway looking into the room. Elsie was lying on a small bed inside. I was prepared to look at her injuries, but she was Elsie, the woman I loved and who loved me.

She was alive, and that was what mattered most. I thought of the things I had to tell her. Would she want or need me now?

She looked up at me and the smile on her face warmed my soul. "Oh, Laurence, you came for me," she exclaimed.

I almost fell as I rushed to her side. "Elsie, I am here and will always be here!" Her arm and side were heavily bandaged. I took the delicate hand that was not injured in mine. Suddenly, my gallant plan to release her evaporated. As her gaze met mine, I knew that, in one way or another, I would be at her side forever.

"Laurence, you are hurt! Bring that chair over and sit by me."

I mumbled, "It is nothing."

As I brought the chair to her bedside, I realized this was the moment I dreaded. Sitting down, manipulating my leg, I took her hand again.

"How are you feeling?" I asked to forestall her questions about my leg.

"Much better. I have been here for what seems like forever. Yesterday, I was taken outside for the longest time. They tell me I can go home soon. Have you been to Oldham and seen my parents? I haven't been able to write to them."

"They are well and send their love."

"And you, are you doing well? Laurence, you are a dream to see, but you are in pain. You forget who you are talking to." A look of gentle kindness came over her face as she spoke.

I hesitated. "I am no longer whole, Elsie. I was hurt on the front and they took my leg."

"Just seeing your face is all I need. We will get better together."

"But," I stammered, "you cannot want me hobbling around, unable to care for you, to provide for you."

Elsie's eyes looked straight at me. "That is nonsense and you know it. Laurence, I love you. I want to spend my life with you. You lost a leg and I was badly burned. Did you forget that together we always said we could accomplish anything? Stop thinking you are not whole. You are the man I love dearly. Now, no more of this."

I could tell I had upset her. "Elsie, you know how much you mean to me. I will never desert you. I only felt you deserved more."

"Laurence, do you still love me?"

"Oh yes, Elsie, and I always will."

"That is all that matters, Laurence. Kiss me."

I leaned over and gently kissed her. I was home again and with the most important person in my life. With her good arm, Elsie pulled me close and whispered in my ear.

HEATHER GRAHAM

HOT SUMMER NIGHT

Guns were out, aimed at them both.

Nelson Taylor turned and looked at Vanessa Mero, into her eyes, and he knew that *she* knew.

She knew what he was planning.

And they could not be in a more desperate situation.

There was just one chance, one chance to save her life, and probably his life as well. He prayed that the look she was giving him meant that she understood what was on his mind, that she might know what his next desperate move might be.

Because he knew something about the beautiful Vanessa Mero that these drug smugglers didn't.

"Bitch!" Nelson roared, as if he was in a homicidal fury himself. "I'm going to kill her! No damned guns, we're not shooting her, that would be too easy. This witch can melt in the water, just like the monster in *The Wizard of Oz*, the way every such traitorous witch can die!"

With that, he flew across the deck and pushed her, pushed her far, with calculated strength to send her over the aft section of the hull and into the water.

She screamed, of course. And she screamed really well. Since her hands were tied behind her back, she'd be in trouble. Incapable of swimming, of grabbing hold of the boat, and since her ankles were bound as well . . .

Her scream, desperate, terrified . . .

Cut off as she hit the water and appeared to sink.

Her performance was, thankfully, Oscar-worthy.

Around Nelson, the men who had taken aim at Vanessa—and maybe him—had lowered their guns.

"Well, go figure," Ben Stafford said dryly. "Imagine that! Nelson, who knew? You can be one tough cookie yourself, boy. You've got it right—you can't suffer anyone to live who can possibly bear witness against you. Bravo. I thought you had the hots for her, that you may have tried some kind of a dramatic martyr movement, trying to save her."

Nelson didn't look at Ben, he just shook his head as if disgusted. Ben was grinning. It wasn't easy to think of him as a hardcore criminal; he had the look of the perfect, striking, young businessman. Tall, blond, capable of charming just about anyone. On the outside, he was perfect. On the inside, he was the most broken example of humanity Nelson had ever encountered. He didn't have an ounce of empathy within him, and he was totally incapable of caring for another human being.

"Maybe he likes them pliable," Javi Martinez said. "She'll pop up somewhere if a few sharks or other creatures don't take a few bites out of her. But if they dish her out later . . . well, she won't fight him, that'll be for sure."

Javi wasn't quite as bad as Ben. He was shorter in stature, and if he'd had the right influences growing up . . .

But he'd fallen in with Ben, who knew how to use him.

Ben walked to the hull and looked out into the water. It was night, and the boat's lights were low.

"Looks like she sank or drifted already. Maybe we should have shot her, too," he said.

"Maybe. She'd have been more appetizing to the sharks if she'd been shedding some blood," Nelson told him.

That drew laughter from them all.

Nelson shrugged, shaking his head. He blinked against a bead of sweat that dripped into his eye.

It was one damned hot summer night. And they were out on the water! Well, no cooling bay breezes were going by tonight. Of course, the sweat on him was being caused by more than the night and the heat, he thought. He'd grown up down here; a Miami kid, long accustomed to the heat of the summer.

Hey, he'd even grown up with these guys.

He'd never figured that they might get their hands on Vanessa, or that she might have decided that she just had to explore the boat's hold!

Why the hell had she agreed to take a boat ride with them to begin with?

The four of these human monsters.

Ben and Javi, along with Greg Anderson—their great and fearless leader—and Fred Garcia, the Latin lover. All of them had been hardcore kids, escaping the principal's office by blaming all their antics on other kids who were too terrified of being beaten to a pulp to argue with them.

And, as Nelson had discovered, they'd been learning from the start through Alfred Espinosa, a longtime supplier of cocaine, heroin, psychedelics, and opioids. Perhaps a natural progression since Espinosa was Greg Anderson's uncle on his mom's side. In their research, agents had traced all kinds of records. Greg had been taught lessons in intimidation the hard way, being beaten to a pulp a few times himself.

And now, good old Uncle Alfred Espinosa was due anytime,

meeting them on the open water for an exchange of goods—and money. Greg had always said that there was little choice when your family had a major league business going.

Those around them had always assumed it just meant his parents' apparel shop. And, of course, he did work there . . . at least one day a week.

Nelson hadn't known everything he knew now about the foursome when he'd started on this assignment.

But he had known them. And it hadn't been much of a shock to discover what they'd been doing as adults.

Which, of course, knowing them had made it easy for him to scrounge his way into their operation. As far as they knew, he was still the nerd they'd liked to taunt in high school. And, yeah, they probably had considered him to be a nerd—his interests had been different from theirs. They'd always treated him with scorn and threatened violence upon occasion. Surprisingly, his folks had always said, he'd made it to adulthood with his confidence in himself intact. For some reason, a strange quirk in his personality, he just hadn't given a damn. He'd always known what he wanted for himself and what he needed to do to get to where he wanted to be.

So, he'd known them and ignored them.

Then graduation and years in which they hadn't seen each other.

Pursuing different *business* interests.

Then Nelson had come back to Miami.

And they'd realized they needed someone just like the person they thought him to be.

And as far as logistics, computing, and money went, they'd needed a man like him on the team.

And now he was in, while before . . . he had been someone to taunt.

He grinned inwardly as they all stared at one another. Yep, he was still a lesser human being in their eyes.

Well, it didn't help much that his parents had named him Nelson. Of course, it might have been worse. They could have named him something like Poindexter or something even more awful.

And now they were adults.

Some of them had gone on to a local junior college—one that was actually known for its excellence. But that was it. Some, like Greg, hadn't gone to college at all. Nelson was the only one who had managed the grades—and an excellent scholarship—to head to a prestigious, Ivy League school.

Maybe—since they'd apparently been lost themselves when trying to incorporate certain logistics into a plan or work out monetary arrangements—the years out of high school had taught them all that studying, learning, and finding a way to get a decent job for the remainder of one's life might not have been a bad thing.

They'd needed someone with more abilities than just those to sell drugs out on the streets.

So, he'd gotten in. They must have decided that he was desperate enough for friends to do anything he was told. And, of course, if he erred in any way . . .

They'd still beat the pulp out of him.

Or simply shoot him.

Because, he knew, he still wasn't considered to be one of them. He was more like the hired help. That's why the guns trained on Vanessa had been ready to turn toward him at any time. And why he'd been given the task of binding Vanessa's wrists while the four of them had kept their weapons trained on her—and him, perhaps, if he'd appeared to have been doing anything other than tying her hands.

Ben looked at the water again. Javi walked over by him, then Greg, and lastly, Fred. The foursome stared into the water.

"She couldn't have gotten far, hog-tied," Fred murmured. He laughed. "No hot air in that one, man, what a pity—she was one nice piece!" He turned to Nelson. "Guess it's a good thing you flipped out—thought I'd be fighting you for her later."

And to this ass, it was amusing that he'd killed her.

"Ah, come on! You guys were going to shoot her!" Nelson said.

"Maybe. But we might have had some fun first," Greg said. "Still, she had to go, so . . . we'll let it slide on this one. And my uncle is due any minute now."

He looked out over the water again.

There were no lights on the water yet. But Espinosa would come with low lights; they were quiet on the water, careful. If Greg's crew was seen by a Coast Guard vessel, they would appear to be a group of guys just out fishing—the poles were always out, just in case they were seen.

"There's something out there," Javi said suddenly. "There, at a distance."

"Low lights, and, yeah, at a distance," Nelson commented.

Greg swore. "Could be Coast Guard."

"So?" Nelson countered. "Just stay cool! What are they going to see? Just a bunch of drunks out fishing."

"I thought you were supposed to be so damned brilliant!" Greg shouted, walking toward him with his fists knotted at his sides. "My uncle is coming by any minute!"

No, he wasn't. There were several Coast Guard vessels out on the water that night.

"Okay, okay, but he's not blind!" Nelson argued. "If he sees them, he'll keep his distance. And if we just act cool, we'll be fine," Nelson argued.

"It's definitely not my uncle—he'd flash the light so that we would know," Greg murmured.

"Ah, man!" Javi said.

"What?" Greg snapped.

"The broad. The broad in the water. What if she's still alive?"

At least Greg laughed at that. "No way in hell. Even if she was a damned dolphin—or a mermaid—she couldn't have gone this long without breathing. Naw, the girl is dead," he told Javi.

"Okay, so, I'm going to run down and get a few beers," Fred told them. He pointed at Nelson. "You. New boy. You don't get a beer, you get a soda. You're captaining the boat when we move."

"Yeah, fine," Nelson told him.

Greg sank onto the bench near the helm. They were at anchor, and, of course, if they'd decided that Nelson needed a beer, too, they could have said that they were anchored for the night. And he sure as hell wouldn't have met the criteria of a BUI—Boating Under the Influence—from just one beer.

But, hey, he was the new guy.

"What the hell made you pick up Vanessa tonight anyway?" Javi asked, obviously still worried about the woman in the water. "You talk about Nelson here! What, you've had a crush on her forever, too?"

Greg started by telling Javi just what he could do with himself.

Then he added, "Like you didn't have a thing for her, too? Everyone did—including Nelson here, who so rudely and quickly disposed of her for us," Greg said.

"Well, what the hell were any of us supposed to do? She saw the stash. Nosy broad went exploring where she shouldn't have been. So much for using her head!" Javi commented dryly. "Oh, wait. Don't forget. You're the one who taught us that the only witness who could be trusted was a dead witness."

Fred had returned with beers for himself, Greg, Javi, and Ben.

And a soda for Nelson.

Greg lifted his can and said, "Here, here! Tonight, we collect the dough!"

"Yeah, because Greg learned from the best! Hey, his uncle Espinosa has been out there almost twenty years getting rich and getting away with the biggest drug-running operation in the whole South, knocking off a few nosy people here and there . . . so . . ."

Nelson lifted his can like the others. Time to act like good old boys, just out fishing for the night. Except . . .

Well, it was all a play, wasn't it?

"Doesn't look like they're after us at all," Fred murmured after a while.

"I've looked up their duties," Nelson said. "Sometimes they're just out—seeing what they can see. If we panic and try running, they'll come after us."

"Right," Greg said, staring at Nelson. "And when have you ever seen me panic?" he asked.

"Nope. I've never seen you panic," Nelson assured him.

"Okay, so, while we're just sitting here . . ." Ben mused. He laughed suddenly, then took a long swig of his beer. "Nelson! Why were you such a twerp in school? You're a good-looking guy, what, about six foot three? Fit enough, but never on the football team. Never learned to fight, I guess, but, hey, you're okay with us, we're always armed. But why didn't you get into the swing of things, be a cool kid?"

"Hmm," Nelson said, shrugging. "I like *watching* football!"

"You would have made a great tackle or guard!" Ben told him.

"Yeah, maybe. You mean I'm big enough for people to beat on without going down too fast," Nelson said.

Greg laughed at that. "Come to think of it, you steered

clear of us. We never had to give you a beatdown. Just give you a warning now and then to look away or keep your distance."

"Yep. I know how to listen," Nelson assured him.

"It's moving!" Fred shouted suddenly. "That vessel over there—it's moving. And it's moving toward us!"

Greg leaped up, throwing his beer can overboard and looking at the boat coming their way.

And, yes, it was a Coast Guard cutter, and it could only mean one thing.

They already had Espinosa.

"Get to the helm and get us the hell out of here!" Greg raged to Nelson.

He stood, ready to obey.

But Ben furiously headed to the wheel, drawing his gun.

"No! No, no, no! None of this ever happened to us until he was part of the gig! Time to say goodbye, nerd boy!"

"What?" Greg demanded. "I call the shots around here!"

"Oh, yeah, you're the tough guy, leave no witnesses, all that crap. But you're trusting this idiot—" Ben argued.

"The man who threw the girl we all pined for throughout our youth into the water, all hog-tied?" Greg asked.

"He probably can't get anything up anyway!" Ben shouted.

"You jerk," Nelson said to Ben. "I didn't play football because I didn't feel like going through life as a cripple like some kids wind up being, and I knew I never wanted to go pro! I studied sea charts, history, the police, you name it—stuff you all need now! I wanted to make money—"

"Oh, yeah, right! Pro football players don't make money?" Fred put in dryly.

Javi looked uncomfortable.

"That ship is coming. Ben, come on, cool it—we can outrun

the thing with Nelson—he does know boats and the sea! C'mon, man, yeah! We all had the hots for Vanessa and go figure that she was at the club before we left tonight, and too damned bad she had to snoop around. But—"

"Screw this BS!" Ben raged. "We don't need him!"

It might be time for him to make his departure, though it wasn't going to be exactly as planned.

But Ben had his gun out—it was a Glock he'd stolen from an agent that the techs at headquarters determined had been helped to an early demise when he'd been closing in on Espinosa and his cartel.

Ben knew how to use the gun.

But then again, he didn't expect anything from Nelson.

Before Ben realized what was happening, Nelson had moved like a flash, headbutting him so that he fell back, stunned—his Glock flying across the bow.

"What the hell! Kill the freak!" Ben shouted.

"Why?" Nelson demanded.

"It's him! It's him! That's the Coast Guard, and it's his damned fault!" Ben raged.

Greg was reaching for his gun.

He might not believe Ben.

Yet.

But he just might in the next few seconds.

Nelson swung around, moving again with the speed of light, diving into the water.

Deep. Deep, deep . . .

At first.

Because, of course, now that he had made his move, they were going to shoot at him and make sure of his demise in the darkness of the bay.

Even the water at this depth was warm, it was such a hot

summer night. And, of course, he was nearly blinded by the fact that it was night in deep, salt water.

But he knew the water and knew the bay. He even knew that, yes, there were sharks out here. Maybe not a megalodon or a ravenous great white like in the movies, but there were hammerheads, lemon sharks, makos, and more. Seriously, with this kind of heat, while a great white had wandered the area now and then, it sure as hell wasn't when the water was this hot!

It didn't matter. He wasn't afraid of the water. He respected it, but he wasn't afraid. He was far more worried about the men on the boat overhead—them and their Glocks and Smith & Wesson firepower.

They'd never trusted him with a gun.

One smart thing on their part.

Deep, deep . . .

And even then, he knew that it was luck that kept him from being hit by one of the bullets they were pounding into the water in his wake.

He was good. After high school, he joined the navy and made his way straight into the SEALs.

While others had been playing football, he'd spent his life in the water. He could hold his breath for over five minutes.

But what then?

He was good—but was he good enough? They were now determined on his extermination.

As he plunged deeper and deeper into the dark water, he prayed that he'd been right about Vanessa.

He was the one who had hog-tied her.

And he'd known her in a way that they hadn't—they had both been in a swim club that hadn't been part of the school curriculum, rather an outside institution. Actually, a club run by the very yacht club where they had been that evening before setting out in the boat. Ben's family had a membership.

As did Vanessa's.

Nelson's family did not, but his dad's boss at the car dealership where he worked did, and because of that, Nelson was allowed to join the swim club.

One thing was true. Like all of them, he had once harbored a serious crush on Vanessa. She was popular, beautiful, a cheerleader—and kind. Kind to everyone. She had the best smile in the world.

He'd caught her off guard at one point that night. She'd been staring at him, frowning, trying to determine how he had come to be with Greg and his gang.

Of course, he hadn't been able to explain. But he'd been wondering what the hell she'd been doing with them as well.

She'd almost gotten away with her curiosity, pretending to be a little lost, opening the hatch to the hold and slipping down while the others had been on deck. She was on her way out when Javi went to the galley for something . . .

And cried out with surprise, seeing her arise. A few seconds' difference . . .

No. Greg had planned on sending her to a watery grave from the moment he had picked her. Because the plan that night had been to meet up with his uncle out in the bay and do their trading where such things could be done with no one to see for miles and miles and miles.

He wouldn't have had her see what was happening.

Why had he planned on killing her?

Because she'd never fallen for him. She'd dated a guy named Joe Connolly through their junior and senior years. Joe's dad had been a cop. While Greg, Ben, and the others might have all had their crushes on her, they'd stayed far away from anyone associated with law enforcement.

Nelson was good, but . . .

Not even he could stay underwater forever. If Greg had decided that they were going to battle it out with the Coast Guard rather than run, the boat wouldn't have moved much. He had to come up beneath it, carefully, carefully, head to the aft section and dare to take a breath.

They'd been firing off the bow section of the boat—a craft that was bizarrely, or perhaps confidently, called the *Lucky Sun*.

Tonight, that seemed to be a total oxymoron.

As he kicked against the warm water to rise, he blinked against the sting of the salt water and saw that the boat had remained where it was.

As he rose far enough to touch the hull, he found himself worrying more about Vanessa than himself.

She had known what he was doing, he was certain.

He couldn't imagine anyone with the talent he had seen in her years ago in high school would have forgotten how to manage herself in the water.

And his so-called hog-tying hadn't been anything that would hold her back at all; one of his instructors at the academy had shown all of his students how to fake a good binding.

Of course, she had known then that he wasn't with them.

At least, not really.

Maybe she thought that they had taken him in just in the way that they had—the world had become a place that was just about run by computers, the internet, and those who knew how to use them.

She had to know he had done what he did to save her life.

And he could only hope that she had done what he had done, gone deep, shed the ropes . . .

And hopefully made it to the Coast Guard cutter. She would have surfaced far from the *Lucky Sun*.

Why was the Lucky Sun *still where it had been? Didn't the foursome know that there were about nine officers and about forty-six enlisted members on a Coast Guard cutter? They should be running. With their speed boat, they'd have a chance of outrunning it! Well, running right into another boat waiting for them since this sting had been planned, but they didn't know that.*

His five minutes of not breathing were almost up, Nelson knew.

He carefully, carefully moved along the boat's hull to the far aft and there, near the motor, he dared to lift his head and breathe.

They were all still toward the bow; he could hear them shouting at one another. It was difficult to make out their words—except that Greg was shouting at Fred, telling him that he was going to wield one of the grenade launchers, and Ben would shoot the other.

They intended to do their best to blow up the Coast Guard ship. They weren't idiots; they knew they couldn't fight a crew of over fifty with just guns.

Had Vanessa seen the arsenal in the hold? Had she made it to the Coast Guard cutter and been able to warn the crew?

That was hoping for a lot. He was going from praying that she was alive to praying that she could save dozens of other lives.

Maybe he couldn't count on that.

He took long breaths, making his determination. There was a rear entrance to the rooms and galley and from there . . .

He'd need to watch, to wait.

Get down to the hold and get a weapon himself. Then hope that he could wield it quickly enough against four men also wielding weapons.

But . . .

What if Vanessa had made it to the Coast Guard vessel? And did that matter? There were fifty-plus souls on that cutter.

After three more deep breaths, he caught hold of the trim on the hull and carefully, carefully pulled himself up. Staying low, he saw that the four were at the aft, and he dared to lift the rear door and slip into the cabin.

None of them were inside. They were watching the other vessel, talking about the most strategic areas to strike.

He hurriedly let himself down into the hold and looked quickly through their cache of weapons.

He found a Glock 18. It was a damned good gun, one that was supposed to be among the fastest-firing weapons on the market. All he needed was ammo.

He found it.

Again, he did his best to move silently and invisibly, hoping that Fred or one of the others wasn't coming back down for something.

More grenades, hell, they might even have a torpedo launcher.

He came up the rear way again, sliding along the starboard side toward the bow.

Just in time, the Coast Guard cutter was almost in firing range.

And Greg and Ben were both aiming at it, ready to shoot it full of grenades.

He saw Greg move and shout, "Now!" to Ben.

Nelson fired. The Glock 18 was damned fast. Greg screamed and fell back, half his shoulder gone as he catapulted over the side.

Ben went straight down.

Javi screamed, throwing his weapon down and turning to look around desperately as Nelson appeared.

Fred started to lift his weapon but suddenly and strenuously shook his head and dropped it.

"Don't shoot, don't shoot!" he screamed desperately.

Nelson moved forward, watching the two of them carefully, but they had apparently decided that prison was going to be better than dying or finding themselves maimed for life.

Nelson moved closer, kicking the men's weapons far from them, keeping an eye on them as he knelt by Ben, throwing his weapon overboard before checking to see if he had a pulse. He did. Whether they could make it to a hospital in time or not . . .

"Ahoy there! This is the US Coast Guard. You're about to be boarded!" someone shouted from a megaphone.

Nelson knew the voice. It was Captain Avery Clark, a man who had been in the meetings before this night had come to fruition.

One of the cutter's lifeboats was in the water, heading their way.

"Special Agent Nelson Taylor!" Nelson shouted. "Situation under control. One man in the water, Captain!"

A minute later, the small boat had roped onto the *Lucky Sun*.

And to Nelson's incredulous relief, not just the captain and three of his crew stepped aboard, but Vanessa Mero as well.

Someone had given her a dry shirt and jacket. Her sweeping long hair was still wet, but her eyes were as bright a green as ever, even in the pale light, or perhaps more so because of it.

"Greg—" Captain Avery began.

"Maimed and overboard, I'm afraid," Nelson said. "No choice, he had—"

"One of the grenade guns," Vanessa said. "We were afraid of that—small boats were already launched."

"We'll send a diver in," Captain Avery said. "You're all wet," he noted, frowning at Nelson.

"Yeah, I had to take a dive and come in the back way," Nelson said. "We need medical assistance—"

"Crew is on the way. We'll take those two into custody, and if we find Greg, we'll do what we can for him, too," Captain Avery said. "You can get aboard the cutter, Special Agent Taylor," he added. "Looks to me like you did your work for the night. As did you, Agent Mero."

"*Agent* Mero?" Nelson said, stunned.

Vanessa just smiled. "Sorry, not FBI, Nelson. Florida Department of Law Enforcement. And I almost failed to the extreme tonight. Credit where credit is due—Special Agent Taylor saved my life."

"Med techs arriving. Diver in the water. You two—out of here," Captain Avery said.

And soon, they were. They were greeted with congratulations on a job well done when they reached the cutter.

And it was a while before they were left in a galley room alone, drinking hot coffee—Nelson in dried, borrowed clothing as well.

"So," Nelson said, still confused, "you were on the *Lucky Sun* tonight to—"

"Scope out the goods and make a quick exit. We have a boat out here tonight, too. I'm out of the office in the Keys. We've been trying to catch these goods for a long time. Since I'd gone to school with this crew, it seemed the best bet was to make sure we had something to fight for before getting a bunch of people killed. I was going to make the same escape you managed for me—except, of course, my plan had been not to get caught. I was trying to play the part of an old friend, acting how cool it was to be back. I slipped down into the hold, and then . . . and while you saved my life, I may still be the brighter one!" she said.

"Oh?"

"I knew you'd never have really been a member of that crew!" she told him. "And when they ordered you to tie me up . . . well, I knew I had a chance. Also, just before this all came down tonight, my boss got word that the Coast Guard was going after these guys, too, hoping to catch Espinosa himself along with some of his gang."

"And they got him, right? I didn't know if he'd catch up with the *Lucky Sun* first, or if they'd see him before he did so," Nelson told her.

"I didn't know myself," she said. "But, yes, they got him!"

"A hell of a night."

She smiled. "You know, swim club really did prove to be an awesome thing! You definitely could have played football, but I am so glad that you didn't!"

He laughed. "Me, too." He shrugged. "I had an uncle in the FBI. I always wanted to be an agent. I haven't worked undercover that much, but then again, this was working undercover as myself, so . . ."

She grinned. "Me, too!"

Captain Avery poked his head into the galley. "Another forty minutes, and we'll have you ashore!"

They both thanked him.

"Good night's work! We've been after Espinosa for years and years! And I have the rest of this covered. There will be paperwork for you—"

"Always!" Nelson said.

"But you can do it tomorrow. Get some sleep tonight. We'll have an interagency meeting tomorrow, too."

"Did they find Greg? Alive, dead?" Nelson asked.

"Alive, but I imagine he'll be glad that taxpayer money will wind up getting him a prosthetic arm. But he's damned lucky to be alive, too. You are one hell of a shot—knocked that thing that could have blown up a hell of a lot right out of his hand. Amazing that a shark didn't come at him—lots of blood. But our divers are the best. They got him in. Alive. And it's good—he's going to be in a desperate enough position and situation to share a lot of needed information with us."

He lifted a hand, gave them a nod, and left.

"A good night indeed," Nelson murmured after the captain had gone. He smiled at Vanessa. "We're both alive."

"Thanks to you," she reminded him.

"Well, that makes it my best day of work ever!" he assured her.

They talked. He'd been living in Northern Virginia. She was stationed at an office in the Upper Keys.

They laughed about school. "I always liked you," she told him. "You were good to other people. Helped kids . . . but I thought you'd be some kind of a tech genius. Never thought you'd be in law enforcement!"

"I thought you'd be a swimsuit model or something like that," he told her.

She laughed. They kept talking. He discovered that after high school she'd gone on to study criminology. She loved the Keys, and straight out of school, she'd known what she wanted to do, though she had wavered between a more local police department and the FDLE.

She had a cat named Cicero; he had a dog named Groucho. Oh, but she loved dogs, too. Yeah? And he was fond of cats. No, he didn't have a wife—his next-door neighbor was watching his dog.

A cat was a good pet because she could be gone overnight, and Cicero looked after himself.

It was nice. Well, of course, again, just being alive was nice. But . . .

He was sitting there, talking with—*no, flirting with*—Vanessa Mero.

But it wasn't until they reached shore that she told him she had an extra room—and a couch—and he was welcome to stay at her place.

And the way that she said it . . .

Well, he knew he wasn't going to be sleeping on the couch.

Really incredible things could happen on a hot summer night!

ABOUT THE AUTHORS

ANDREW CHILD was born in Birmingham, England, in May 1968. He went to school in St. Albans, Hertfordshire, and later attended the University of Sheffield where he studied English literature and drama. After graduation, Andrew set up and ran a small independent theater company which showcased a range of original material to local, regional, and national audiences. Following a critically successful but financially challenging appearance at the Edinburgh Fringe Festival, Andrew moved into the telecommunications industry as a "temporary" solution to a short-term cash crisis. Fifteen years later, after carrying out a variety of roles including several which were covered by the UK's Official Secrets Act, Andrew became the victim/beneficiary of a widespread redundancy program. Freed once again from the straitjacket of corporate life, he took the opportunity to answer the question, what if?

RICK BLEIWEISS has been a successful musician, songwriter, music producer, and record company executive. He has worked as a social activist and journalist and is currently a publishing executive. His novel *Pignon Scorbion & the Barbershop Detectives* was selected as an Amazon Editors' Pick for Best Mystery, Thriller, and Suspense, as well as being chosen as one of the year's Best New Debut Mystery Novels by *Publishers Weekly*. Rick lives in Gig Harbor, Washington, and is at work on his next Pignon Scorbion novel. Follow him and Scorbion at RickBleiweiss.com.

DAVE BRUNS took advantage of the COVID pandemic to begin a second career as a writer. Thirty-six years spent working in child welfare prepared him for a walk of life as a storyteller. His clients included drug dealers, smugglers, and murderers, and his Carl Boyd series reflects that experience. Bruns lives in Toledo, Ohio, with his wife, LouAnn Frey, and an obnoxious Portuguese Water Dog named Roscoe. *Rule Number Four*, Bruns's debut novel, was published in the summer of 2024.

When **JOHN GILSTRAP**'s first novel, *Nathan's Run*, hit the market in 1996, it set the literary world on fire. Publication rights sold in twenty-three countries, the movie rights were scooped up at auction by Warner Brothers, and John changed professions. A safety engineer by training and education, he specialized in explosives and hazardous materials, and also served fifteen years in the fire and rescue service, rising to the rank of lieutenant. That "first" book was really his fourth, and that one call from an agent (after logging twenty-seven rejections) changed the trajectory of his life. Twenty books and seven movie projects later, it's been a good run, and it's still running. Outside of his writing life, John is a renowned safety expert with extensive knowledge of explosives, hazardous materials, and fire behavior. He lives in Fairfax, Virginia.

DON BRUNS is an ad executive and a *USA Today* bestselling author. As a former road musician, he performed with Ricky Nelson, the Four Seasons, Ray Charles, and others. Bruns has authored seventeen published novels including the Quentin Archer Mystery series. *Casting Bones* has been optioned for a motion picture by Nine Ton Entertainment. He makes his home in Southern Florida.

A third-generation military kid, fiction author **C. J. KUDLACZ** grew up all over the USA and strives to incorporate this atypical perspective and sense of place into his characters and settings. He has worked as a bartender, a stage and voice-over actor, and has traveled the world flying jets for both military and civilian organizations—all outstanding ways to find and tell stories. A 1997 graduate of the University of Notre Dame, he also has an MA from the University of Oklahoma and is a twenty-five-year Air Force veteran. He lives in Utah.

CHARLES TODD is a pen name used by the American authors Caroline (1934–2021) and Charles Todd, a mother-and-son writing team who write the Inspector Ian Rutledge mysteries and the Bess Crawford mysteries, as well as stand-alone novels. Their novel *Proof of Guilt* was a *New York Times* bestseller, and *A Test of Wills* was named one of the Independent Mystery Booksellers Association's 100 favorite mysteries of the 20th Century and was a New York Times Notable Book of the Year selection. Their novels have won the Agatha Award, the Barry Award, and the Anthony Award, as well as being finalists for several other awards. Charles is continuing the series.

HEATHER GRAHAM, a *USA Today* bestselling author, has written more than a hundred novels. She has been awarded the

Thriller Writers' Silver Bullet Award, the Thriller Master Award, and Lifetime Achievement Awards from the *Strand Magazine* and from Romance Writers of America. She is an active member of International Thriller Writers, Horror Writers Association, RWA, and Mystery Writers of America.